BEDDIN

This bad boy is ready to work some magic...

Identical twin and Las Vegas performer Max Dalton has always been the number one bad boy in his family, and he's appreciated the women and fame that comes along with his reputation. Now, with his brother married to the love of his life and expecting a family of his own, Max sees what being a playboy has cost him.

Grace Sinclair is on a mission when she comes to Vegas, one that involves asking Max, her best friend's brother-in-law, to give her the pleasure no man's ever been able to. She suspects Max has more layers than he lets people see, but she's determined to keep her heart safe even as she offers him her body. After all, Max can give her what she wants, but not what she needs–her own family. For that, she has a plan that doesn't include Max.

Will Grace see beyond Max's bad boy façade long enough to trust him with her heart? And will Max figure out what he really wants before he loses the one woman who makes him believe in love again?

BEDDING
The Bad Boy

BEDDING THE BACHELORS, BOOK TWO

by
VIRNA DEPAUL

PROLOGUE

Max's Magic Rule #1:
The only way to convince people to believe in magic
is to first accept it doesn't exist.

Twenty-two-year-old Max Dalton knocked on his girlfriend Nancy Morrison's apartment door. As he waited for her to answer, he rubbed the promise ring in his pocket. He'd bought it for her last week and carried it with him ever since, something his identical twin brother, Rhys, took great pains to tease him about.

"Finally, a girl who's got you whipped," Rhys crowed before Max left. "Try not to fawn all over her when you see her again. You'll ruin your heartthrob image. Hell, you'll ruin *our* image."

Max didn't give a shit about images, his or theirs. He'd missed Nancy the past two weeks. He'd dated plenty of girls before her, but Nancy was the first to truly understand him. To make him feel special, not like an extension of his loving but crazy showbiz family. She was sexy and smart and deep. She understood he was more than a performer or jock. Even though they'd only been dating two months, he'd told her things he'd never told anyone before, including how he sometimes hated performing. How he sometimes wished he'd gone off to live on his own so people wouldn't constantly be comparing him to his brother.

Now he had something else to share with her: he loved her.

He'd suspected it before, but being away had confirmed it.

He rapped on her door again.

As the minutes ticked by and Nancy didn't answer, unease morphed into worry. She'd called him less and less lately, and she hadn't been around to answer most of his calls. Of course, he'd assumed she was just busy with her studies, just like he was busy on the road with the Dalton Family Magic Act, but—

He heard her voice coming down the hallway before he saw her. His heart sped up when she rounded the corner, her blond hair floating around her shoulders and her pretty green eyes sparkling. He grinned—

Until he saw she wasn't alone. Her arm was around the waist of a dark-haired guy with glasses. She froze when she saw him.

"Max? What are you doing here?" Her brows drew together and she dropped her arm from around the other guy.

But she didn't move closer.

"I told you I was coming home today. Who's he?" He jutted his chin toward her companion.

The guy shifted his feet uneasily then said to Nancy, "I'll catch you later," before walking away.

Nancy crossed her arms. "Don't make a scene, Max."

His eyebrows shot up. "That implies there's a reason I would. Are you seeing that guy behind my back?" His voice sounded steady. Annoyed. Righteously indignant. But inside his heart hurt and he had to work to make sure his words didn't quaver.

He gripped the ring in his pocket. This couldn't be happening. She wouldn't betray him like this.

"Don't look so surprised. You knew it could never work between us. I'm just me. And well... you're Max Dalton. Hot magician. The guy whose magic wand every girl wants."

He stepped toward her. "I've never played around on you." And he could have. Lots of girls came on to him on the road, but he'd never been tempted, not once, to cheat on her.

"Maybe not yet," she said. "But it would happen eventually. I know you want to believe you're more than that, but..."

Her trailing words felt like daggers. She believed all the hype about the Dalton Brothers after all. Believed he was all flash and no substance. "You're wrong about me," he said. "The way Rhys and I are on stage, it's an act—"

"I'm not talking about Rhys. You might look exactly like him, but you're not your brother. Even though Rhys likes to have fun, he's solid. He's dependable. One day he'll have a wife. A family. But you'll—"

"I'll what?"

"You'll keep having fun. Just like I'm going to have fun while I'm in college. The difference is I'll move on after I graduate. You're a professional magician—your whole life's about fun and games. So go back on the road and don't act like you want to be chained down."

A vise squeezed his heart, pain radiating everywhere. "Nancy—"

"Goodbye, Max Dalton." She shrugged away his touch, slipped inside her apartment then quietly shut the door behind her.

Max stood in the hallway for minutes. Hours. He didn't know. Finally, he walked away in a daze.

He was twenty-two and they'd only been dating a couple months—it wasn't like he'd been considering marrying her or anything. But he loved her, he was committed to her, and she... what? Thought fun and games was all he wanted?

Anger built inside him.

Rhys was a professional magician, too. So was his dad. But that obviously didn't matter. Something about *him* made girls only want him for a good time.

How often had his family and friends referred to him as "Max, the fun one"? "Max, the chick magnet." "Max, the charmer." They never spoke of his intelligence or his ambition, or his ability to care about others.

Maybe that's because they knew something he didn't.

Maybe they saw him for what he truly was.

And what he wasn't.

Unless he wanted to hurt like this again, he needed to start thinking the same way.

1

Max's Magic Rule #2:
The bigger the risk, the louder the applause.

Las Vegas, NV
Eleven years later

Max took his second bow of the night. The audience was on their feet, clapping and whistling, impressed by the show's final trick, which he and his brother recently invented.

Glancing stage left, he saw Rhys standing in the wings, grinning. Of course, his grin probably had less to do with the crowd's reaction than it did the woman standing next to him. Melina, Rhys's wife, was beautiful, but six months pregnant with twins? She glowed with vitality, blushing when Rhys bent to whisper something in her ear. Max had never seen his brother happier.

When the curtain came down, Max strode toward them, laughing when Melina threw her arms around him.

"That was an amazing set, Max. Brilliant."

He pulled back and flicked her nose, and his affection for Melina—whom he and Rhys had known since she was fourteen and they were sixteen—swelled inside his chest. Back then she'd already been in love with Rhys. Max had known it. Rhys had known it. Hell, everyone had known it. When Melina turned sixteen, Rhys had finally decided to ask her out but Max messed things up by kissing her. It had been a shitty thing to do, one motivated by jealousy, and because of his rash behavior they'd all paid a heavy price. Rhys and Melina essentially stopped speaking to one another, and Max often sensed his brother's resentment towards him. Luckily, last year, Max had the chance to make things right. By forcing Melina and Rhys into a sexually charged situation, he'd gotten them to confess their true feelings. Soon afterward, they'd figured out how to meld their different lifestyles, which is how they'd all wound up in Vegas. Now Rhys managed the act and continued to invent tricks while Max took the stage solo.

Max looked around but didn't see Melina's best friends, who were visiting her from California. "Where are Lucy and Grace?"

Lucy's name rolled off his tongue with ease. Grace's not so much. It never did. Something about the woman got to him, even when she was just a voice on the phone.

Melina's eyes flickered slightly. "They said to tell you they loved the show. Lucy had a Skype date with Jericho, and Grace decided to head back with her. She has a lot on her mind. A few things she needs to work out."

Well, that was certainly vague. And intriguing.

Lucy was a redheaded spitfire with a smart mouth but a kind heart. She also had a penchant for dating younger men, brooding artists with lots of passion but little stability. Her new guy, Jericho, was hitting it big in California's Napa Valley and had an art opening tonight.

Grace was quieter than Lucy. Not shy exactly, but definitely more restrained, with a hint of a southern drawl and a propensity for idioms that called to mind hot sultry nights and smooth bourbon. She had an irreverent kind of humor that sometimes sneaked up on him, but on the few occasions he saw her, Max felt the wall she put up between herself and others. Each time, he was tempted to climb it. Partially because he was curious, and wanted to appease that curiosity. Mostly because she was so damn beautiful. The combination revved him up. Made him think of all the ways he could rattle her. Challenged him to explore just how long it would take to melt her reserve and have her clawing at his back, clenching around his cock, and screaming his name as she came.

Imagining her spread and under him had become a small obsession, one he sometimes had difficulty hiding.

The last thing he needed was to jeopardize his relationship with his brother and Melina by screwing one of Melina's best friends. Grace wasn't like him or the women he dated, out for some fun while it lasted. Besides, she wasn't impressed by Max's sex appeal or his notoriety. Hell, she barely seemed to notice him at all.

Still, she was Melina's friend so…

"Anything I can help Grace with?" he asked.

Max could swear Melina blushed before she shrugged. "I'll let her know you offered but she probably just needs a good night's sleep."

He was feeling tired himself. So tired, he wanted to go home, shower and sleep for three days straight. But he had a date. A big one. One that might reverse a shaky situation that was casting a pallor on his family's happiness.

Despite tonight's enthusiastic applause, the theater had only been half-full. Their show had been spectacularly successful since they'd moved to Vegas last year, but sales had plummeted the past few months thanks to their new competition—a dance and acrobatic revue—that had opened in the casino next door. Jeremy Pritchard bought the building with the theatre six months ago. Like the owner before him, he now got a cut of the proceeds from every show in addition to rent. Two weeks ago, he'd threatened not to renew their lease unless they brought sales back up dramatically. They'd upped their promotion budget and marketing efforts, but so far it hadn't paid off.

Now they only had another month until their lease was up. While having to find a new venue for their show wouldn't be the worst thing in the world, it could generate weeks of missed performances, lost income and unnecessary stress for his family and crew. His parents, who were about to leave for a brief second honeymoon in Hawaii, would feel compelled to cancel or cut it short. Most importantly, Max refused to allow anything to mar Rhys and Melina's pregnancy, which was going well but was still high-risk due to her small stature and the fact she was having twins.

"Did Jeremy show?" Max asked.

"I sure did," Jeremy called from behind them.

They all turned.

Jeremy was of average height with a stocky build. He had graying light brown hair and a mustache. His ruddy complexion would bring to mind Santa if you didn't know the guy was a blow-hard and a schemer.

He slapped both Max and Rhys on the shoulder. "Great show tonight, guys." He nodded at Melina. "You're looking beautiful as ever."

Melina smiled politely. "Thank you."

He looked at Rhys. "Great applause, Dalton, but still not a packed house. For your sakes, I hope that changes soon. Goodnight," he said before walking away.

Melina glared at him. "I do not like that man."

"With the exception of the casino owners, not many do," Max said. "Rumor is he's got a gambling problem and has mortgaged this place to the hilt."

Rhys sighed and rubbed the back of his neck. "It's too bad we didn't get a say on who bought the building."

Max's already considerable anger at Jeremy flared as he turned to his brother. "I don't want either one of you worrying about Jeremy or the lease." Rhys opened his mouth to reply, but Max interrupted before he could. "I've got it under control. Concentrate on getting ready for the babies. Now, I'm off to Lodi's. You two heading home?"

Lodi's was one of Vegas's hottest new bars. The

owner, Rick Lodi, was a huge fan of the act and referred a lot of customers their way. Max often stopped by the bar for drinks after the show, which usually led to a late night with a sexy vacationer or showgirl. Tonight, however, he was going to be focused on Elizabeth Parker, his ex-girlfriend and current Hollywood "It" girl who, for her own reasons, had suggested exploiting both her celebrity status and Max's reputation as a playboy to bring buzz to Max and his show.

Rhys pulled Melina closer to his side. "Yep. Ladybug here's been yawning all night so I want to tuck her in."

She gazed up at him, her eyes filled with love and adoration.

That, Max thought. That's why he'd kissed her all those years ago. Because he'd wanted a woman to gaze at him the way Melina had always gazed at his brother.

It's what he'd wanted from Nancy Morrison.

It's what part of him still wanted.

But as always, he squashed that part of himself down.

He had a good life, with only the occasional blip, like the one Jeremy was causing by threatening not to renew their lease. Hopefully that was something he could rectify. As for wanting what Rhys had with Melina? Why mess things up by dreaming of things he couldn't have? He simply wasn't the kind of man women wanted to settle down and have kids with, but hey, that had its perks, too. If he sometimes forgot that, more women were always there to remind him.

So off to Lodi's he went. Within minutes, Elise, a

gorgeous brunette he'd dated a few times, clung to his side and made it clear she'd be down for more of what they'd shared. He chatted with her while he waited for Elizabeth, and the paparazzi that would inevitably be following her.

The more time that passed, however, the more he found himself thinking of a different woman altogether.

Melina's friend, Grace.

What problems were stressing her out?

And why had Melina blushed when Max had offered to help?

* * *

Max Dalton was an orgasm waiting to happen.

According to rumors, the famous magician, who just happened to be Grace Sinclair's best friend's brother-in-law, delivered the goods every single time.

The question was could she convince him to work his magic on *her*.

Grace sneaked another peek at Max's reflection in the mirror hanging behind the bar at Lodi's. She'd been watching him for more than an hour, feeling green around the gills whenever she thought of approaching him.

She caught the bartender's eye. "Can I get another lemon drop please?"

A minute later, the bartender set the drink down on the counter. "Here you go, sweetie." She tucked her bleached blond hair behind her ear to reveal a tattooed chain of roses covering her neck. "Get you anything else?"

"This is good for now, thank you." Closing her eyes, she tossed back her drink, then slapped the glass onto the bar with a loud *thunk.* She always counseled students at the university to aim high when it came to their career goals. Why shouldn't that rule apply to her? And why shouldn't they apply to an orgasm? She was almost thirty and, thanks to Logan Cooper, she was dealing with an ugly sexual misconduct charge at work. More importantly, while she was thrilled that Melina's dreams of love and family were coming true, she also couldn't deny she was jealous.

She didn't like feeling jealous of anyone, particularly her friends but she was determined to deal with her issues in as practical a manner as possible. This entailed acknowledging her jealousy, dissecting it and making a plan.

Of course she was jealous of Melina, who was now building a life with the man of her dreams, and that included the imminent arrival of their babies. But Melina hadn't gotten where she was without taking risks, and Grace had to admit she'd gotten far too comfortable with her safe life in California. She'd put everything into her job and hadn't dated in months, convinced if a man couldn't satisfy her in bed and was just going to leave her eventually because of that, what was the point? Now her career had been hijacked and she had extended periods of time with nothing to do but contemplate her failures. If she didn't want to spend the rest of her life alone, she needed to do something about it. Like Melina, she needed to take some risks.

The first thing to address was her inability to orgasm with a man. That particular problem had dominated her life and her actions for so long, however, that this was the final hurrah. She was willing to give it one more shot, but if it didn't happen this time, she was moving on to more important things. That's why she'd finally decided to recruit Max Dalton for the task.

She'd secretly crushed on him from the moment she'd first talked to him on the phone more than a year ago. More importantly, while he might be a tomcat, Melina trusted him completely. As such, so did Grace. She trusted him to be discreet. She trusted him to be kind. And she trusted him to give her what she needed in the end.

Turning slightly on her stool, she scoped him out. As usual, he wasn't alone. The brunette he was talking to was the antithesis of Grace, who was slender and blond with pale skin. Grace dressed to flatter her body but still exuded magnolia blossom more than vamp. The brunette was beyond overt, with hair down to her waist and a voluptuous body poured into a tight midnight blue dress. It showed off her ample breasts and mile-long legs to their best advantage. She looked confident in her sexuality, as did Max, who was grinning broadly—although his smile seemed to dim a little when the woman ran her finger down his arm.

When Grace imagined it was *her* touching him, a current of desire zipped through her chest and settled low in her tummy. Good Lord, he did it for her, but who *didn't* he do it for?

He dressed formally when he was performing on stage. Now that the show was over, he'd lost the jacket and rolled up the sleeves of his button-down shirt, exposing the corded length of his forearms. Even with most of his body covered, it was apparent he was strong, with broad shoulders, hard thighs and a sexy ass. He moved with confidence and, despite his sandy brown hair and sparkling green eyes, he exuded a tall, dark and handsome vibe.

Experienced and more than capable of giving a woman exactly what she needed in bed—and then some.

Last year, Melina had even asked Max for sex lessons. Granted, he and Melina had been friends for years, and Max had only pretended to agree as a ploy to finally get Melina and Rhys together. While Max and Melina hadn't had sex at the appointed time (the same couldn't be said for Melina and Rhys), Grace would bet he'd had sex with *someone* that night. Sex for Max was like breathing was for most people. Natural. Comfortable. Bountiful.

She faced the bar again. As she did, the fabric of her blouse rubbed against her nipple piercings. The friction caused by the dainty gold hoops with tiny silver balls exacerbated the tight achiness she already felt staring at Max. The piercings, including the one between her legs, had been one of her more desperate attempts to feel sensual and maximize her sexual pleasure. They turned men on plenty. As for the pleasure they'd given her, the piercings actually lived up to their promise. Manipulating them brought her to orgasm much faster when she was masturbating. When she was with a man, however? Great for ratcheting up her arousal but just like everything else she'd ever tried, useless when it came time to bringing it all home.

She turned back to look at Max.

He was finally alone. Now was her chance. But still she hesitated.

That's what came with being a little too self-aware.

What made her hesitate was fear of rejection, yes. But more than that, it was the knowledge that while she was here to ask Max for an orgasm, that was the least of what she really wanted from him. In her heart of hearts, she knew asking him to get her off was just an excuse to get closer to the man who had steadily begun to fascinate her more and more. And that man wasn't the one with the playboy reputation or the electric charisma on stage. It was the man she'd gotten glimpses of over the past year. The one who was so affectionate with Melina. The one who pumped his fist in the air when Melina and Rhys walked down the aisle as man and wife, and danced with his mother at that same wedding, then boogied with the crowd to "YMCA." The man whose gaze she sometimes felt on her and wondered if perhaps... just maybe... he was as attracted to her as she was to him.

He was the man she wanted to get to know better, but she knew it was dangerous to think that way. No matter how many layers he seemed to have, Max was the quintessential playboy. He wasn't going to magically transform into a monogamous family man who fell hopelessly in love with her simply because she had sex with him. If she was going to do this, she was going to have to do it knowing the most she would get out of the experience was release, not happily ever after.

She could do that, right?

Finally, when she was able to answer that question in the affirmative, she braced herself to stand. Just then, someone sat on the stool next to her and touched her arm. It was the brunette.

"So you decided to go for it?" The woman didn't even try to flag down the bartender. She just looked at Grace, a definite challenge in her eyes.

"Excuse me?" Grace asked, even though she knew exactly what the woman was referring to. *Who* she was referring to. Good Lord, had she been that obvious? Stalking Max like he was some kind of prey?

The brunette smiled. "Don't worry. He hasn't noticed you."

Right. Gloves off, Grace thought, as her spine stiffened.

"Chill out. I didn't mean it that way. You're gorgeous and Max does like variety. He's obviously done with me. I just want to make sure you know what you'll be getting into, that's all."

Hmm. Still on guard, Grace remained quiet. The brunette was going to have her say, so what was the point? Besides, Grace always did have too much curiosity for her own good.

"See, Max only has one speed. Fast and furious. He's

really good at showing a woman a good time. Multiple times. All night long, if you get what I mean."

A rock would get her meaning and the woman's words were making her regret coming. Which was undoubtedly what the other woman wanted. Max might be done with her, but *she* was obviously not done with him. Her next words confirmed it.

"You seem a little... delicate... for what Max dishes out. I'd think twice about taking him on. But even if you can handle him, don't expect it to last long. It never does with Max. Just thought I'd do my duty for the sisterhood and let you know."

Mentally, Grace told the woman what she thought of her advice in southern terms: *Opinions are like assholes, some are just louder and smellier than others.* What she actually said was, "Well, bless your heart," while deliberately exaggerating her southern drawl. "You must think I don't have the sense God gave a goose to be making a play for Max. Good thing I've always relied on the kindness of strangers." Her tone was sugary sweet, but as she held the woman's gaze, it was apparent they understood each other. The brunette had warned Grace off. Grace wasn't about to give the other woman the satisfaction of listening.

After the woman left, it took Grace a couple of minutes to gather her courage again. The fantasy of Max doing her—hard and fast and furious, all night long—was both a temptation and a deterrent. If things went as usual for her, he'd spend the whole night *not* getting what he normally did out of a woman. But…

She took a deep breath and spun her stool in Max's direction yet again.

Instead of catching his eye, she caught him staring at the ceiling. The energy he'd had while talking with the brunette earlier had seeped out of him. Unsmiling, he tilted back his head and seemed to let out an audible sigh. His facial muscles relaxed and he appeared to be relieved. Grateful to finally have a moment alone.

It was yet another layer to add to the others she'd already witnessed.

Max Dalton might very well be a celebrity and a player, and a man who could give a woman multiple orgasms, but at that moment he was just a man craving some peace and quiet, something he obviously didn't get enough of.

Who was she to intrude?

He glanced over and met her eyes. Surprise flickered across his face—he knew she was in town visiting Melina but he was probably wondering why she was here alone— just before he lifted his chin, his facial muscles tightening. She saw the tension come over him and she heard his thoughts loud and clear.

What now? What the fuck does someone else want from me now?

Grace's belly heaved to and fro.

Her cheeks heated and she shot him a small smile before spinning around. Her crush aside, she didn't know the real Max Dalton. She'd only met him a few times.

Melina asking him a favor was one thing, but her? She'd been viewing him as some kind of sexual object, expecting him to do her an insanely intimate favor just because he happened to like sex in general. The brunette's words proved there were some who viewed Max as a means to an end, and she was no better.

"Hey."

She glanced up at the bartender.

"Were you waiting to talk to Max? He's alone now, but that's not going to last. If you want a shot at him—"

She nearly winced. How much of her conversation with the brunette had the bartender overheard? Shaking her head, she smiled slightly. "He looks tired so I don't want to disturb him. I'll chat with him some other time."

"You sure? Because he's actually coming this way."

"What?" She glanced over her shoulder and stiffened. Max Dalton was indeed headed straight for her.

Damn, damn, damn. What was she going to do now?

Her heart pounded, pushing her into panic mode. Jumping to her feet, she searched her bag for her wallet, then dropped a few bills on the counter.

Suddenly, a redhead with boobs spilling out of her strapless sequined top grabbed Max's arm. He glanced at Grace, his jaw tightening and his eyes reflecting impatience as the woman blocked him.

Grace used that opportunity to escape. Holding her purse tightly against her, she wove through the crowded nightclub, feeling Max's gaze on the back of her neck.

"Grace!"

She stumbled slightly when she thought she heard Max call her name but didn't stop. Finally, she pushed out the door, her heels clicking along the crowded Vegas sidewalk. Her heart pounded wildly as tears burned behind her eyes but she blinked them back.

Then strong fingers gently clasped her arm and she swung around. With a feeling of dread, Grace looked up and met Max's gaze.

"What the hell, Grace? Why are you running from me?"

She gulped. The feel of his hands gripping her arms—gently, but firmly—made her shiver. She pasted a smile on her face. "Oh, hi Max. I'm not running, Sugar. It was just time for me to leave."

He let her go and crossed his arms over his chest. "Uh-huh. And you didn't hear me calling you?"

"You called me?" she asked, eyes wide, her tone obviously forced. Lord, she was such a horrible liar.

Slower than molasses going uphill in January, his gaze traveled down her body, taking in her outfit. A rose-colored halter, black skinny jeans and heels. Definitely club worthy and sexier than anything he'd ever seen her wear. When his eyes finally met hers again, she couldn't help but gasp.

His expression was hot. Scorching. And unless she was mistaken, he looked like he wanted, really *needed*, what the brunette had said he was very good at providing. Fast and furious sex with a woman all night long. Sex with *her*.

Before she could stop herself, her gaze traveled to the front of his pants where sure enough…

The evidence of his obvious desire ignited her own.

She'd come here for a reason and now she had her opening.

The question was whether she was going to reach out and take it.

The answer was a resounding no.

She couldn't.

Couldn't endure being in Max's arms only to have him witness her inability to do what so many other women seemed to do so easily. Besides, although he'd checked her out and seemed to like what he saw, it was probably just reflex. She was dressed up. He was on the prowl. More importantly, she'd actually been running from him. His hunter instincts had kicked in was all.

She started to back away. "I'm sorry, Max, but I have to go. It was good seeing you again."

"Damn it, wait."

At the commanding tone in his voice, she instinctively stopped. She held her breath as he walked toward her. That breath whooshed out of her lungs when Max lifted a hand and cupped the side of her neck. She gasped at how delicious his touch felt, how it was both tender and inescapable, and his eyes darkened to a deep burnished jade.

"What's going on, baby? Why are you here?"

The way he stared at her, intense and deep, coupled with the way he called her baby, almost made her knees buckle. They certainly quivered, as did that tender spot between her legs. Heat washed over her then exploded when he skimmed his thumb across the line of her jaw. The way he was looking at her… as if he saw something in her that others didn't, as if he liked what he saw and wanted to spend some time exploring it and hoped that's what she wanted too… made a foolish hope start to bloom.

"Grace," he said. "Answer me."

"I—" She licked her lips, noting how his gaze dropped to her mouth as she did so. "I came to ask you…"

When she paused again, he leaned closer, until she could feel his breaths on her mouth, like tender air kisses teasing her with all that could come next. "Grace, I know you're having a problem with something. You don't know me well, but I think you know I'll help you if I can. So tell me. What did you come to ask me?"

She took a deep breath and wondered if she was really going to say it, right here on the street. But the way he was looking at her, the way he was touching her… she wanted more of that. She wanted it too much.

Her gaze flitted away from his. "Max, I can't…"

He raised his other hand so he was cupping both sides of her neck now. It made her feel boxed in. Trapped.

And she never wanted him to let her go.

Instinctively, she gripped both his wrists.

"Grace. What did you want to ask me?"

"You're being far too bold, Max. I'm not going to—"

"What did you want to ask me, Grace?"

"Will you please stop—"

"Dammit, just tell me."

"I want you to give me an orgasm!"

They both gasped.

Oh God, she'd actually blurted it out.

Max looked shell-shocked. But she had to admit, he didn't exactly look turned off by the idea.

His expression softened, if softening and burning could happen simultaneously, and he moved even closer, covering the throbbing pulse at her neck with his thumb. "Baby—"

"Max."

They both jerked at the sound of someone calling his name.

Grace looked over Max's shoulder at the gorgeous blonde gliding toward them while a bevvy of what appeared to be reporters trailed after her. A few people on the street stopped. Stared. Pointed.

Max cursed under his breath, stepped back, dropped his hands, and turned away from her. Grace felt the loss of his touch like a slap. He cursed again and said over his shoulder, "I'm sorry, Grace. I have to—" His words cut off as the blonde threw her arms around him and kissed him. Grace felt like she'd been run over by a train. Twice. Mortification flooded through her flattened remains and her skin turned as cold as a cast iron outhouse on Christmas day.

Oh God. Oh God.

She'd just said she wanted him to give her an orgasm and he was obviously dating this gorgeous woman.

Oh God.

Camera flashes went off.

Paralyzed, Grace waited for Max to pull away and acknowledge her. Waited for his attempt to ease the embarrassment and humiliation he had to know she was feeling.

Instead, he wrapped his arms around the blonde and kissed her back. Passionately.

The crowd hooted and hollered, and more camera flashes went off.

Finally, the couple pulled apart. The blonde buried her face in his neck, now seeming embarrassed by the attention she garnered. Max darted Grace a quick glance, a slightly strained smile on his face. But then he turned back to the blonde, shielding her even as he maneuvered her through the reporters hurling questions at them and towards Club Lodi.

Even after they disappeared into the crowd, Grace stood there for several minutes. People on the street bumped her as they passed. Abruptly, she began to laugh.

It was either that or cry. And she'd already made a big enough fool of herself. Despite what she'd tried to convince herself, she'd obviously still harbored hope that there was more to Max Dalton than met the eye. That he could give her more than sex.

That she could give him something special in return.

That he could at least be a decent human being.

All it had taken to get her there was him coming after her, calling her baby, and asking her what she'd wanted and she'd virtually stripped herself naked in front of him.

At which time he'd kissed another woman and left.

She was such a fool.

Without looking back, she walked away, checked Operation Orgasm off her mental list, and forced herself to contemplate what came next.

2

Max's Magic Rule #3:
Cover up mistakes and turn them to your advantage.

The day after seeing Grace at Lodi's, Max dropped by Rhys and Melina's house. When he got there, the newspapers on the dining room table jumped out at him. Each one folded to reveal a photo of him and Elizabeth kissing on the street. Their plan had worked. He was now being heralded as the actress's new love, the one destined to heal the wounds recently inflicted by her cheating husband, a famous Hollywood director. Another paper had gone with pictures of Max and Elizabeth walking into his condo later that night.

Soon, the Internet would probably be flooded with pictures of him kissing her goodbye at the airport this morning. Their hope was the photos would give Max, and thus his show, the increased sales Jeremy wanted, while also giving Elizabeth's husband the impression his wife was moving on. In truth, she was still grieving their separation. Temporary solutions, both of them, but enough to buy them more time so that better alternatives could be explored.

Nothing to feel guilty about. He was single. Elizabeth was legally separated. There was no reason kissing Elizabeth in front of Grace should have made him feel like shit.

But that's exactly how he felt.

Max helped himself to some beer from the fridge. He still couldn't believe Grace had come to him for sex in the first place, let alone that she'd admitted it to him. But the fact that she had, and the memory of how vulnerable she'd looked when she'd said it, told him he was an asshole for walking away with Elizabeth last night.

His only excuse was he'd been shocked by Grace's admission and feeling pressured to fulfill the bargain he'd made. How would it have looked to those reporters if he'd pushed Elizabeth aside to continue his conversation with the beautiful Grace Sinclair?

So he'd stuck with Elizabeth, showed her to his guest bedroom later that night then tried calling Grace at her hotel. She hadn't answered. When he'd gone by the hotel to see her after he'd dropped Elizabeth off at the airport this morning, she hadn't been there.

Which was part of the reason he was now here.

According to Rhys, who had called him early this morning to grill him about Elizabeth, the women were out shopping. He'd told Max to use his spare key and meet him at the house.

When the girls returned, he was going to explain why he'd walked away last night, apologize and get Grace to talk to him. Then, after making sure he'd actually heard her correctly, he was going to give her what she wanted.

What they both wanted.

Hell, part of him still wondered if he *had* heard her correctly or if hearing the word orgasm come out of her mouth had been wishful thinking. How many times had he fantasized about making Grace come? Too many to count.

Grace always looked good, but last night she'd looked *hot.* Not only because her hair had been big and her clothes had hugged her body just right, but because of the look in her eyes. Nervous but aware of him as a man. As if she'd wanted to get down on her knees and pleasure him, right then and there on the street. As if she'd wanted him to do the same to her. Later, even with Elizabeth bunked down in his guest room, Max had gone to bed reminding himself all the reasons he'd fought his attraction to Grace in the first place. Then, after falling asleep, he'd promptly fantasized about his hands on Grace's body and her mouth around his cock. He'd woken up sweating and on the verge of coming. From that moment on, staying away from Grace made no sense at all.

They were both adults. He'd never tried to convince her he was anyone but who he was. If Grace was into him in spite of his reputation, and if she remained into him despite what had happened the night before, then why shouldn't they explore what they felt for each other?

"I'm raising the white flag, girls."

Max choked on his beer when Grace's voice came out of nowhere. He whirled around, expecting to see her standing next to him, but the kitchen was empty. So was the family room.

What the hell? He sure as shit wasn't hearing ghosts.

Max scanned the room, finally spotting the baby monitor sitting on the counter by the toaster. Melina must have been testing it and forgotten to turn it off, which meant Grace, and probably Melina and Lucy, were in the upstairs nursery. He stepped up to the monitor, reaching out to turn it off, when he heard Melina speak.

"You can't, Grace. You swore you'd never give up."

"I was wrong. I'm a sorry excuse for a woman. I've given it my best shot, but my 'get up and go' has got up and went. I'm never going to have an orgasm with a man," Grace said.

The air whooshed out of Max's lungs.

He felt like he'd been sucker punched.

Grace Sinclair—Melina's smart, gorgeous and amazingly hot friend, the one who had him hard and aching on several occasions, including all of last night— had never had an orgasm with a man?

How the fuck was that possible?

And even worse, she thought that made her less of a woman?

Max dropped his hand. How could he be expected to do the right thing after what he just heard?

He placed his beer bottle next to the monitor then braced both hands on the counter, willing Grace to speak again.

"You know, Melina," Grace said. "I like both fabric patterns. What do you think, Lucy?"

Fuck the fabric patterns, Lucy. Are you going to just sit there while your friend resigns herself to a life that doesn't include the ultimate sexual pleasure? You're a fucking feminist, for God's sake.

"I think your sexual frustration has reached unprecedented heights," Lucy said. "Time to come back down to sea level. You're not giving up, girl. You need head-banging, ear-splitting, crazy-inducing sex. And we're going to find the guy to give you an orgasm that will send you to the moon."

Yes, Max thought, mentally giving Lucy a high-five. Though he had to admit, picturing Grace with some faceless jerk as said jerk bent over backwards to pleasure her didn't sit well with him. In fact, it pissed him the hell off.

"I'm frigid," Grace said. "I have to accept it but I'm not giving up on love. I'm just moving forward with my life."

Max mentally snorted. Grace saying she was frigid was as ridiculous as Melina thinking she needed lessons in sex because her ex-boyfriends were ass-hats. Rhys had disabused her of such silly thoughts, and now it was Melina and Lucy's job to do the same for Grace.

Only... only...

"You're not frigid because there's no such thing. But..." Melina hesitated, then sighed. "You *have* given plenty of men a fair shot at pleasuring you. Why continue to force things? Until the right man comes along, maybe you should—"

"Jesus," he muttered in disgust. He wanted to charge into the nursery and say, "What the hell are you thinking? You're a beautiful, responsive woman. There's absolutely nothing wrong with you, other than needing to be fucked, long and hard, until you're screaming out in pleasure. If the men you've been with have been too incompetent to accomplish it, then I'll—"

Before he knew what he was doing, he took several steps toward the kitchen doorway, stopping only when Grace spoke again.

"I've wasted my adult life trying to find a man who can pleasure me so I could move on to the good stuff— marriage and a family. Well, I don't need a man to get me off sexually, and I don't need one to raise a baby, either."

"A baby?" Lucy gasped. "That's your new plan? Are you crazy?"

Max winced. He could practically hear Grace's hurt in her silence.

"Oh Grace, I didn't mean it like that," Lucy said quickly. "I think you'd be a wonderful mother. But you *do* need a man to have a baby."

"Unless you plan on going the turkey baster route?" Melina asked.

"No," Grace said, her voice trembling slightly. "I want a loving and stable father for my baby. I just don't want a boyfriend, lover or husband."

"So no sperm bank but no personal connection between you and the father either. You just want a baby daddy?" Melina clarified.

"Exactly. He lives in his house, I live in mine. Shared custody. I still have time to do the things I enjoy. Dance. Even date. And my baby gets the benefit of an involved, loving father."

Well, that sounded stupid as hell, Max thought. If she was going to bother having a baby with a man, why not try for the whole package? A woman like her deserved that. Plus, did she really think she could trust her child and her own happiness to a total stranger? Whether they lived in separate houses or not, her father's baby would be in her life and would have an impact on almost everything she did. Just who was she planning on…

A crazy idea made him suddenly lightheaded.

She'd asked him for an orgasm. Was it possible she'd been going to ask him to father her child, too?

Granted, he didn't have the kind of reputation or lifestyle that would make most women want babies with him, but maybe, despite what had happened with Elizabeth last night, Grace had seen beyond all that. Maybe there was finally a woman who saw more to him than others did.

"When did you decide this?" Melina asked.

"To have the baby? I've been thinking about it for a while. But I made the final decision to forgo Operation Orgasm for Operation Baby around one a.m. "

About an hour after she'd seen him with Elizabeth.

"Grace," Melina said quietly. "I know you went to see

Max last night. He talked to Rhys this morning and told him. Were you thinking of asking him to be the father—"

"What?" Grace's high-pitched laugh was incredulous. "Are you crazy? Of course not. I was going to ask him to have sex with me, but that was before he kissed Hollywood bombshell Elizabeth Parker and they wound up with their picture splashed all over the papers."

"Grace," Melina said, probably intending to tell Grace about Max and Elizabeth's arrangement. Max had explained things to Rhys, and he had no doubt Rhys had shared the details with his wife. But Grace kept talking.

"I had a weak moment. But not *that* weak. Max is the last guy I'd want to have a baby with. No, I've done a bunch of research on co-parenting options and—"

The rest of Grace's words were drowned out by bitterness. The *last* guy she'd have a baby with. That hurt. But fuck, why was he surprised? The whole reason he and Elizabeth had gotten together last night was to reinforce his reputation as a playboy. And apparently, that was the only reason Grace had come to him as well.

With an abrupt move, he switched off the monitor. Pressing his palms in his eye sockets, he took a deep breath. Then grabbed his beer again.

Fine. Grace didn't want him to father a child. He should be relieved. And it wasn't exactly small potatoes that she *had* come to him thinking he could get her off. So why did it leave a bad taste in his mouth to have confirmation, once again, that a woman saw him only as sex on a stick? At least before, he'd thought she wanted sex with *him*. He'd thought she found *him* attractive. But no, she'd spoken the truth last night. She hadn't wanted *him*. She'd only wanted the orgasm she believed he could give her.

"Max," Rhys yelled from the front door. "You here?"

Max glanced at the now-silent monitor before calling back. "In the kitchen."

"Hey," Rhys said as he appeared in the doorway. "Elizabeth on her way back home?"

It took a minute for Rhys's words to penetrate and for Max to switch gears and take his mind off Grace and everything he'd heard. Finally, he put down his beer, rubbed the back of his neck the way Rhys often did and shrugged. "Yeah."

"Has she heard from her douchebag of a husband?"

"He tried calling her last night. She didn't answer." Even though she'd wanted to. She still loved the guy and was doing her best to get over him, starting with convincing him and the rest of the world that she *was* over him.

Rhys grinned and shook his head in amazement. "So your plan worked like gold. For her and you. I checked online and the next ten performances are sold out."

Max smiled tightly. "That's great."

"What's wrong?" Rhys asked, and Max silently cursed. His brother didn't miss much, and now that he'd shown a chink in his armor, Rhys would probably be all over it. "Nothing. Just a late night. You know how it is." He grinned and punched his brother in the arm. "At least

Jeremy will stay off our backs for a while. The key is to make sure we can keep ticket sales up until we sign the new lease. Then we'll have time to strategize our next move."

"And in the meantime?"

"I'll keep doing what I do best—"

"Hi, you two," Melina called just before she stepped into the room.

Rhys's expression immediately softened.

"We finished shopping early for once. Can you believe it?"

At the obviously forced cheer in her voice, Rhys's eyes promptly narrowed. His brother and Melina had fought a long, difficult battle to be together and Rhys would do anything to ensure his wife's happiness. Add the fact she was now pregnant with his children? Protective didn't come close to describing his brother.

Sometimes it still shamed Max when he thought about the part he'd played in keeping Rhys and Melina apart for so long. It had taken almost ten years to make things right between them again.

Watching Rhys kiss Melina and cup his palm around her rounded belly, Max ruthlessly pushed away a small pang of jealousy. They were happy here in Vegas. It was up to Max to make sure they *stayed* happy. Plus they had a responsibility to the show's crew and their families, and that was something neither he nor Rhys took lightly.

"Hey, Max," a feminine voice called. Max turned to see Lucy, her deep red hair longer than he'd ever seen it, standing just behind Melina. Next to her stood Grace. As Melina pulled away from Rhys's kiss, she glanced back and forth between him and Grace. Grace's gaze flitted to the baby monitor and her shoulders relaxed slightly.

"Hi, Lucy. Grace," he said, his gaze locking with hers.

Maybe it was because he'd dreamed of her all night. Maybe it was because of the conversation he'd just heard over the baby monitor. Whatever the cause, he instantly envisioned the two of them together.

Naked. In his big bed. Both of them on their knees, arms wrapped around each other, his head pressed against her breasts as her hands caressed his hair and she sprinkled kisses on his face.

He felt her. In his hands. His chest. His head. His dick. Her soft skin enclosed him. Her sweet smell surrounded him. His mouth watered, certain she'd be the sweetest thing he ever tasted.

Her screams of pleasure as he got her off would make his ears ring.

The sting of her nails digging into his back as she shook with the force of her orgasm would set him off, making his lunging hips pick up speed and his balls tingle as he prepared to—

"Max? Were you talking about Jeremy and the lease? *Max*."

He jerked at Melina's voice, feeling shell-shocked and struggling to keep his breaths even. What the hell? He'd always been attracted to Grace, but never, not even last night, had he so vividly pictured them together. He'd never pictured claiming her, shooting his load inside her, covering her with his cum until having a child was not just a possibility but an inevitability.

Apparently her confession that she'd wanted an orgasm from him but not a child had changed things in a big way. He wanted to do her. He wanted to accept the gauntlet she'd thrown down, too.

And she seemed to be right there with him, her composure smashed to smithereens, her face cherry red and her hand covering her throat as if to protect herself from... *him* he supposed. He'd probably looked like he wanted to drag her down and drill her into the ground, not caring who was watching them.

With great effort, he ripped his gaze away from hers and turned to answer Melina. But as he spoke, he spoke mostly to Grace. "Being seen with Elizabeth has paid off, just like we planned. Her dick of an ex is sweating bullets and the next ten magic shows are sold out. How about that?"

Melina picked up one of the newspapers on the table. She glanced at Grace, who was staring intensely at something on the floor.

"Grace," Max said softly.

Startled, she glanced up.

"I'm sorry I didn't get a chance to explain last night. I was playing a part and with the reporters there—"

Grace airily waved her hand. "No need to apologize, Sugar. It wasn't exactly a surprise seeing you with one of your women. It didn't bother me a bit."

She was lying, Max thought, just like she'd been lying, if only to herself, about no longer wanting to find release with a man. The fact she'd come to see him last night proved it, but so did the way she'd looked at him then and just now. With passion. Desire. Yearning. What he'd seen in her, what he'd felt when he'd touched her last night, all pointed to the fact she wasn't a woman who was okay with trading in good sex for a baby, but one who'd resigned herself to a life without good sex and was settling for something else because she was desperate. It didn't matter that a baby could ultimately be a blessing. Settling was still settling, and a woman like Grace shouldn't have to settle for anything.

"Elizabeth's such a sweetie," Lucy said brightly. "It sucks what happened to her, but it was so nice of her to fly down here to help. You sure you have no interest in getting back together?"

Max and Grace still stared at one another, and Grace didn't flinch at Lucy's question. Playing the game right along with her, he said, "You know me, Lucy. Why settle for one woman when there are so many who need what I can give them?"

Grace stiffened. Good, he thought. Why should he be the only one feeling uncomfortable here? She obviously needed to be shaken out of her comfort zone—*hard*.

"Now what?" Melina asked, her voice strained, indicating she felt the tension zipping between Max and Grace.

Rhys rubbed her back. "Max will keep up his presence

in the press. Maybe make a few more public appearances with Elizabeth. Once we sign the new lease, we'll have the time we need to get the show back on its feet."

Even though it made perfect sense, Max wanted to snap at his brother that he wasn't a damn performing monkey.

But that's exactly what he was. What he'd always been.

It was what Grace thought of him, too. Just like every woman out there, with perhaps the exception of Melina. Max was all flash and no substance.

But he was smart enough to know what Grace needed. And honest enough to know he needed it, too.

So she didn't see him in baby daddy terms. Big deal.

She needed to come. He needed to be the man that gave that to her. He also needed to stop her from making a colossal mistake by trying to have a baby before she was really ready for one. After all, she was Melina's best friend. Melina was family, and he didn't want her expending precious energy worrying about what trouble Grace was getting into.

Grace had made it clear when she was talking to Lucy and Melina that she wasn't looking for any kind of long-term romantic relationship. Rhys and Melina wouldn't have to know about their arrangement. Even if they found out, there would be no reason to think Max was hurting their friend.

Resolved, he gave his brother a fist bump.

"Elizabeth is filming this week, but we're supposed to

touch base when she returns. Until then, I'll hit the clubs like normal. Make sure I'm seen and keep the buzz we've started going. I'll start right after tonight's show. Speaking of which, I've gotta head out. I'll catch you all later." He hesitated a moment, then turned to Melina's friends. "See you next time you're in town."

Lucy waved.

"Bye now," Grace said before quickly shifting her attention to Melina, looking like she'd already put him out of her mind.

Of course, he had no intention of letting that happen. She didn't know it yet, but she wasn't flying back to California anytime soon.

Not until he gave her the orgasm of a lifetime *and* convinced her that having a baby with a stranger wasn't good planning on her part, but a cop out.

3

Max's Magic Rule #4:
If all else fails, distract the audience with sex.

"Max heard," Lucy said after Max left and Rhys excused himself to work in his office.

Grace was feeling a little weak at the knees. *Had* he heard their conversation? He'd hinted as much. But *how much* had he actually heard? The baby-making part, the I-was-on-the-hunt-for-an-orgasm part, or both?

"Maybe he didn't," Melina said.

Lucy pinned Melina with an incredulous stare and she winced.

"Okay, you're right," Melina said. "I left the baby monitor on in the kitchen. He heard everything."

"Yah think? He practically stripped her naked and climbed her with all of us watching, then bragged he was good at giving a woman what she *needs*. Clearly, Grace, he's into you. I've always suspected as much but—"

Grace shook her head. "Even if you're right, he's not

into me. He's into the challenge I represent. He overhears me saying no man has ever given me *le petite mort*, and of course he's going to imagine himself doing the deed." It was the same reason—the *only* reason—he'd come after her last night—male instinct. She'd been dressed up and fleeing. He'd been on the chase. As soon as Elizabeth Parker had shown up, she'd been easy enough to dismiss. She didn't care what scheme they'd planned beforehand. Being dismissed by Max *hurt* and she wasn't setting herself up for it again no matter how much heat she thought she'd seen in his eyes. "It's reflex, is all. Exactly what you'd expect from a man like Max."

"What's that mean, a man like Max?" Melina asked, clearly protective of the man she'd loved like a brother long before he'd actually become one.

Now it was Grace's turn to pin Melina with a look of incredulity. "Says the woman who asked him for sex lessons because who else would have more experience than him?"

Melina winced again, conceding the point.

"Who cares if he mentally stripped you because you represent a challenge?" Lucy asked. "Now that you know that kiss with Elizabeth Parker was staged, you should do what you'd planned to do last night and ask Max to *deliver the goods*."

No way, Grace thought. Sex wasn't her priority anymore. She didn't care how many times she had to remind herself of that. She was not falling back into that vicious cycle again. "My priorities have changed, Lucy. I told you, I want a baby, and it's as obvious as fried chicken and lemonade at a picnic that Max can't help me with that."

"Fried chicken and lemonade...?" Melina giggled then shook her head. "Anyway, you implied that about Max before but I think you're wrong. Yes, Max has a reputation with the ladies. His unwillingness to commit to one woman aside, he's wonderful. He'll make a great father so long as he has a partner who can work with his unique lifestyle."

The sheer certainty in Melina's voice made Grace's belly do a weird little somersault. Melina knew Max better than any of them. And last night, when he'd stared into her eyes, she thought she *had* seen a glimpse of the man behind the playboy mask. The loyal brother and loving son. That man *would* make a good father. But that kind of thinking was heartbreak waiting to happen. It was the kind of "a good woman can uncover the bad boy's heart of gold" thinking that got women all over the world in trouble. A man with a heart of gold wouldn't find it so easy to call in his ex-girlfriend and kiss her on a crowded street, thus capitalizing on said ex-girlfriend's celebrity status in order to gain the upper-hand in a business situation. So Grace scoffed and looked to Lucy for a show of support.

Lucy shrugged. "If we were talking life mates here, I'd agree Max isn't a safe bet. You and he are too different. As I learned the hard way, when it comes to long-term relationships, like should be with like."

At Lucy's words, Melina and Grace glanced at each other. That was Lucy's refrain lately, her excuse for once again dating over-the-top creative souls. Grace and Melina knew it was an excuse to deal with her recent heartbreak. Lucy didn't. At the very least, she wasn't going to admit it.

"If we're talking about someone to co-parent with," Lucy continued, "I don't think it's necessarily a foregone conclusion that Max wouldn't fit the bill."

Grace instantly forgot what Lucy was fooling herself about. "You're both crazier than a road-running lizard," she said. "I want my baby's father to be stable. Comfortable. Someone who has his priorities straight. Not someone who beds a different woman every night. Not someone who is looking to put himself in the press even if it is only to drum up interest in his magic act. I want a baby and I'd like my two best friends to be behind me on this."

Now it was Melina and Lucy who looked at each other. Grace's stomach dropped when neither of them managed to even fake a show of support.

"In light of Logan Cooper's actions, I know why you're doing it," Melina finally said, "but you're running away from your issues. You can't just ignore your desire to find Mr. Right, with part of Mr. Right being someone who can give you an orgasm—"

"I'm not running away," she said, even as she pictured Logan's face and wanted to cringe. He'd been an undergraduate student when she started counseling him about academic and career options. He could be charming when he tried but he also blamed the world for anything that went wrong in his life. When he'd propositioned her, she'd declined as politely as possible, but he'd obviously harbored a grudge. Later, at a university mixer with faculty and graduate students, Grace did something stupid and played right into his vindictive little hands. Wearing a wrap-around dress, she'd let it slide apart enough to flash Steven LaBrecht, a professor she'd slept with several times. Logan used his camera phone to take a picture, told the dean she was "flirting" with him, and filed suit against the university. Now she was on academic leave pending the board's ethics hearing. Eventually, she'd be a star witness in Logan's suit against the university.

But she wasn't going to dwell on all that right now.

"Instead of running away," she said, "I'm running to something far more important than an orgasm—which I can give myself anyway. Whether the ethics committee dismisses Logan Cooper's charges against me or not, I won't be returning to the university. I'm moving forward with my plan."

Lucy scowled. "You can't let that little twerp drive you away."

"I'm not. Not completely. I liked my job, but the truth is I haven't been truly happy for a while. The idea of having a baby? That makes me happy. I'm not rich by any means, but I can afford to take some time off. I want a new start. A family before it's too late."

"Too late?" Lucy said. "You're only twenty nine years old."

"My parents had me when my mama was forty and my daddy was fifty-two. I was *ten* when they died."

"We know, honey, but your mom died in a car crash. And your dad died of a known heart problem. It wasn't necessarily age that took them from you. Can't you wait a little bit? See if someone special comes along?" Melina's tone was pleading.

Grace shook her head. "I've gone almost twenty years without a family. I don't want to wait anymore. I want to move on with my life and that means having a child."

"Without love. Without passion." Lucy's voice held a dark tone.

"Passion is just the foam on a latte. Nice, but it's not the actual latte."

"Lord, Melina," Lucy said. "She sounds a lot like you before Rhys."

"Not quite," Grace said. "I've had passion in my life. I'm just saying I don't need to focus on a man as the be-all, end-all. I want a family of my own. One that's going to be there even without orgasms in the picture. In a way Logan Cooper did me a favor by forcing me to get my priorities straight."

Melina scowled. "How dare you say the guy did you a favor? He's dragging your professional reputation through the mud. The ethics committee will see how ridiculous his allegations are."

"Maybe. I hope so. But either way, I'm not going back. I'm going to make a completely fresh start. This morning I contacted several surrogacy services to see if an arrangement can be worked out, and one agency has set up an interview for me two days from now. The man's from South Carolina."

"You're going to move to South Carolina?" Melina asked.

"I figure being open to where I live only increases my chances of finding the perfect baby daddy, right?"

Melina and Lucy said nothing, which meant they still weren't on board with her plan. Grace forced a smile. "Let's just table this for now. I'm going to a gym by the hotel in an hour, but tonight... Are we still having dinner before Lucy and I leave tomorrow?"

"Screw that," Lucy said. "You have our support but we're still going shopping."

"For what?" Melina asked.

"For a bustier, see-through bras and a black garter belt and silk stockings," Lucy said. "You intended to get your big O here in Vegas and you're going to get it. Whether it's Max who gives it to you or not."

"Lucy, you're not listening to me. I'm not interested in sex anymore. I need to focus on what's important."

"You can find a baby daddy tomorrow. You have one night left in Vegas. Make that night count. If you do, Melina and I promise we won't mention the O word again. We won't even mention the words Mr. Right."

Melina hesitated, bit her lip then finally nodded. "That's right. One more night. What can it hurt?"

Grace studied her friends and wondered if they truly believed what they were saying. But they only wanted the best for her. And the chances of her meeting someone who'd make her forget her baby plan was nil. Even Max couldn't convince her to get back on that roller coaster again. "Fine. One more night."

* * *

"I feel like an idiot," Grace said a few hours later. After leaving Melina's, she'd taken a drop-in class at a nearby gym and returned to her hotel feeling pleasantly exhausted and achy. She'd wanted nothing more than to shower and lounge by the pool, but Lucy and Melina had dragged her to one lingerie store after another. Now she was at a hip new club, squirming on her stool at the tall bar table, trying to adjust the silk stockings that kept threatening to pop off the garter. Somehow Kevin Costner had made a seductive show of taking garters off a woman in that '80s movie *Bull Durham* but as for her, well, she felt all trussed up like one of those Budweiser horses strapped to the big beer wagon.

"Stop squirming." Lucy was dressed up, too, working her red hair and compact, curvaceous body, and eradicating all hints of girlishness by covering the freckles on her face with make-up. Despite how sexy Lucy was dressed, Grace knew her friend wasn't looking to score herself. While she and Jericho weren't necessarily exclusive, Lucy barely drummed up enough interest to keep that relationship going as it was. Whether she wanted to admit or not, her heart had been broken. By a nice guy, no less.

Last year, Lucy—who'd always been drawn to bad boys and moody artists, had accepted Grace and Melina's challenge to give a nice guy a shot. A women's studies professor at the same California university where Grace and Melina had worked, Lucy had spent months denying her attraction to Professor Jamie Whitcomb. To everyone's surprise, she'd abruptly given in and the two had dated several months before he'd broken things off. The breakup had crushed her. She denied it, of course, but Lucy was like that. She'd sooner eat worms than admit—even to her best friends—that a man had the power to hurt her.

Lucy pushed Grace's dirty martini closer to her. "Drink up, Grace. We're at one of the best clubs in Vegas, and men are looking at you. Men who probably want a night of Vegas fun before going back to their boring lives. They won't want your phone number, or to see you again. These guys want to give you a night of sexual pleasure. Just pick one."

Lucy acted as if picking up a guy for a one-night stand was something Grace did all the time. Sure, it had happened a time or two in her life, but she wasn't a pro. And she'd enjoyed the sex on those instances even less than normal. Sleeping with guys that didn't care about her as a person? Men who cared most about getting laid and the pleasure she could give them? She hadn't been able to truly relax, never mind being comfortable enough to share what she enjoyed or thought she *might* enjoy.

Grace was only here to placate Melina and Lucy. She

wasn't going to pick up a guy. She was going to stay focused on her plan.

Grace scanned the room. The place was so crowded she wouldn't be able to cuss a cat without getting fur in her mouth. Where did all these people come from? Women were eyeing men, men were eying women, as if the nightclub was a true meat market. Sheesh. She should hang a sign around her neck: *Single and Willing to Go at it for One Night Only*. But that would hardly make her stand out in the crowd. It was like a pack of wolves in here. One man's pants were so tight she could see his…religion. She knew the Dalton brothers worked their image as sexy single performers. Was this what Max—and before he got married, Rhys—lived with on a constant basis? Being perpetually hunted?

"It fries my rear end to have to be here," she murmured, then downed the rest of her martini. "Give me colic and dirty diapers any day."

"None of these men are here looking for a woman they actually want to get pregnant, that's for sure. But you're not here to set your Grand Plan in motion. You're here because you deserve to experience at least one rocking orgasm with a man before you tie yourself down with a baby and shared parenthood."

Grace didn't disagree but she wasn't keen on Lucy's plan either. Pick up a guy, go through the motions of awkward flirtation and the getting-to-know-yous, and finally have sex only to be disappointed in the end.

Been there, done that.

It was just too bad Melina wasn't here. Having a pregnant woman along as her wingman would have been the perfect excuse to cut the evening manhunt short. But although Melina had come along to the lingerie store and helped select the outfit Grace was wearing, her back had started aching and she'd gone back home to rest.

Grace envied Melina big time right about now, and not just because she was six months pregnant.

"Lucy, I think we should just go back to the hotel."

"But the pickins are ripe," Lucy said, then pointed toward a group of men. "Look at that one—the guy in the grey suit. He's hot. And he just looked at you. Show him some leg."

"What?"

"You're sitting with your toes and knees all pressed together like some prim and proper matron. Cross one leg over the other—your skirt will slide back a bit and he'll be able to see the garter. He'll be here in less than a minute, offering to buy you a drink."

At Lucy's urging, Grace felt a tingle of interest. She knew most people viewed her as a fragile hothouse flower, not as a woman who'd ever get a tattoo let alone body piercings. Even if she hadn't shared her deepest fantasies, each of her lovers had been surprised by how adventurous she was in bed, and she'd enjoyed revealing herself to them one shocking secret at a time. Unfortunately, her willingness to do so had started to fade more and more as she began to view her own sexuality as false advertising. Sure, she could cross her legs and give Grey Suit a peek of her garter, but if it worked and he wanted to get together, the evening would simply end the way it always did, with her doing whatever it took to get him off even as she knew it wouldn't happen for her.

Plus, she'd tried to flirt by exposing her body before, and look what a disaster that had turned into…

"Grace," Lucy said over the noise of the crowd. "No one knows you in Vegas. You're free to do what you want. There will be no consequences. No one's here to set you up. Now cross your leg."

"Lord, Lucy. If I do, can we get out of here?"

"If you do and he comes to talk to you—and I *know* he or some other guy is going to come and talk to you— and you give him a fair shot and decide you're not into him, and you do that maybe a dozen times and get the same results? Then we can go."

A dozen times? Eating worms was sounding really good. "Lucy—"

"You promised one more night before you start your plan, Grace. One night to find a man who will at least *try* to give you that orgasm you've been complaining about for all these years."

"I don't complain," Grace said, startled. Did she? The fact that she'd had a few lovers but had never achieved orgasm with them bothered her. It did. It hot-and-bothered her. Enough that she'd contemplated asking Max Dalton for help. But she hadn't thought she'd brought the problem before her friends *that* much.

"You hardly ever complain. You almost take it like

it's a given. Now cross your fucking leg."

Grace crossed her leg to shut Lucy up.

And her skirt slipped. Enough to show the lace edge of the silk stocking and the strap that led to the edge of her garter.

She glanced across the room at the man in the grey suit. He was staring at her—not at her face, but firmly at her leg, where the silk stocking left off and her bare skin began.

She felt a little quiver between her legs, further proof of what she already knew: she had a bit of an exhibitionist in her. It's why she'd flashed Steven LaBrecht at the university mixer. She liked teasing a man in public. Loved the idea that he or she could get aroused in a room full of people. The fact that it was a *little* quiver told her she wasn't all that interested in the guy staring at her. Now if he'd been Max?

The little quiver turned into a rolling pulse that made her gasp.

Heat flushed her neck and face.

Why had she let her friends talk her into this? What she'd said earlier was true. She was used to getting herself off and right now she could be back at her hotel room, doing just that while thinking about Max. She did it a lot, and it never failed to make her come hard.

The man in the grey suit finally caught her gaze. He smiled—not a *bad* smile, per se, but his teeth weren't as strong and white as Max's, and his lips were thin and stretched too far back, showing his gums. He had nice shoulders and seemed tall enough. Hot, just as Lucy had said. He turned back to his friends, and Grace quickly did the same.

"I think Grey Suit is coming over here," she whispered, desperation starting to form. She wanted to leave. But she also didn't want to let cowardice drive her the way it had last night at Lodi's. She didn't want to regret her life to the point she spent the next few decades *complaining* about it. She never wanted that.

She could do this.

No, she couldn't do this.

Yes, she could do this.

But she didn't want to do this. Not with *him*.

Oh, for heaven's sake.

"Excuse me," a deep male voice said from behind.

Her insides went to jelly, and not in a *wow, I'm about to get laid and isn't this fantastic* way, but more like a *crap on a cracker, what have I just done* way. She forced her muscles to work, and turned to face Grey Suit.

"Sorry to interrupt," he said, smiling down at her, "but I couldn't help but notice you the moment I came in. I've been standing there with my friends for a while, trying to get my nerve up to come over and introduce myself. I'm Blake Jordan." He held out his hand for her to shake.

Well bless his heart. That was sort of sweet. He'd been watching her, and had been nervous about taking the first step. Even if she didn't sleep with him, she could still make small talk with the guy.

4

Max's Magic Rule #5:
Convince females in the audience you only
have eyes for them.

M ax was pissed for two reasons.

First, he was close enough to hear the scumbag currently trying to pick up Grace. The guy had hit on at least three different women before her, and had only focused on Grace when she'd shown her garter.

Second, Grace was showing said garter while wearing a mind-boggling short skirt. Her outfit was *come fuck me* wear most places, but especially in Vegas.

That meant even though Grace had been ready to ask for his help last night, she was now more than ready to give herself to another man. It was one thing for her to trust and respect Max enough to ask such an intimate favor, quite another to see him as just another dick that might get the job done. If that's all she saw him as—

But even as Max's anger continued to build, he saw the strain underneath her game face. No, coming to him last night hadn't been easy for her. And the only reason she was here right now was because Lucy had encouraged her —Melina had said as much when she'd told Max where to find them.

Neither Grace nor Lucy had seen him when he'd arrived. And now he stood behind them as they faced the jerk-off—what was his name? Blake. Probably a fake name to go with the fake persona. Under the neon lights of the nightclub, the tan line on the man's ring finger told him everything he needed to know. Max pulled some bills out of his pocket, handed the money to a passing cocktail waitress, then scooped two martinis off her tray. She gave him a crooked look, but then shrugged and walked off.

He came around from behind the girls' table and held the drinks out—one for Lucy, and one for Grace.

"Hi, Dixie. Sorry I'm late with the drinks. Took forever to get them from the bartender," he said, smiling broadly at Grace, who looked puzzled, and—though she hid it quickly—pleased to see him.

"Max," she said slowly. "What are you—"

"Oh, sorry, babe. Did I get you the wrong martini?" He turned to the married jerk-wad and took his hand, shaking it before the man could walk away. "Hi. I'm Max Dalton. I'm the headliner at the Portofino. This is my date, Dixie. And you are?"

Next to him, he heard Lucy snort and mutter under her

breath.

"Just leaving," the man said. He pulled his hand out of Max's tightening grip, turned and walked off. Leaving Max alone with one visibly annoyed and probably horny woman and another who was laughing hard enough to pee her pants.

"Dixie," Lucy said. "I totally get it. Grace is a sweetheart and she's from the south. Heart of Dixie."

"You read my mind." Max winked at Lucy then turned to Grace. "The guy was married," he said. "And he'd tried picking up on three different women before you caught his attention with..." He stroked the outside of Grace's thigh, tracing his hand up from her knee, past the tip of her stockings. Then, with one finger, he lightly flicked the garter strap.

Grace gasped.

Without taking his gaze off Grace, he said, "Lucy, you know I adore you, but Grace and I have something we need to discuss. Think you could make yourself scarce for a while?"

"Um, yeah. Sure. I'll be at the bar. Grace? Find me when you're done, um, *talking* to Max."

After Lucy left, Max took his hand off Grace's oh-so-sexy thigh and sat on Lucy's stool. "We didn't finish our conversation last night," he said, getting right to the point.

"Oh, we finished it," she said. "I've moved on."

"So I heard," he said.

Her face flamed, but she tilted her chin up, apparently not willing to be intimidated by him. "You did *not* overhear our conversation on the baby monitor."

He just looked at her.

Exhaling loudly, she rolled her eyes. "Okay, fine. But you did not hear the entire conversation." She scrunched up her nose, which he found adorable. "Did you?"

"Answer this question first. Why are you willing to settle for having a child with a man you don't love?"

Her brow furrowed. "*That's* what you sent Lucy away to discuss?"

He shrugged. "It's a bleak way of going about making a family."

"Not all of us are about passion, Sugar."

"Do you realize you only call me Sugar when you're trying to pull the wool over my eyes? Newsflash: It's not working. You overflow with passion."

"I have reasons for being… practical," she insisted.

"I'm aware of that. That's what brought you to the club last night, looking for me. It wasn't that you just wanted me to give you an orgasm. You *needed* me to give you an orgasm because no other man has been able to get you there."

She'd been pink before, but now she blushed so red she practically glowed. "Okay, so you obviously heard everything I said over that baby monitor. But me coming to you last night? Call it a case of temporary insanity. Or massive sexual frustration. I wasn't thinking clearly."

"I'm not worried. But I'm not stupid, either. I'm not going to let you brush off what you said as unimportant."

She refused to answer, but for the first time, dropped

her gaze from his to stare at her hands in her lap.

He leaned in close to her, mentally willing her to stay put. She held still. When he got his mouth to her ear, he whispered, "Last night, you told me what you wanted. Tonight, I'm telling you I'll do it."

She didn't pull away. Instead, she turned her head until her mouth was even with his ear, and whispered back, "You're a true gentleman, Max, but I told you what I *wanted*. I don't want it anymore."

He leaned back then, settled in his seat and grinned at her. "Liar."

Her eyes darkened and he could swear she shifted, pressing her thighs together under that miniscule skirt. "It won't work," she said. "You made your choice when you walked away from me last night. I made mine. You know about my little... issue. I wish you didn't, but you do. So you have to know how sick and tired I am of dealing with it. Elizabeth interrupting us last night was a sign. I'm finally receiving the message and moving on to more important things."

"Bullshit. You're embarrassed because of what you told me and pissed because I walked away. But I already explained why I did, and it had nothing to do with not being interested in giving you what you want. You know that's not the case. You know how damn attracted I am to you, right?"

"Max—"

"Tell me you get how attracted I am to you, Grace."

"You seem to be attracted to me, yes."

"I have been for a long time. And you've wanted me, too. You need an orgasm? Then you've come to the right man. As for moving on to more important things, with said things being a baby and a stranger to be your baby's father—"

"Will you please lower your voice," she hissed, looking around. Luckily, no one seemed to be paying them any attention.

"—we can talk about that idiocy later."

"It's *not* idiocy. And it's none of your business."

"You made it my business last night. You made *you* my business."

"Like I said, I trusted you last night. I don't anymore. You walked away from me, Max. You left me there, feeling like a complete fool."

He covered her hand with his. "I know I did. And I'm sorry. I promise, Grace, that won't happen again."

She shook her head, obviously not letting what he was saying sink in. "You're my best friend's brother-in-law. It would complicate things."

That's exactly what he'd thought. Why he'd never come on to her. Now that he knew Grace *needed* him, things had changed. "It won't complicate things between the four of us because Rhys and Melina don't have to know. Between you and me? I like complicated."

"I don't."

"That's right," he said, placing a hand on her knee and skimming the top of her stocking with a finger. "You like things practical. It's why you came to me last night.

Because common sense told you if any man could give you what you need, it was me. Here's a word of advice, Grace. When if comes to sex, trust your instincts." His finger traced a little higher, insinuating itself just under the hem of her skirt. Damn, her skin was soft. So much softer than the silk of her stocking. Heat washed through him and his dick strained against his pants. He took a shallow breath and told himself to get it under control. Practicality, he reminded himself. That's what they'd been talking about.

"Tell me the truth," he said as his finger traveled even higher up Grace's thigh. With a stifled moan, she caught his wrist, stopping him from going father. "Before you came to Lodi's, did you make sure your hotel room was spotless, and stash condoms and lube in the bed stand?"

He was just teasing her, trying to get his own raging desire under control, but she glowered at him and pushed his hand away. "I was wrong. You, sir, are no gentleman."

"And we've already established you need a good lay. I'm here to give it to you. The condoms we'll use. The lube you won't need. I'll make you come, Grace. I'll make you come so hard you won't know if you're still on this earth or in the ether."

"Better men than you have tried," she said.

He grinned, reached out and stroked a finger against her cheek. "See? That was your first mistake, Dixie. Because no one's better than me. And I won't stop until I've performed whatever magic it takes to make you scream my name."

"You arrogant—"

He hadn't been planning it, but he couldn't resist. Cupping the back of her head, he pressed his mouth against hers. Not aggressive. No tongue. But not tentative or shy either. He sipped at her lips as if she was a fine wine, and it was true—she was intoxicating. She tasted like peaches, soft and ripe and succulent.

He immediately wanted more.

So did she.

Her lips parted. Her tongue sought out his, taking his breath. Angling his head, he took the kiss deeper but only briefly. Even so, by the time he pulled away, they were both breathing hard. Staring at each other in a way that screamed encore.

He leaned his forehead against hers, stroked back her silky blond hair, and whispered, "Think about it. And don't get on that plane tomorrow. Fly with me instead."

Then he left.

She knew where he lived and it was important she trust him enough to come to him. If they didn't have that, Max knew no amount of sexual technique was going to get Grace off, not when having an orgasm was obviously so difficult for her in the first place.

Either she'd show up at his place later, or Lucy would get her safely back to the hotel. But even as he left, Max was pretty certain he'd see her soon.

Grace was fighting it but she knew what she wanted.

She wanted *him*.

* * *

Struck by indecision, Grace watched Max walk away.

Her mind told her to let him go.

Her body screamed to run after him.

His kiss. His words. Neither had been completely over the top, but they'd been just bold enough to get her attention and prove what she'd always believed. Max Dalton would be a spectacular lover.

Good Lord, the sound of his voice alone, cajoling her to *fly* with him while they were in a crowded bar, where anyone might overhear him, had her soaked and pressing her thighs together to ease the ache.

She refused to think of Operation Baby as idiocy, no matter what he or Lucy or Melina or anyone else thought. She knew what she wanted. But she also couldn't deny she still wanted what Max was offering, too.

"You're kidding, right?"

Lucy's voice caused Grace to jerk.

"You're actually still sitting here when I saw Max Dalton just make his move?"

Grace turned to face her friend. "I'm scared, Lucy," she whispered before she even knew what she was going to say. But it was true so she didn't bother trying to take it back.

"Why?"

"Because—because I trusted him last night and he hurt me, even if I understand he didn't mean to. Besides, what if I do let him—" She waved her hand in a small circle. "—you know. If Max Dalton can't give me what I want in bed, no one can. And if he can, how will I ever live without him? I'll be screwed either way. If I concentrate on family first, there's always the chance that later... "

When her words faded into a prolonged silence, Lucy reached out and hugged her. "Grace, there's nothing wrong with you. So many women have the same problem and for many different reasons. You don't need to rush out and have a baby because you think you're defective."

"I know," Grace said, resting her cheek against Lucy's shoulder for a moment, even as she admitted to herself— she *did* think she was defective. All she wanted was to be normal. She was so tired of reaching for something she couldn't have. Of enduring the psychological pressure and the physical frustration that came with repeatedly getting turned on only for it to go nowhere. Great sex should come naturally. The only thing that might come even more naturally was procreating. If she couldn't have the first...

But she wasn't going there. Not with Lucy, who already saw too much. Maybe her motives were slightly mixed up, but in the end it didn't matter. Taking a deep breath, she pulled back. "I don't want to have a baby because I think I'm defective. Not completely," she said swiftly when Lucy opened her mouth to argue with her. "I just want a baby. I want one while I'm still young. I want one even without a man in my life. And I'm ready to have one. Honestly. But you were right. If I can... find what I'm looking for with a man beforehand, it would ease my mind about the future. And you're also right about Max. He did make his move."

Lucy looked like she wanted to respond to several of Grace's comments but contented herself with simply saying, "So what are you waiting for then?"

Grace looked in the direction Max had gone. Her heart thudded like a runaway train in her chest. "Do you think I can still catch him?"

"I'm betting he's walking *really* slowly, just in case. Now go for it, girl. And remember, no matter what happens, you are fabulous, Grace. You are fierce. You are an amazing woman. And Max isn't doing you a favor here. He's reaching out for what he's wanted for a long time. You've just given him a great excuse to do so."

Grace stood but looked at Lucy with confusion. "Why would he need an excuse to proposition me? Anyway, you're wrong. This *is* a favor Max is doing for me. At most, he's bored and this is a challenge he can't resist."

"You keep telling yourself that," Lucy said. "But we'll see where we are in a few weeks."

"This is one night. Then I'm moving on with my plan."

Lucy nudged her in the side, silently encouraging her to go after Max. "We'll see," she repeated. "Just don't think you're getting away with not giving me details afterward."

With another gentle nudge from Lucy, Grace began walking toward the exit. Part of her felt like she was a robot on autopilot. The other part of her felt incredibly human, her tummy dancing to the hum of people in the bar and her teeth unable to keep her lip still.

Nervous.

Excited.

And yes, hopeful.

This was Max Dalton they were talking about.

The Max Dalton.

But more importantly, it was the man who'd promised he'd do whatever it took to make her fly. Even if in the end he failed, she knew everything leading up to that moment would be the best she ever had.

* * *

Max was just unlocking his car when he sensed someone behind him.

He turned and saw Grace.

She looked about ready to bolt and he automatically raised his palms, as if she was a small animal he didn't want to scare off. "Grace," he said with a smile. "I—"

She took several jerky steps closer then said, "I want a baby. I mean, I know you know that. And I'm not asking you to have anything to do with that. Of course I'm not. But you have to understand, that's what I want most. More than good sex. And that's not going to change."

"Okay," he said, not knowing where she was going with this.

"You might think I'm making a mistake, but it really is none of your business. Aside from what you're offering me, *I'm* not your business. So I don't want to hear any more about my baby plan being idiotic, okay?"

Fuck, what could he say to that? He still had every intention of convincing her to rethink her plan, if only because he owed that to Melina. But she didn't wait for his response.

"I'd made up my mind that I was focused on the wrong thing. Because sex has been good for me, even without... all that." She waved her hand in a small circle, obviously referring to her ever-elusive orgasm. "I've never believed sex is the be-all, end-all."

Did she seriously think he was going to agree with her? He remained silent.

She rubbed her arms together, appearing frustrated that he wasn't responding the way she obviously wanted.

"Maybe it's not the be-all, end-all," he finally said. "But it sure makes life worth living."

Her mouth twisted and she looked away. "Spoken like a man," she said.

"No," he said. "Spoken like someone who's actually had sex."

Her head whipped up. "I've had sex. Good sex."

"You haven't come with a man, Grace. In the end, how good could the sex have been?"

She licked her lips and shuffled her feet, looking as uncertain and tentative as he'd ever seen her. "And you really think you can change my mind about the benefits of sex?"

What was going on here? Was she testing him? Did

she expect him to say, "Hell, yes. No problem"? He wasn't that naïve. He couldn't just touch Grace and make her come, but he would keep going until they found the magic ticket. Hell, he imagined he'd die trying, and it wouldn't be such a bad way to go. Only he couldn't do it by himself. "Depends," he said.

"On what?"

"On whether you'll actually give up control."

"I give up control."

"No. You don't. Because if you did, you'd have had an orgasm long before now."

She seemed stumped for an answer. "Have you ever… been with a woman who's had trouble with all that?" Again, the hand wave.

He dragged his hands over his face, trying not to smile. Somehow he didn't think she'd appreciate it. "Sure," he said. "It's not that uncommon for women, Dixie. But those women trusted me. They embraced the idea that *that*—" He waved his hand. "—was possible and let me run the show. And we always worked it out."

Her face transformed. She practically pointed her finger at him and shouted, "Ah ha." Of course she did neither, but he read her all the same. "How do you know? They could have faked like a possum."

His brows furrowed at the suggestion he'd allow a woman to leave his bed without being completely satisfied. "Did you fake it?" he asked.

She immediately sobered, giving him his answer even as she took several steps back. He sighed. Not exactly what he was going for. He'd have to push her to talk, of course, but he'd have to do it when she was closer so she couldn't run away and hide.

"Most men have fragile egos," she said.

"Well, I don't, so you don't have to worry about playing possum. But let's focus on one thing at a time here. It seems you're accepting the offer I made inside. If that's the case, stop using delay tactics to cover up your nerves and come here." He said it gently, but with the obvious intention that she obey. He wondered if she'd balk. He liked to dominate in bed, and instinctively he knew that was exactly what Grace needed from him.

Only she wasn't through fighting whatever was keeping her ten feet away.

"Wait. Before... it's only fair... You have to know I enjoy sex. I like pleasing a man. I like being pleased. And despite what you said, I do give up control. But the chances of it happening for me are zero. Below zero."

He immediately wanted to deny her claim. Hell, he immediately wanted to take her in his arms and kiss away the nonsense she was spouting. Instead, knowing she was all jazzed up and needed to say what was on her mind, he leaned back against his car and crossed his arms over his chest. "In this context, I'm not sure a below zero chance is even possible."

His relaxed posture seemed to calm her and she stepped closer. *That's right, baby girl. Come to me.* A strange sense of lightness overcame him, as if a burden he was carrying and didn't notice until now was lifted. It confused him, but he was too focused on Grace and her next words to analyze it.

"See, that's where you're wrong. I mean, you're right. I did come to see you last night to ask for... that. But part of the reason I chickened out, well, I can't let this go any further until you know exactly what a burden it's going to be for you, Sugar."

Max felt a fierce frown overtake his face. "Burden?" he said, straightening. Suddenly he remembered her telling Melina and Lucy she was a sorry excuse for a woman. "That's how you think of yourself? Damn it, Grace—"

"Please," she said. "Just listen to me. Let me say what I need to say or this can't go any further."

Seeing she was serious, Max forced himself to lean back against the car again. "Fine. But don't refer to yourself as a fucking burden. You're a beautiful woman and it would be my honor to be with you. It would be any man's honor."

"That's what several men before you thought. Before they tried to give me what I wanted and couldn't. And before you say what I know you're going to say, it wasn't them, it was *me*."

"Dixie—"

"My first boyfriend was an all-star quarterback in college. He was handsome, popular, smart. And he was a good lover. He took his time. He liked sex. He liked me. But we went out for two years. Two years, Max, and nothing."

She was speaking fast now. As if she had to in order

to get it all out. Max straightened and took two steps toward her. "That doesn't mean—"

She took exactly two steps back, causing him to narrow his eyes and stop. He'd stayed away from her for more than a year, but already he was damn tired of her backing away from him.

"After that, I tried a couple of times… with guys I just met and…" She was clearly embarrassed to be admitting she'd had casual sex. He wanted to shake her. As if she had anything to be embarrassed about, considering he was a veritable master at casual sex. "Those times, it wasn't even good. Not any part of it. I could barely relax and I learned it wasn't worth it, trying with someone who didn't care about me and whom I didn't give a hoot about either. I just ended up feeling worse about myself."

"That's not what's happening here. I care about you. And I've—"

She interrupted him again, and it started to piss him off even as part of him was finding her more and more adorable. "I didn't have a serious boyfriend again until a few years later. I met a guy when I was out celebrating my twenty-fourth birthday. He was a college professor, but far from a nerd. Again, handsome. Again, sexy. Again, he cared about me and I cared about him. He had—he had straight, white teeth. Great hair. He was funny. He was kind. He came from good people. I tried to fake it but eventually he caught on. And after three years together, three years of him trying and trying and trying, and me failing and failing and failing…" Her breath hitched and

Max had had enough.

He moved quickly toward her, not letting the fact she backed away deter him this time. "Grace," he whispered as he gathered her in his arms. She was shaking, he realized. Totally eating up that shit about her being a failure. Or maybe she was just reliving the sheer frustration she'd felt time after time, caring about a man but not being able to totally let herself go sexually. Reliving the heartache of those men walking away from her because of it.

Only she wasn't seeing things clearly. With the amount of pressure she was putting on herself, of course it had been impossible to let go. And that's what this was about, he was sure of it. She hadn't been able to let herself go with those men. He was going to find out why and help her past those barriers.

"It happened again and again, just like that," she said. "Good men. Men I was attracted to. Men I let tie me down or blindfold me. Men with hard abs and big biceps and some with big—"

She abruptly stopped talking and he found himself no longer able to hide his amusement. Laughing, he hugged her tighter. "White teeth. Good hair. Hot bods and big dicks. I got it. Message received, Grace." She shook her head and started to pull away, but he held her tighter. "You were with quality men. They were with a quality woman. You don't have to worry that I don't know what I'm getting into. You've warned me this isn't going to be easy. What I need now is for you to get that shit out of your head." He pulled back and held her gaze. "This isn't just about me doing you a favor. I've wanted you for a long time."

When she started to look away, he cupped her chin and refused to let her. "I think you're beautiful. You turn me on more than any woman has in a long, long time. I need this, Dixie, just as much as you need it. Something's been missing from my life. I don't know what it is, but what I do know is the idea of being with you, and yes, the idea of proving to you there's not one damn thing wrong with you, has me jazzed up and excited. Very excited," he whispered. "You with me?"

"Max—"

"Are you with me, Grace?"

She hesitated, her anxiety and doubt apparent. Then, tentatively, she nodded.

"Good," he said, feeling like he'd crossed over some kind of finish line when in reality the race had barely begun. "Now, I'm assuming Lucy knows you're with me and is heading back to your hotel on her own?"

She nodded again, seeming to have gone mute. He smiled and kissed her forehead. "Have you ever parked?" he asked.

"Parked?" she asked with a crinkle between her brows. She looked over at his car, a sleek black Audi.

"Yeah, as in, made out in a car. Until the windows got all steamy. Until you were ready to rip off your clothes and do it regardless of who might come along and find you."

She swallowed hard, and Max couldn't help himself.

He reached out and lightly caressed her throat with the pads of his fingers. She shivered.

He clenched his teeth to contain his own moan.

She was as responsive as hell. He couldn't wait to see what else made her shiver. And shake. And scream.

"In college," she whispered, her eyes getting drowsy with memory.

"Then let's get in the car, Grace. Because I want to hear more about what you were like in college. Including what you liked then, what you like now, and what you think you might like but have been too embarrassed to admit."

5

Max's Magic Rule #6:
Always leave them wanting more.

Good Lord, Grace thought. I'm in a parked car with Max Dalton. And he told me he needs me. He wants me to give up control so he can give me a big O. So why am I sitting here pressed against the passenger door? And why isn't he reaching over the center console and touching me?

Max, who'd just pulled his car into a lookout point with a stunning view of the Las Vegas Strip, turned toward her. "Locals call this place Love with a View. I've never actually been up here but I've meaning to check it out."

She gazed at the twinkling lights and far-off desert scape.

"It's pretty," she said. She tried to relax and started with unfolding her hands from her lap. Her palms were sweaty but she resisted wiping them on her skirt.

She wasn't sure how he planned on starting to steam

up the windows, but when he asked, "So, what were you like in college?" she blinked in surprise.

"You really want to talk about that?"

"It's a good place to start."

"Start what?"

"Start talking, Grace," he said gently.

"I thought you wanted to make out and steam up some windows."

"We'll work our way up to that. You said you had your first sexual experience with your college boyfriend. What was his name?"

Grace just stared at Max, not sure why they were working their way up to anything. And really not sure why working their way up meant telling Max her ex-boyfriend's name.

She shifted uncomfortably in her seat. "He's really not relevant."

"So humor me."

"His name was Neil."

"And you said Neil was a good lover. That you enjoyed sex with him for... two years, wasn't it?"

"A little less than that considering we went out six months before we actually had sex, but that's about right, yes."

"Since you waited until college, waited six months with Neil, sex is meaningful to you. Did you wait for religious reasons?"

"No."

"Then why?"

She shrugged. "I didn't want to give myself to just anyone."

He nodded, his eyes darkening, and she wondered what he was thinking. She was obviously willing to give herself to *him*. "Before that, before you had a boyfriend, did you experiment with sex? Make out in high school?"

"Not really," she said.

"Did you masturbate?"

She felt her face getting warm but tried to appear composed. "Sure."

"You never had any problem getting off by yourself and that's still true?"

"Yes, it's still true. But I've got to tell you, Max. This is starting to feel like a routine doctor's appointment. And I'm not turned on at all. I—"

She gasped when Max reached over, put his hand on her thigh and leaned in close. "Concentrate, Grace. Because I'm betting if I put my hand down your panties right now, you'd be wet. Shall I find out?"

She swallowed hard, concentrated and realized he was right. She'd been in her head, focusing on the seeming mundane questions he was asking her, but her body was obviously going where Max wanted. She was wet. She actually ached. But that didn't mean she wanted to talk about sex with him.

Listening to him say sexy things to her, fine.

But her? While she could surprise people with her sexuality and her piercings and her other secrets, one thing she'd never been good at was talking about sex. The only thing that mattered during sex was action, whether she could make a guy feel good and whether he could do the same for her.

She covered his hand with her own. "Max—"

"I was going to spend a little more time exploring your sexual history, but I certainly don't want this encounter to seem clinical. So let's change the subject. What gets you off?"

She tried to move back, but he caught her hand. "Why do we have to talk about mechanics?"

Without preamble, he slipped his free hand into the crease between her thighs. His hand didn't get far between her closed legs, but it got far enough. "Because talking about sex gets you hot."

"No, listening to *you* talk about sex gets me hot, but I'm not any good at it."

"Or maybe it just makes you uncomfortable. And what we're going to be doing isn't about comfort. I'm going to push you, a lot. Contrary to what you might think, I'm not just a sex toy and sex isn't just about the physical. It's psychological. Emotional. It's about tapping into a woman's fantasies even if she doesn't know what they are or is unwilling to admit them to herself. I'm going to find out your fantasies even if I have to drag them out of you. Now what gets you off?"

"I—I'm not sure what you're asking. And can you move your hand, please," she asked, her voice high and breathy. "I—I can't think straight when you're touching me."

"I'm going to be touching you a whole lot more. Get used to it. Now let me rephrase my question so you understand. When you're pleasuring yourself, how do you do it? Do you use a toy?"

Okay, fine. He wanted to push her to talk. She could do that. "Some—sometimes. Most of the time."

"What kind of toys?"

"A vibrator?" Oh no. Was she asking him or telling him?

"Do you ever use a dildo?"

"No."

"Why not?"

"I—I don't know. I don't need it. I can make myself come with the vibrator and my—my…"

"You use your fingers?" It was the barest movement, but he rubbed against her center. She gasped and automatically reached out with her one free hand to grab his wrist. She didn't pull him away, however. She just held him. Waiting.

"Yes." She closed her eyes, focusing on his touch. Her words.

"So you focus on your clit and fuck yourself with your fingers. And how long does it usually take to make yourself come that way?"

"Not long. Maybe… ten minutes?" More like five since she'd gotten the clit ring, but she wasn't about to tell him that.

"What do you think of while you're doing it? Who do you think of?"

Her eyes flew open.

"Max—"

"You ever think of me?"

With the barest of movements, she nodded.

"Ah, Grace. That's good. That's fucking fabulous. In your fantasies, what am I doing to you?"

Again, she tried to pull away. Again, he wouldn't let her. "What's wrong? What are you embarrassed of?"

"Nothing." Everything.

"Then tell me what I do to you. Do I eat you out?"

His words caused such a spike of arousal that she automatically flinched away from it. Maybe this had all been a really bad idea. "Why are you being so crude?" she asked. He must have sensed the panic in her voice because he straightened and took his hands off her. She barely stopped herself from whimpering in protest.

"You think I'm being crude?"

"Aren't you?"

"Haven't men talked dirty to you before?"

"Yes. But with you… I don't know… I just thought you'd have more finesse. That you'd be more… romantic."

"When it comes to sex, Grace, I'm whatever a woman needs me to be."

"And you think I need a man who's crude?"

"Baby, I think you need a man who's willing to talk straight. One who's willing to move beyond what one might expect and get down to business with giving you what you need. To know what you need, I need to ask questions and not be held back by your sense of modesty. I want to give it to you good, Grace, and that means knowing what'll make you come."

"Nothing," she said quickly. "Nothing makes me come with a man and it isn't as if I haven't tried. I've never been good at talking about sex, but I'm not a prude. I've tried plenty of things, with plenty of men, and all of them have failed."

Max grinned. "You forget you're in Vegas. And you forget how motivated I am. Make no mistake. You're about to get lucky."

"Does that mean we're actually going to stop lollygagging around and have sex now?"

"I think I've got a pretty good handle on what you need and how we're going to get you where you need to go."

"What exactly do I need?"

"A partner who wants to play. One who's willing to push you while at the same time holding off giving you his dick until you're wild for it. One who's going to prove he's not settling, but enjoying every fucking second of that exquisite torture right along with you. There's no end goal, because you're not in control of when intercourse actually happens. He is. *I am.* And my whole goal will be to string things out. Find out how far we can go without coming. For us, sex is going to be about experimenting and feeling and getting jacked up hot, but not giving in. We're going to go for broke until one of us loses control and takes the other. And I'm going to let you in on a secret. *You* are going to do the taking, but *I'm* going to control when it happens."

She was breathing so fast she was afraid she was going to pass out. She struggled to form coherent speech. "So what you're saying is the way you're going to give me an orgasm is by refusing to let me orgasm?"

"By building it up then controlling when it happens. For you and for me."

"Sounds frustrating for both of us and I've had enough frustration as it is."

"Any frustration you suffer during the process will be worth it, don't worry about that."

"Don't worry about totally placing myself in your hands?" She snorted. "You don't ask a lot, do you?"

"I'm asking for what I think you need. And Grace that includes canceling your flight tomorrow."

* * *

Max watched Grace squirm in her seat. He knew appearances could be deceiving, but damn if she didn't look like she was about to come without the aid of his fingers, tongue or dick. God knew he felt close to coming himself.

It was beyond fun rattling Grace and tempting her inner vixen to come out and play, even as she struggled to retain that blasted control of hers.

The control she was still clinging to.

"And stay how long?" she asked.

"A week should do the trick."

She laughed nervously. "I—I can't stay in Vegas that long."

"Why not? Melina said you were taking time off from work."

When she remained silent, he said, "Grace, you've got a plan for yourself. One that doesn't involve California or career. You want me to give you something before you start your plan, but you have to give me a fair shot. One night to give you something all your lovers haven't been able to? One night to make you feel pressured and like a failure if it doesn't happen? No way. The way to get you where you want is to keep you in the dark, literally and figuratively."

"So you plan on keeping me locked in a dark bedroom?"

"I know what I've got planned. Other than what I've already told you, you don't and you're not going to. That's the point. If we're going to do this, we're doing it all the way. And that means total trust by you. And total openness to whatever may come."

"I don't know if I can give you that. Total openness? Come on. I have no idea what kink you're into." She was obviously striving to be funny, but he didn't give her the out.

"I'm into a lot of things. But the only thing we're going to do, or I'm going to do to you, is what you're into. I will push you to stretch your boundaries and inhibitions, but I will never do anything you don't like or cause you pain. If I do, all you have to do is say no and I'll stop."

"So no is my safe word?"

He paused and studied her. "Sounds like you know a thing or two about kink. You ever need a safe word before?"

"No. And I didn't mean—"

"I know exactly what you meant and we'll explore it later, quite thoroughly. What's your favorite fruit?"

"What?"

"A safe word is one you wouldn't normally say during sex but one you can easily remember. What's your favorite fruit?"

"Mango."

"Then that'll be your safe word."

She was tempted to give in. He could see it in her eyes. In the way she bit her lip and looked at him as if he was a big slice of chocolate cake—and she was starving. But she held back. Out of fear. Out of honesty. Given her reluctance to talk dirty and verbalize her desires, he was getting that words meant something to Grace. She didn't use them lightly. And she *really* didn't want to say she'd give him total control when she wasn't sure she actually could.

"What about your plans?" she asked, obviously trying to buy herself some time. "Back at the house—you said you need to draw more attention to your show by drumming up press. How will you have time for that and me?"

"I'll make time."

"I wouldn't feel comfortable. That is, I wouldn't want…"

"You wouldn't want me to go from touching you to touching another woman?"

"More like the other way around."

"That's not a problem. You said it yourself, what I'm going to be doing is about drumming up press. That means being seen with women not having sex with them."

"You kissed Elizabeth," she reminded him.

"And I won't be seeing her for another week. When I do, we might pretend some more, but we're certainly not going to have sex."

"Even so…"

"You're the only woman I'm interested in right now, Dixie."

"What if that changes?"

"It won't."

"But what if it does?"

"I'll deal with it. And that will mean talking to you before I betray your trust."

"I don't want press," she said. "I'm dealing with stuff you don't know about, Max. Stuff that means I need total privacy. If you can't give me that…"

He immediately wanted to grill her about what "stuff" she was talking about.

One thing at a time.

"I promise I'll keep you out of my business. We're the only people who will know we're seeing each other. With my performance schedule and having to work the bars, we won't have tons of time together, but the time I do have, I'll devote to you."

She thought about it then seemed to come to a conclusion. "Okay. Under those conditions, I'll try to be open to whatever you suggest."

He wished he could let it go at that, but he couldn't. She was waffling, and he needed to be very clear about what he was asking for. And what she'd be agreeing to. "*Trying* to be open isn't going to be enough. You place yourself in my hands completely—with the exception of anything that you don't like *after* you've given me a fair shot at persuading you. You have to commit to letting me do everything I can to pleasure you and trust I'll know when the time is right for you to go all the way."

Her expression turned mutinous. "That doesn't make sense. *I* already know what I like. *I* already know what works for me. I don't mind giving up control, but only to a point."

"And it's that point I have to push you past, Grace. *I* don't have a problem with you being in control, but I'll sure have a problem when your control cock-blocks me. Better to reach an understanding now."

"Cock-blocks you?" she practically choked out.

He leaned into her. "Yeah, because given your past, it will happen. And my cock wants what you're control is hell-bent on blocking. Let me have it. Let me have all of you or tell me what you're afraid of. Because it shouldn't be this hard."

She flushed, looked away, then forced herself to meet

his gaze again. "Easy for you to say. Have you ever given your body and your orgasms over to someone else?"

"I've never had the issues you do," he said quietly, to which she had no response. "So are we going to do this or not? You know I won't hurt you. You know what I want to give you. I can't unless you trust me in a way you haven't trusted any of your partners."

He was saying it straight out so she couldn't misunderstand. She looked scared as shit but tried to rally. "I did trust them. I trust you..."

"Words are easy, Dixie. You might think you've trusted your lovers because you've let yourself be topped. Because you've let a man blindfold and tie you up. But I'll bet anything you maintained control even then, no matter how it looked. If you think you trusted them with all of you, you're wrong. And it'll be my job to prove it to you."

He saw the conflicting emotions in her eyes and felt her pain. The fact she was still clinging to the very *idea* of control told him she more than liked it. She needed it. Just like she needed to keep some part of herself from others even out of bed.

She shook her head and he knew he was losing her.

"I don't know. Maybe this is a bad idea. Let's just—"

"What if I give up control to you?" he asked abruptly.

She looked startled, then intrigued. "What?"

He hesitated. Cursed himself. What the hell was he doing? But he'd already said he wouldn't allow himself to come unless she did. Why not go all the way if it made her feel better about what she was going to be giving up?

"You said it was easy for me to tell you to give up control, when I haven't done the same thing myself."

She nodded.

"So before you place yourself in my hands, how about I place myself in yours?"

"What does that mean?"

"You say you're adventurous. Show me. Control my pleasure and decide when it's time for me to come. Who knows, maybe that's what'll get you off. If it doesn't, then we'll try things my way."

Silence stretched between them as she thought about it. He practically saw the gears turning in her head.

"I need to think about it. Can—can I take the night? To make sure I can clear my schedule, I mean."

Disappointment crashed through him, but he nodded. "Sure, Grace."

He drove her to her hotel and pulled up in front. To his amusement, when they got out of the car, she held out her hand. "No matter what, thank you, Max. I mean it."

His mouth tipped up and he shook his head. "I think we can end this night with something better than a handshake, don't you?"

"Um…sure," she said.

She waited for him to move toward her. When he didn't, she leaned closer and kissed him.

She was complex and so was the way she kissed. She started slow and easy, a whisper of soft caresses that drew him in. Then when he started to relax, she amped things up. Nipped. Sucked. Made him groan and bury his hands in her hair and, before he knew what he was doing, start to take over. He tipped her head to the side, giving him better access to her mouth and plunged his tongue inside her. Pushing her back against his car, he lapped her up and pressed against her until a car honked and someone whistled.

He pulled away.

Her breath hitched and puffed against his mouth. She wanted more. And so did he.

It took everything he had, but he took several steps back.

She'd said she needed time and he was going to give that to her.

"Take tonight, Grace. If you decide you can accept my terms, let me know. Otherwise, catch that plane tomorrow and know that I wish you well."

6

Max's Magic Rule #7:
Never let a beautiful woman upstage you.

"Melina told me you were concerned about Grace. You finally track her down and make your move?"

Max blinked. Considering he was right in the middle of bench-pressing two hundred and fifty pounds, he didn't answer his brother, who was spotting him, right away. It had been less than twenty-four hours since he saw Grace, but for all he knew, she was heading to the airport to catch her flight right now. To make sure he didn't do something stupid like try to stop her at the airport and fall to his knees begging for another chance at bedding her, he'd called his brother to meet him at the gym. Like he'd told her, he needed Grace's total trust if he had any hope of giving her what she wanted. Without that...

After he settled the free weights in place, he sat up and cocked a brow at Rhys. His brother already saw too damn much. On the off chance Grace didn't get on that plane today, he needed to throw him off the scent. "Make my move? What are you, in sixth grade?" he asked, injecting an "as if" tone into his voice.

Rhys rolled his eyes. "Right, like you haven't wanted a piece of her since you heard her voice? She's gorgeous. Her accent is sexy as hell. And all those little Southernisms she spouts?" He paused, obviously waiting for Max to fill in the blank.

"Adorable," Max said. They were just one more thing he enjoyed about Grace. One second he wanted to shove her against a wall and fuck her hard, the next he wanted to laugh at the crazy things coming out of her mouth. He wondered how many southern idioms she had in her back pocket.

He choked back a laugh when his brother scowled. "I don't get you, Max. You hit everything else, why not Grace?"

Max took the towel lying around his neck and wiped his brow. "She's Melina's friend. I fuck her and that fucks up everything." He shrugged, again suggesting his disinterest rather than lying flat out.

Rhys's shrug mimicked his. "So what's the plan for tonight?"

Max frowned. He hadn't expected Rhys to accept his excuse so easily. He found himself wanting to continue talking about Grace. To give in and do what he always wanted to do but never had—grill Rhys about what he knew about his wife's friend. He wanted to know what her hobbies were. What kind of movies she liked. What her favorite ice cream was. All he had were the little bits of information Melina had dropped in conversation over the years and what he'd learned about Grace last night, which wasn't enough. But he contented himself with the knowledge that he probably knew things about her that Rhys didn't—like the fact she'd dated guys with big dicks. And that she made out like a porn queen.

Just thinking about those lips she'd laid on him last night had him wanting more and getting hard—not a good thing when he was wearing thin, dry-weave shorts at a gym.

He forced himself to answer Rhys. "Same as usual as far as I know. Rehearsal. Show. Promoting the show." Unless Grace had decided to stay in town and grant him the opportunity to add something even more spectacular to his agenda.

"You heard from Elizabeth?"

"Only a voicemail, thanking me again and checking in."

"She's a good friend. Now that her husband's out of the picture, you think anything might happen between you two again?"

Not at all, Max thought. First, because her husband wasn't out of the picture. Not as far as her heart was concerned. Second, the only woman Max was interested in right now was Grace.

"Hey," Rhys said, nudging him with his elbow. "Look who we're *not* talking about."

Max followed his brother's line of sight and barely stopped himself from pumping his fist in the air.

It looked like Lady Luck was sidling closer and closer.

Grace stood at the check-in counter, dressed in black spandex shorts and a pale pink sports tank that left a few inches of her lower back exposed. Her head was bent as she signed some papers, her ponytail revealing her neck and upper back. Above and below her tank, Max could see tattoos, which had always been covered before. The tattoos were curved lines, spaced about an inch apart. The lines, at least what he could see of them, created a shape that resembled half a feather. He had no idea whether all those curved lines met in the middle of her back to form some kind of recognizable image but he wanted to find out. More than that, he wanted to trace the patterns with his tongue, then work downward until he could kiss, suck and bite the curvy flesh of her ass and explore the buttery-soft skin between her legs.

The tattoos were just another facet of Grace. Bold yet mysterious. Trendy yet subdued. She wasn't hiding them, but she wasn't revealing them either. Just like she wasn't hiding her desire for an orgasm, but—despite the fact she was right here in front of him—he'd still bet she wasn't willing to bare all she was, *give* all she was, to get it.

Not unless he continued to push her.

In a moment, she straightened, dug around in the large workout bag slung over her shoulder, and produced what Max figured was a credit card. The young woman helping her at the counter took it and swiped it through a register.

"She's staying in Vegas for another week," Rhys said. "But you knew that already, didn't you?"

"What?" Max said absently, keeping his eyes on Grace as she headed toward the women's locker room. He could feel the grin trying to take over his face.

Then he remembered he'd promised to give her total control and it tempered his feelings of victory and anticipation. His unease grew the longer Rhys stared at him. Was his brother going to say anything, or burn him with laser eyes all day?

Max finally turned toward him. "She's staying for a week? Why would you think I already knew that?"

"You called Melina last night and found out where she was. Next thing I know, Grace has decided to extend her trip. Quit bullshitting me, Max. I need to know *you* know what you're getting into. Because somehow I don't think you do."

"I'm not getting into anything." Besides Grace's pants, he thought. But Grace wasn't some conquest to bed. She was one of his sister-in-law's best friends. He was determined to take care with her, and that meant respecting her desire for privacy. Too bad it would be creepy for him to follow her. It'd be fun to watch her bouncing up and down doing aerobics, or displaying her ass as she did a Downward Dog.

"Max," Rhys said.

"Don't you have a pregnant wife to get home to?"

His brother sighed. "I most certainly do. And to tell

you the truth, she hasn't been feeling well."

Max's good humor immediately fled. "What's going on? Do you need to take more time off?"

"She and the doctor assure me it's just normal aches and pains. And believe me, I'm taking plenty of time off to be with her. So much she's worried she's interfering with work."

"Well don't let that stop you."

"Of course not. But you know the baby blankets Mom's been working on? She finished them early and wants me to pick them up before they leave for Hawaii. I'd planned on driving there today. Only…"

"No problem. I'll swing by and pick them up for you."

Rhys's expression turned to one of relief. "That would be great. I'll head home and watch a movie with Melina."

"Is that all?"

When Rhys hesitated, Max understood. "Wait. Are you that concerned? That you're afraid to—"

Rhys shook his head. "We've been cleared to have as much sex as we want. Only she's so tired lately. So fragile…"

"If Melina heard you say that, she'd kick your ass. Besides, even if most of her old clothes don't fit her right now, I'm betting a certain bikini still does. Break it out and neither one of you will be tired for long."

Rhys laughed and rubbed the back of his neck. "You're right. She *would* kick my ass. Thanks, Max."

"No problem. Now run along and have sex with your hot pregnant wife. Magician's orders."

The hand Rhys clapped on Max's shoulder said it all. After Rhys left, Max headed toward the check-in counter.

The young woman who'd helped Grace a few minutes earlier smiled at him and leaned against the countertop, not so surreptitiously pressing her breasts together with her elbows. "May I help you, Mr. Dalton?"

He flashed her a mega-watt smile. Even counter girls expected him to flirt with them. All women did.

But right now, all he wanted was peace of mind. And that meant figuring out why Grace hadn't yet come out of the women's locker room.

"Hiya, sweetheart," he said smoothly, leaning against the counter and getting close to the girl, who giggled nervously. "I'm looking for my friend, Grace. She was supposed to meet me but I'm not seeing where she went. Maybe she got the time wrong?"

The girl—Kenya, according to her nametag—pulled back a little but her smile widened. "Yes, she was just here. She told me you might be joining her. That you're working on something for your show?"

What the hell? Why would Grace have told her that? "Sure. Something for the show. So where is she waiting for me?"

He looked around. The main gym, with various elliptical and treadmill machines, and a weight-lifting circuit, sat surrounded on three sides by glass-walled rooms. In the first room, sweaty women jumped and rotated to music, and in the second room, a combination of men and women were in the middle of a yoga practice.

The third room was empty.

Kenya giggled again, the sound grating on his nerves. He wasn't sure he'd ever heard Grace giggle, but he was pretty sure it wouldn't annoy him. Everything about her fascinated him. That wasn't bound to last, but right now...

"She's in one of the private dance studios. Probably took the back door through the women's locker room. You can get there through that hallway." She tipped her head behind her. "It has everything you'll need," she said with another giggle.

"What do mean?"

"It's set up for pole-dancing."

His combined shock and excitement nearly staggered him.

Grace was in a studio meant for pole dancing. Just the thought sent blood pounding everywhere but his brain, where he needed it the most. Instead, he stood there in total guy mode, with a major hard-on and his knuckles practically dragging on the ground. But then he jerked into action and headed down the hall.

He did so with a huge smile, feeling like he was following the yellow brick road.

* * *

Bluesy pop music was already playing on Grace's smart phone, the lyrics echoing her hopes to soon have Max Dalton begging her for mercy.

She'd had no clue he'd be at the gym. The moment

she'd seen him and Rhys, she'd wanted to turn and run. Her own cowardice had appalled her. It didn't matter that she'd gotten up the nerve to cancel her flight. She'd felt shaky and unsure of herself, and by reserving the gym's pole dancing studio, she'd hoped to exhaust her body and clear her mind, at least for an hour.

A minute after seeing Max, so damn sexy in his workout clothes, his biceps bulging as he lifted weights, her nerves completely disappeared. An idea formed instead. Why not let him watch her on the pole? Surely that would help her regain the upper-hand in the small game they were playing. But she wasn't about to invite Max directly, not with Rhys there. She figured if he was interested enough to track her down, however...

She peeked outside the studio window, which was tinted so she could see out but no one could see in. Her pulse accelerated when she saw Max heading up the hallway toward her.

She scrambled to the metal pole at the front of the room. As she did, she caught sight of her image in the mirrored wall. She looked decent in her workout clothes but not terribly seductive. Her expression, however? Even she could see the excitement. She looked youthful and daring and free. How had Max managed to significantly diminish her stress and anxiety over Logan Cooper and her baby plan in one night?

She'd taken enough pole-dancing classes back home to know exactly what she was doing. In a matter of seconds, she'd climbed up the pole, hooked her calves around it, then lowered herself until her chest was pressed against the pole and she was hanging upside down in a basic inversion. Then she braced her elbows and gripped the pole with her right hand about two feet higher than the left. Her instructors called it a split grip.

When she heard his footsteps just outside the door, she kept her right calf hooked around the pole but released her left leg and pressed it behind her, keeping her knee bent so the toes of her left foot pointed toward the floor. The position stretched her thigh muscles and her pant fabric pressed tight against her body, stimulating her clit ring. It felt good. It felt twice as good because she knew Max was coming.

She heard the door open. "Grace? *Jesus*."

A quick glance confirmed he looked shocked... and aroused. With a loud click, he shut the door behind him and locked it.

When Max stepped toward her, she said somewhat breathlessly, "Sit. And just watch, Max. No talking. No hands."

He saw the chair in the corner. And sat.

Then watched as she proceeded to do the rest of the routine she'd learned. It involved contorting her body in ways that sparked her imagination. She'd bet it did his, too. That was the whole point.

She squatted and spun, undulated, frisked the pole, and even managed to pull off a crescent—an advanced move that ended with her sliding down the pole with her body contorted into the shape of a crescent moon.

By the time she was done and standing with both feet on the ground, his expression was tight. Lids heavy. His fists clenched. Hot flags of color rode his cheeks. He looked thoroughly aroused. And she felt like she was going to go off like a firecracker.

He obviously hadn't believed it himself, but maybe he'd been right the night before, when he'd said controlling his arousal might be the thing that got her off. She'd hurt when she'd lain in her bed last night. Ached for him. And even after she'd made herself come, she'd still ached.

She ached *now*. Her body fairly throbbed and she could almost smell the arousal—hers and Max's—in the air.

More than ever she needed to convince him she was no shrinking violet when it came to sex. That he could trust her to give both of them something good even if she didn't give him everything.

He sat rigidly, sucking in breaths as if he'd just run a marathon, waiting to see what she'd do next. Her plan had been to blow his mind, then blow him a kiss and walk out, leaving him to suffer. Instead, instinct moved her toward him.

The way he sat, thighs slightly spayed, eyes glued to her, was so hot, so tempting, she couldn't end things here. Only she had to keep the upper-hand.

"Do you want more?" she asked, her voice dark and raspy.

Instead of speaking, he inclined his head slightly, a

facsimile of a nod.

"Do you go to strip clubs?"

He hesitated only slightly. "I have."

"Have you ever had a lap dance?"

"Yes."

She liked his honesty, as well as the fact he didn't look ashamed or embarrassed. "I assume you looked but didn't touch?"

"That's right. But…"

"But what?"

"But if you dance in my lap, Grace, I'm not sure I'll be able to keep myself from touching you."

His honesty stole her breath. It made heat spread through her. Made her feel powerful and sexy and in control. See? She liked this. She didn't need to give up control in order to get turned on. In fact, the more control she wielded, the hotter she got. She'd prove it to him.

"But you *will* have to keep yourself from touching me. I'm in control here. That's what you promised me and that's what I want."

For a minute, he looked ready to argue with her, then the tension seemed to seep out of him. He slouched lower in his chair and made a production of putting his hands behind the back of his head. The position emphasized his muscled shoulders, biceps, and chest, making her think of a predator. "Go ahead and have your fun, Dixie."

Dixie. She loved that something as simple as her southern roots had created an intimate bond between them, even if it was only a nickname.

Max continued speaking. "Just remember you asked for it when you're the one being controlled."

She refused to acknowledge how her core clenched with need. That's never going to happen, she told herself. It doesn't have to. Not if I do this right. She stole a quick glance at the one-way window and locked door. Could she actually give Max a lap dance, then make him come right here and now?

"Don't worry about my memory, Sugar. Worry about yours. Because right now I'm going to make you forget everything but me."

She advanced to within three feet of him. With her back arched, feet slightly more than hip-width apart and her toes turned out, she began a slow grinding circle. Max's gaze stayed glued to her hips as she bent her knees then straightened. She repeated the movement before turning her back to him. With straight legs, she bent forward slightly, looked over her shoulder at him then slapped first one ass cheek then the other. "Have you ever spanked your lovers, Max?"

He visibly swallowed. "I've told you before, Grace. I've done whatever my lovers needed. Do you enjoy being spanked?"

"As I think I'm demonstrating, I prefer to be in charge."

He smiled thinly. "Keep telling yourself that, baby."

She frowned. She wasn't getting her message across. Determinedly, she danced into the triangle made by Max's open legs, back still to him, feet together. Bending her knees but keeping her back straight, she placed her hands on Max's knees. His body immediately tensed at her touch. Slowly, she lowered her bottom toward his lap until she just made contact. Then, keeping her hands on his knees for support, she grinded down, moving her hips in a circular motion.

"Doesn't that feel nice as pie, Max? When I'm done playing with you," she said, "I'm going back to my hotel and I'm going to take care of myself in a way that's guaranteed to get me off. Next time, if you want to be the one to give me an orgasm, trust that I know what I need. Stop making things so hard on yourself. Whether we label it control or not, let me direct you so you can get me there. And I promise I'll give you what you need, too."

When he didn't respond, she turned and looked at him over her shoulder.

He was breathing hard again. He remained still, but he looked ready to explode. He smiled evilly. "Oh, I'm going to give you what you need, Grace. I guarantee it. And when I have, you're going to dance for me again. Only you're going to do it *naked*. You're going to do it while I have my hands and mouth on you. And you're going to know exactly who's in control."

Her movements faltered before she got going again. "You're spoiled. Too used to getting your own way. But I can see how much this is working for you, Max."

"It's definitely working for me," he said. "Everything you do works for me. Kiss me."

She turned back again, having to block his look of

need since it reflected everything she was feeling herself. "Uh-uh. This is my thing, remember? I get to give instructions."

"Then tell me what you want."

"I'll show you instead."

Turning to face him, she moved closer, gently leaned forward, and placed her hands on either side of his chair. Slowly, she pressed her breasts toward his face, then brushed from side to side, stroking the end of his nose with her nipples. The gentle pressure against her piercings made her nipples instantly harden into tight points. As if connected by an invisible cord, sharp tingles traveled from her nipples to the piercing at her clit. Her body involuntarily jerked, and she rubbed her nipples against him even harder.

He groaned and she felt a rush of victory sweep through her. Before she knew it, however, he'd opened his mouth and covered one nipple through her top. The heat and suction was so sudden and so amazing that she cried out.

Their gazes locked, giving her a perfect view of his cheeks hollowing as he sucked her. She should have moved back and scolded him, but she hesitated. What he was doing felt good. So, so good. But she could see by the gleam of satisfaction in his eyes that he thought he'd won, stealing control away from her.

She dropped her hand to his groin and cupped him through his shorts. His eyes widened even as his mouth loosened. She tried to move away, but his hands came up and gripped her hips.

She stroked him harder. Tighter. "I'm in charge," she said breathlessly. "Let go or you 'n me are gonna mix."

He laughed. "Is that a promise or a threat?"

"Both. Let go, Max."

"Only if you promise you won't," he said.

She smiled at the naked need in his voice and, without realizing what she was doing, agreed. "I promise."

When he released her she kept her word, continuing to explore his length and rigidity.

"Show me your piercings."

"Later," she said, rubbing against his face again while gripping him tightly.

He tipped his head back, and she couldn't resist licking and nibbling at his throat. Getting more frantic, he arched his hips into her touch but she could tell he wasn't anywhere close to coming.

Time to amp things up even more.

She dropped to her knees.

His head tilted down, eyes narrowed, and he watched as she teasingly traced his waistband with her fingertips.

"Do you want to come?"

"I want you," he said.

Those three words dripped with such yearning that she almost caved. Almost told him to take whatever he needed. She wouldn't care if she came or not. It would feel so good to hold him. To feel him slide inside her.

"I want to see your tattoo and your piercings. I want to see where else you're pierced. I want to feel your nipple piercings against my tongue even as I fuck you. But this isn't about what I want. I'm yours to control, remember? For my pleasure. For yours. You want to suck my dick? Suck it. But only because it will make you hot."

She was already hotter than blue blazes yet she knew sucking him off would indeed make her hotter. She wanted to feel him against her core even more. She ached so badly. And he'd said he'd give her anything she wanted. No, he'd implied she could take it.

Without conscious thought, she straddled him, resting her hands on his shoulders. Swiftly, she began grinding down on him, their thin clothes barely any protection against the delicious friction that sent ripples of electric sensation zipping through her veins. She was sure he could feel how wet she was, and how much wetter she became with each second that passed. She could barely resist tearing their clothes off and shoving him inside her. But that would require breaking contact with him, and right now... right now...

Their breaths soughed together, loud and erratic. His deep groans mingled with her high cries of excitement. He gave her the illusion of control, not touching her, but the piercing intensity of his gaze kept her trapped as surely as the feel of his body did.

She closed her eyes, focusing on the rise of pleasure inside her. She could feel it building and building and building. But at some point, it faltered and she almost cried out in despair.

"You gonna come, baby?" he asked, causing her eyes

to pop open. "You going to get what you need like this? Cause this is all for you."

His heated words of encouragement made her body tighten and desire surged through her again. Her movements grew almost frantic as she sought release.

But it remained outside her grasp.

It wasn't going to happen. No matter how badly she wanted it, no matter how determined she'd been to make him hot and take control of her own sexuality, she was going to fail again.

With a small whimper, she stopped moving and collapsed into him, burying her face in his neck. Her fingers clung tightly to his T-shirt as frustration thrummed through her. Immediately, he wrapped his arms around her, one hand cupping the back of her neck while the other rubbed soothing circles on her back.

She was so frustrated and embarrassed that she wanted to cry, but somehow she managed not to. Minutes passed. Eventually, she tried to pull away, but he stopped her.

She refused to look at him, instead staring at the floor. All she could think about was escaping his intense gaze. If she'd only stuck with her plan, directing and controlling his pleasure, she wouldn't have to deal with having another talk about her sexual defects. Maybe it wasn't too late…

She tried to slip away again, this time to return to where she'd been before, on her knees. His arms tightened, refusing to let her go.

"Look at me, Grace."

With a sigh, she did.

"It's okay..."

She laughed harshly. "Nothing about this is okay."

He shook her slightly. "There's nothing wrong with you."

"How can you say that? I was into it. What we were doing was hot. I should have been able to—"

"Grind against me in a public gym for less than five minutes and make yourself come?"

"Five minutes, five hours, it wouldn't have mattered. It wouldn't matter where we were, either. I was almost there. I always *almost* get there. I just can't cross the finish line."

She used more force to pull away from him and this time he let her go. With a sigh and a teasing smile, he also stood. "Five hours? Really?"

She rolled her eyes. "You know what I mean."

Arms crossed, he leaned against the wall. "What I know is you've somehow gotten it into your head that if you can't orgasm, sexual pleasure isn't worth a damn."

"Like you think any differently? Would you be okay settling for morsels that only leave you starving for a full meal?"

"I wouldn't be okay with it. But I hope I'd appreciate what I could get. And I'd keep working toward more."

"I guess I'm just not as enlightened as you are."

"No. You're frustrated because you've been dealing with the reality of this for years. I get it. But you're also embarrassed and ready to give up as a result. *Again*. And I'm telling you I'm not going to let that happen."

"It's not up to you. Look, I'm sorry for wasting your time but I can't do this again. Not with you. Not with anyone. But thank you for all your help."

She moved toward the door.

He straightened and stepped in front of it, blocking her escape.

He stared at her.

She stared back.

She waited for him to give up and move aside.

He didn't.

"Max?"

"Giving over control to me scares you that much, doesn't it?"

"Max—"

He stepped toward her and she instinctively backed up. He kept coming. She kept backing away. Until her back hit the wall and he caged her in with his arms on either side. He leaned in close, until she saw nothing but the pure perfection of his green eyes. "We had a deal. I gave it up and you enjoyed it. No, you didn't go all the way, but I'm not a quitter and neither are you, Dixie. We've barely gotten started."

She flattened her palms on his chest and pushed, not budging him an inch. Beneath his workout shirt, he was muscled. Hard. Luscious. She curled her fingers into fists. "What's the point in getting started? You want me to admit I want you? That I see you as more than a tool to get me off? Fine. I want you, Max. Y. O. U. But that doesn't matter. Even with you giving me anything and everything I want, I can't even—"

He took hold of her arms and lightly shook her. "I haven't given you everything you want, Grace, because I haven't figured out what that is. Despite your attempts to protect yourself, I will. You want me? Well, I want *you*," he said. "I want to explore you. I want to savor you. And I want you to do the same with me. I want to prove doing those things is a reward in and of itself, and worth any frustration you might have to deal with."

"You're talking in circles. One second you say you'll get me off. The next you're telling me I need to accept getting off isn't necessary to enjoy sex. You really think you're good enough to juggle both those concepts at once?"

"I think *we're* going to be that good. You had your turn at control. It's only fair you give me mine."

She stared at him. "I don't know what you want me to say. All I can say is what I said before. I'll *try*."

He seemed to ponder her words before reaching some mysterious conclusion, after which he released her, stepped back and nodded. "Fine. This time, I'm willing to accept that answer."

"Why now and not before?"

"Because now I'm beginning to understand the reason you came to me the other night isn't because of my reputation as a playboy, but as a bad boy."

"What does that mean?"

"It means you giving up control isn't what you need, Grace. Me taking it away from you is."

* * *

"You're high as a kite."

"Am I?"

"You are if you think I'm going to let you 'take' anything from me. I'm not into the BDSM scene, Max. Whips and chains don't work for me."

"How do you know? Have you ever tried it?"

"I know."

He shrugged. "That's not what I'm talking about anyway. I don't need leather and chains to take what you need me to take from you, Grace. A private room, you armed with your safe word, and the two of us naked, preferably with a bed in the mix, will do just fine."

"And what if I don't want you to take what you're so dead set on taking? You're going to hold me down and make me?"

"Assuming you don't use your safe word? That's right."

"You *are* high."

"And just the thought of me holding you down and taking everything you have to give me, everything you secretly want to give me, has you turned on."

"You're wrong."

"I'm not. The piercings, that damn sexy tattoo on your back—which I am going to see before this day is over—all your talk about knowing what you like and part of that being control, hell even the pole-dancing and lap dance… That's all part of you, yes, but mostly it's a cover to hide what you really want. What you're really most ashamed of. You can try to fool yourself, but you're not fooling me. Lots of women get off on being dominated. It's nothing to be embarrassed about."

"I'm not embarrassed, it's just not true. You can think whatever you want, but if you intend to hold me down and *take* anything from me, that changes things. I'm leaving."

"I thought we already established you're not leaving until I'm ready to let you leave."

His utter gall amazed her. Her own undeniable reaction, evidenced by the moisture that pooled between her thighs and by the near-painful tightening of her nipples, shocked her.

This time, she didn't walk toward the door. She lunged and ran.

Before she knew it, he had her against the wall, his body pressing into hers, her wrists pinned at either side of her head. Instinctively, she fought him. Kicked out and tried to push him away. But he didn't budge, and she was faced with how strong he was. How his suave, sophisticated, civilized exterior was a complete and utter sham. Deep down, he *was* a bad boy. He just didn't need a leather jacket and biker boots to announce it to the world.

Fear trickled through her, but he was right—arousal was there, too. So much arousal that she had to actually go looking for the fear. But she found it, and clung desperately to it. She had to. A grown woman who got off on being dominated by a man? *Forced* by a man?

"Look at me, Grace."

"Go to hell." It was on the tip of her tongue to say it. *Mango*. But she didn't.

Because she didn't really want him to let her go.

He transferred both her wrists to one hand, pinned them over her head, then cupped her chin with his other hand and made her look at him. Even as he did, she was conscious of how gentle his touch was. "What did I promise you last night?"

"You promised a lot of things," she shot back.

"I promised I wouldn't hurt you, and if you didn't like something I did, after giving it a fair shot, I'd stop. You trusted me then and you have to trust me now."

"I'll trust you if you let go. This isn't you, Max. You're not a sexual barbarian."

"I already told you, Grace, I'm whatever my lover needs me to be. A sexual barbarian might not be who I am most of the time, but it's part of me. Just like wanting to be sexually submissive is just a part of you. It doesn't define you. Outside the bedroom, it doesn't mean a goddamn thing."

What he was saying made so much sense, but the fact he was persuading her just freaked her out even more. She struggled some more to no avail. "Max, I'm not kidding. You need to stop. Keep it up and I swear, I'll cancel your birth certificate. I'll cut your tail. I'll slap you to sleep, then slap you for sleeping. I'll—"

With his body pressed against hers, she felt how he shook with laughter.

"This isn't funny," she snapped.

He struggled to wipe the amusement from his expression and finally succeeded. "Calm down and look at me."

"I am looking at you."

"No, Grace, *really* look at me."

She did.

"Am I hurting you?"

"No."

"Then what are you scared of? Besides, as we've already established, losing that precious control we talked so much about."

"I don't know. I'm just—I don't like this."

"You're scared of it," he said. "Of what it's making you feel. You came to me, Dixie, and now I see you came to me because you're tired. You want me to take care of things for you. So let me." He bent and kissed her neck, then nipped at her, the resulting pain contrasting sharply with the way his tongue immediately soothed the area.

She couldn't help it.

She sighed.

He pulled back, awareness and satisfaction in his gaze. "This is your last chance. Decide you're going to trust me or we stop things now and walk away. Say the word, and this is done and I won't bring it up again. But think carefully before you give me your answer. And study what you're feeling right now. Is it fear or is it desire that has your pulse beating so fast?"

It was desire. Pure desire. She liked the feeling of being pinned down by him. She liked the idea of not having to take responsibility of her pleasure, of her damn orgasm, anymore. But she still couldn't admit it. All she managed to get out was, "Tell me what you mean by making me take what you have to give me."

"I mean you're going to take everything I have to give you. Every inch. Every drop. And when the time's right, you're going to come. Because I'm not going to give you any another choice."

Her whole body trembled, all her muscles clenching, including the ones at her core. She felt empty. Achy. She wondered... if he was inside her at that moment, if she clamped down on the hard length of his cock... *Would* she come?

Without loosening his grip on her or lessening the pressure he was using to hold her down, he kissed her, plunging his tongue into her mouth again and again until she felt drugged. His soft lips contrasted so deliciously with his hard jaw, covered with just the beginnings of stubble. She imagined that roughness against the inside of her thighs, and felt her core spasm so hard she bit his lip. He jerked and kissed her even harder. She lost track of how long they went at it. When he abruptly pulled away, she felt dizzy and disoriented.

She whimpered in distress and he immediately kissed her again, this time keeping the pressure light. Savoring. Comforting. Eventually, he graduated to sprinkling gentle, close-mouthed kisses across her face and throat.

Finally, he released her wrists. Pushing back her hair, he cupped her face. "You okay?"

She nodded.

"You still scared?"

"A little," she whispered.

He stepped back. "Too scared to take my hand?"

He held out his hand, his implicit message clear. She couldn't say it yet. She couldn't admit she wanted what he said she did. But by taking his hand, she wouldn't have to.

She couldn't justify it. She couldn't rationalize it. It was just something she felt deep down in her soul. If she was ever going to trust anyone with the hidden parts of herself, it would be him.

It was now or never.

She took his hand.

7

Max's Magic Rule #8:
The best magicians fake it on stage, never in bed.

After Grace took his hand, Max gave her one last light, close-mouthed kiss then murmured he was going to shower, change and meet her up front. Grace did a quick rinse off and clothes change, silently lamenting she hadn't brought make-up or anything fancier than a T-shirt and jeans. Why would she? She'd been planning on working out, not going a few rounds with Max, but now that she had, now that she'd agreed with no-room-for-doubt to let him take whatever he wanted—no, now that she'd agreed to let him take whatever she secretly wanted to give him, and the answer to that was *everything*—she was seriously nervous and longing for some feminine battle armor. If she had some mascara and lipstick, hot rollers, a LBD, and some seriously rocking heels, she'd be feeling a bit more prepared for whatever was going to come next.

When she made it to the lobby, Max was nowhere in

sight so she contented herself with sitting and thumbing through a few magazines. The selection was truly sad. A body-building magazine held no interest, and neither did a magazine on triathlons. She was thinking *Cosmo* and one of those "How To Be Fearless In Bed" articles would do her good. Instead, she found a magazine on parenting, dog-eared and well-worn and looking like it rolled off the printing press when flip phones were still in fashion.

It stunned her for a second. Made her realize for all her talk with Melina and Lucy about moving on to what was important—a family—she'd been easily and thoroughly sidetracked to the point her sole focus was once again on sex. Granted, it was sex with Max, which was particularly distracting given the select samples she'd been treated to, but she needed to be more careful. Hopefully her time with Max would be fruitful, so she could pursue her goal for a baby with a truly refreshed and clear state of mind, but she couldn't forget two things. First, despite Max's undeniably talented hands, mouth and body, she still couldn't erase *herself* from the equation, and that meant actually achieving an orgasm with him was still a long shot. Second, either way, she needed to keep focus on the true prize. While she was staying in Vegas to spend time with Max, he'd be plenty busy doing other things. She needed to do the same, starting with touching base with the surrogacy agency about the interview scheduled for tomorrow. She'd do that as soon as she and Max finished whatever they were going to do next today. It couldn't take more than a few hours.

The thought of doing anything more with Max—and doing it for a few hours—made her tremble with delighted anticipation. Taking a deep breath, she determinedly opened the parenting magazine. Inside were glossy photos of drooling babies, giggling babies and babies sloppily eating, food in their hair and grins on their faces. Deep in her body something tugged—as if her womb had responded to the images. One article featured insight on how to get a baby to fall asleep. The sleeping baby boy in the photo was cuter than a speckled pup and reminded Grace of how Max had looked when she'd caught him in that brief moment at the club two nights before, when he'd thought no one was looking. The same vulnerability on the baby's face had been present on Max's.

It reminded her of something her mama had used to say before she'd give Grace's daddy a kiss. Something about a man being a little boy just grown bigger. Max hadn't always been the confident, sexy man he was today. At some point, he'd been a child. Defenseless. Innocent. Craving love. As an adult, he certainly wasn't defenseless or innocent, but could she really say he didn't crave love? It was obvious his family was important to him. Melina was important to him. And Melina, who'd known him since she was fourteen years old, believed Max would make a wonderful father.

Who was the real Max Dalton, then? If what she'd seen the other night was him letting down walls, then how high did those walls go? How much of himself was he hiding from the world? And how hard was it for him to keep those parts hidden? She kept parts of herself hidden, too, and she often struggled with the need to be seen for her genuine self. Unfortunately, she wasn't always sure who that was. The woman who pole-danced and had one-night stands? Or the university counselor who rarely swore and enjoyed nights at home in front of the TV with her friends Ben and Jerry. Oh, she knew she was both those women, just like Max was both bad boy and good guy, but it was where the line was drawn that was the question.

All Grace truly knew was she was lonely. Her parents had both been only children, whose own parents died before Grace was born. No parents, no grandparents, no aunts, uncles, cousins, second cousins—nothing.

From an early age, she made life decisions. She provided for herself. She pushed forward every day because she had no choice. In the meantime, except for Melina and Lucy, there'd been pitifully few people she trusted. And even then, she never shared everything about herself with her friends.

That wasn't Max's problem. He was surrounded by people who adored him; family, fans and strangers alike. He seemed to truly love his life. The stage. The women. The fame.

Whatever she'd seen in that moment in the club when he'd looked vulnerable, it didn't mean he felt alone. It didn't mean he was yearning for love. Not the way she was. And it certainly didn't mean she'd ever be the woman that could give it to him.

She looked once more at the picture of the sleeping

baby and that yearning she'd been thinking of tore through her. She wanted a baby. *Needed* a baby. She wasn't going to wait until she was older to find the perfect man and hope she survived long enough to see her child grow into adulthood. The others might think she was being foolish, but regardless of what she gave up to Max in bed, she was a woman in control and she had a plan.

Max first, but not forever.

Her baby, her family—that would be something different.

She cast a quick glance at the doorway to the men's locker room. Still no Max. Tapping a toe impatiently, she thumbed through the rest of the magazine, then reached for the one on triathlons. She was reading about various ways to prepare for a race, and idly wondering if the same rules would work when preparing for a marathon sex session when...

"Ready?" The steady and deeply male voice came from behind her.

She whipped around, dropped the magazine and perused Max. Tight jeans that cupped him just right, a white button-down Oxford shirt with sleeves rolled to the elbows and deck shoes. Yummy. He slid an arm across the chair back, his body now angled slightly closer, and his all-male scent wrapped around her. Briefly, she closed her eyes, imagining that scent all over *her* body and all the awesome ways it could get there. With a silent groan, she popped her eyes back open and gave him a bright smile.

"Ready," she said, then immediately spiraled into

panic mode. He looked good. Good enough to eat. To kiss. To caress. To take. But he'd made it clear he was the one going to be doing the taking.

What if I'm not ready? What if he wants to do something truly kinky? Am I going to let him? Am I going to let him see how much I enjoy it?

Suddenly, Max squatted down in front her and took her hands in his. "Breathe, Dixie," he said.

She hadn't even known she was holding her breath, but at his gentle command, she exhaled, then sucked in a healthy dose. He grinned and asked again, "Ready?" But this time he did it in a dark, husky, near-whisper filled with promises that almost made her sigh out loud. She nodded instead and they stood at the same time.

On the ten-minute ride back to her hotel, they chatted about mundane things, like whether the 49ers had a chance of winning the Super Bowl this year, how round Melina had grown, and the magic show. Although the stunt he'd pulled with Elizabeth increased sales, neither Rhys nor Max was confident that would continue. He was right in the middle of telling her about a new trick Rhys was working on when he paused and cursed.

"What is it?" she asked.

He pulled up in front of her hotel, put the car into park, but kept it running and his seatbelt on.

"I'm sorry, Grace, but dammit... I just remembered Rhys asked me to do him a favor. Today. As in right now. Between you showing up at the gym and dancing for me and me looking forward to what was going to happen

next... I forgot what I promised Rhys, but it's important."
He closed his eyes and groaned dramatically. "God, why
couldn't I have been born an only child?"

Despite the disappointment swelling inside her, she
laughed. It was so obvious he was joking and would do
anything for his brother. "It's no problem. I'm here for the
week, remember? We'll have plenty of time for—" she
waved her hand "—all that."

Max laughed. "You do know you make that hand
gesture whenever you're talking about sex, right? It's
gonna get to the point all you have to do is wave your hand
and I'm going to get hard."

She crinkled her nose. "Kind of like a magic wand?
I'll show you mine if you show me yours?"

His eyes unfocused, as if he'd suddenly gone
somewhere else, and his smile disappeared. "Yeah. Kind
of like that."

She frowned. Why did he suddenly look like she'd
slapped him? Her hands twisted together in her lap.
"Max—"

"Anyway," he said. "Can I come by later tonight, after
the show?" He pulled her left hand from her right, lifted
her palm to his mouth and kissed it. "Then you'll have my
full attention."

She nodded, and breathed a quiet sigh of relief.

"We'll continue what we started at the gym. I can't
promise we'll finish it, but I can promise the continuation
will be amazing."

A thrill ran through her at the thought. She tried to

imagine him focusing even more attention on her. Would she be able to handle it? Giving him total control?

Because from what he'd said earlier, he was absolutely certain that's what it was going to take to get her off. And by her body's response at that very moment, by her escalating pulse and hardening nipples and weeping core, she was pretty close to believing it herself.

Odd, how it had taken only a couple of conversations between her and Max—granted, one discussion had happened with her straddling his hard-on—for him to have learned so much about her. She wanted to know more about *him*.

What was it Max Dalton considered an "important" favor?

"What is it you have to do?" she asked, hoping he didn't think she was being nosey.

"Drive to Cedar City, Utah. Then get back in time for my show. The whole trip will take about five or six hours."

He traced the lines of her hand with his thumb, and although she enjoyed the soft caresses, her hand still tingled from when he'd kissed it. She stared at his mouth, wanting it under hers. Wanting it to explore every crevice and dip on her body.

"What's in Cedar City?" she asked, almost wincing at how husky her voice sounded. He released her hand, touched the edge of her mouth with the pad of his thumb, smiled briefly, then let his hand drop before answering her.

"My parents. They're leaving for a trip—a second honeymoon. We already had a family dinner to send them off, but Mom, well, she's been working on something and she just finished, sooner than expected. It's important to her that Rhys and Melina have it before she goes."

The answer startled her and surprise must have shown on her face.

Max frowned. "What did you think I was going to say?"

"I—I have no idea..." she said, stammering. "I just didn't think it would be... that."

Grace had only met his parents once, at Melina and Rhys's wedding, but it had been plain to see how much they loved each other and their sons. So much it had surprised her they no longer helped with the magic act and hadn't followed their sons to Vegas. Melina said she was surprised, as well, but thought it had something to do with them wanting to give their sons space, which they'd missed their whole lives thanks to all the touring the family had done.

"Do you wish they lived closer?" she asked.

"They're close enough that we get to see them often. They've never taken a lot of time for just the two of them, and they probably wouldn't be going on this trip except that Rhys and I surprised them with it before we knew Melina was pregnant. Mom's wanted to cancel several times, but we talked her around. Once the babies are here, nothing's going to tear them away from their grandkids. I know I won't be traveling anywhere far, that's for sure."

Grace was thinking how nice it must have been to grow up with doting parents and how much she missed her own, who'd been loving if not exactly doting, when Max's last sentence penetrated. The knowledge that he'd not only stay close to spend time with a niece or nephew, but relish doing so, once again had her thinking there was more to Max than she'd given him credit for.

Then again, it wouldn't exactly be a hardship for him to stay in Vegas. He'd have his family close. His magic show. And he could build on his reputation by continuing to date one woman after another after another.

The knowledge that she was just one in a long line made her stomach drop, and she swiftly shoved the thought aside. She knew what she was getting into with Max; she couldn't complain now.

"You mind if I tag along?"

He looked surprised and she wanted a hole to form and swallow her. Had he said he wanted company? No, Grace, he hadn't. But she'd still been reeling by his comment about wanting to stay close to the babies. She wanted to spend more time exploring *that* Max and she'd spoken without thinking.

"Not so we can—" She waved her free hand, returning Max's sudden grin. "—squeeze stuff in or anything like that. Lucy's gone, and Melina's home with Rhys. I just thought... You know what? Never mind. Looks like you're going to be busier than a moth in a mitten. I don't have to—"

"I'd love for you to come with me."

She studied him closely. "You sure, honey? Because maybe you'd enjoy the ride by yourself..."

He was looking at her strangely, eyes blazing.

"What is it?"

"You've never called me 'honey' before."

"I haven't?"

He shook his head. "You've called me 'Sugar,' but like I said, you do it to distance yourself. Plus, I've heard you call others that. I haven't heard you call anyone honey before."

"Do you… like 'honey'?"

He grinned. "I love it. And Dixie, I absolutely guarantee you, I would far prefer your company than driving by myself."

She was still glowing at the fact he liked her calling him honey. "Great then. I just need to run up to my hotel. Take another shower so I can wash my hair and then change. Do my make-up. Is that okay?"

"Sure. But why go to that trouble? You always look great and now's no exception. My parents won't care if you're wearing make-up or not."

His statement that she always looked great made her feel even more warm and tingly inside. "Thanks, but I care. The only time I met your parents was at Rhys and Melina's wedding. I don't want them to see me with no make-up, ratty hair and in casual clothes. I just wouldn't feel right."

"You mean you don't want them to see you without your armor on. But you're letting me see you that way."

It wasn't like she'd had a choice. They'd run into each other at the gym. But he seemed to like the idea of seeing her in a way others didn't. That made her feel warm and tingly again, but this time the feeling scared her. She glanced away, pulled her hand from his and plucked at an imaginary piece of lint on her jeans. "We'll just tell them I'm visiting Melina so they won't jump to the wrong conclusion."

"What conclusion is that?"

Her gaze snapped back to his. He no longer sounded or looked pleased. "Well... I mean... it's probably better if your parents don't assume I'm one of your women. It might make things awkward when I see them in the future."

"Because I don't have female friends? Because my parents will assume any woman I'd bring along for a visit with them is a woman I'm sleeping with?"

It surprised her how hurt he seemed by her careless words. A man-whore slash playboy shouldn't care what she thought about him. The fact he did pulled at her heart. "No. I mean, obviously you have female friends." Though there was only one she knew of—Melina—and she was more like family. She always had been. "I just thought... I don't know. I just figured you wouldn't want them barking up the wrong tree."

Max stared at her for a minute longer, then smiled slightly before shrugging. "They're going to get the wrong impression no matter what we tell them, Grace. But we can play it your way if you want."

Puzzled by his cryptic response, she waited for a moment. When he didn't expand, she asked, "What do you mean they're going to get the wrong impression anyway?"

"I've never brought a girl to meet them. Ever. Friend, lover or otherwise. You'll be the first. And you know what they say, Dixie. No one ever forgets their first."

* * *

Max sneaked a long look at Grace before she stepped out of the elevator and into the hall, headed toward her hotel room. Once again, he wanted to tell her not to bother getting dolled up. She looked great without make-up. Younger. Sweeter. Guard down, even if that wasn't actually true.

She looked beautiful and relaxed. Not worrying about her ability to have an orgasm or finding someone to father a child. Not trying to control every step of her life because she was so damn afraid just living it in the here and now wasn't worthwhile.

When he'd remembered his promise to Rhys, he'd been in agony, picturing everything he *wasn't* going to be doing to Grace's sweet body. But now that she was coming along and he'd have a chance to talk to her for several uninterrupted hours... Well, he was hoping he'd learn more about Grace, but also make some headway in getting her to rethink her baby plan.

For a complex woman, she wanted simple things— things most people wanted. Who didn't want to come while actually having sex and *not* because some vibrator stimulated you into climax? And while he knew plenty of people who didn't want children, the majority of people he'd come across did. Grace wasn't alone in her desires. But who went out and found another person for the sole and specific purpose of creating and raising a baby? Who looked for someone they didn't love and never would just because they wanted a child to have a father, but didn't want the emotional complications that came with having a baby the traditional way?

Someone with enough issues around control and letting go to fill an Olympic swimming pool.

Someone like Grace.

She opened the door to her hotel room and motioned him inside. It wasn't messy, but it wasn't exactly neat either. It was how his own hotel rooms often looked, which for some reason made him smile. There was only one bed in the room, but it was a king. "Did you share a room with Lucy?"

"No. I stayed all by my lonesome," she said, putting her gym bag on the bed. "Why?"

"No reason. But you're ruining my fantasy of two women sleeping together," he said, teasing her. "Why not share a room while you were here?"

"I like my privacy. And Lucy is dating Jericho. They tend to get carried away with their Skype calls."

He snorted. Knowing Lucy, he could only imagine what fresh hell Grace would have to endure if Lucy and her latest boy toy were having internet sex in the same room.

"What do you think about this Jericho guy?" he asked.

"He's brooding, passionate, artsy. Seems perfect for her."

He heard the hesitation in her voice. "But?"

Grace dug around in the chest of drawers then pulled out some clothes. "I'm going to shower first."

He looked at his watch. It would be cutting it close, but they had about a half hour before they had to leave. Without her invitation, he stretched out on her bed, palms behind his head with legs crossed. "Leave the door open, and talk to me," he said, mostly to see how she'd react.

For a moment, she hesitated, and he mentally willed her to do as he asked. She'd made it clear that letting others make decisions for her was not something she generally allowed, and he figured baby steps were needed to lead up to what he wanted from her. And for her.

She gave a tight nod of her head, then stepped toward the bathroom.

"Take off your clothes first."

She froze and turned to look over her shoulder at him, mouth open and eyes rounded with horror.

He stifled a grin. She wanted him to make her come. An hour ago she'd been sliding her body all over his hard-on. And yet she was embarrassed to take her clothes off in front of him?

Baby steps, he reminded himself. Baby steps.

"Just strip to your bra and panties. We'll save the rest for when we have more time."

She took a deep breath. "Your parents. You said—"

"We have time. Now do what I said, Dixie. Start with

your top."

She licked her lips, looked toward the bathroom as if she was thinking of running inside, then carefully placed her fresh clothes on the dresser beside her.

Facing him, she pulled her top off. When she dropped it to the floor, she lifted her chin and kept her hands to her sides.

He studied the baby blue lace demi-bra that cupped her flesh to perfection. It looked padded, but he could still see the thrust of her nipples and the slightest hint of her piercings through the thin fabric.

"Nice," he whispered. "Now your pants."

She shifted her legs, but immediately moved to unbutton the jeans. She lowered the zipper. When he glanced up, he saw her eyes on him. As if she was judging his reaction to what she was doing. As if she was getting off on it.

He knew he was reading her correctly when the zipper was completely down but she didn't remove her jeans. Instead, she trailed her fingers across her belly and the edge of her panties in a devious little tease.

He straightened and sat up, no longer able to just lie there. No longer able to pretend this was just a game. "Take them off."

"Or what?" she said.

He narrowed his eyes. "Or I'm going to have to punish you."

She shook her head. "I'm not afraid of you. You're too much of a gentleman to hurt a woman."

He stood, watching as she stiffened and visibly stopped herself from retreating. When he was three feet in front of her, he reached out and gently freed her hair from her ponytail holder. He skimmed his fingers through the golden strands, loving the way she leaned into his touch. Then he dropped his hands.

"You don't know me, Grace. We don't know each other. But we're going to. And you're going to learn I'm the type of gentleman that makes a woman hurt really, really good. Now take off your jeans."

She licked her lips. Swallowed hard. Then did as he said.

Her panties were blue lace, too. Unlike the skin on her back, the rest of her body was bare of ink, her skin smooth and creamy.

He reached behind her with one hand and unclasped her bra.

"Max," she said, her breath starting to hitch.

"Shh. Let me," he said. "I want to see you."

When she remained quiet, he tugged her bra off, letting it fall to ground.

He sucked in a breath. Her breasts were just as graceful as the rest of her. The perfect size. Not big and overblown, but still womanly and lush. Her nipple piercings were gold hoops with a tiny silver ball. Forcibly keeping his hands off her, he leaned forward. Kissed her throat. Kissed down her chest. Then sucked her nipple into his mouth. Hard.

She immediately buried her hands in his hair and

arched closer. "Oh God. Oh Max."

He repeatedly flicked the ball dangling from the hoop with his tongue, then moved to the next nipple, sucking it good while his thumb and forefinger played with its mate. Whenever he pinched her nipple, she gasped. Whenever he tugged lightly on her piercings, she moaned.

He wanted her to scream.

Wanted to nibble his way to her belly and to the moist, delicate flesh between her legs. He wanted to bury his face there. Rub her cream all over himself until all he could see and taste and smell was her. He wanted it so damn bad he was shaking.

A half hour, he reminded himself. Not enough to do what he wanted by a long shot.

So he forced himself to pull away.

She reached for him, but he grabbed her, kissed her hands, then let her go. He returned to the bed, hands once again behind his head. Enormous erection on display so she couldn't miss how aroused he was.

"Do what you need to do, Grace. But first turn around."

She was flushed and breathing hard, her eyes dazed. At first, she didn't seem to understand what he was saying.

"Show me your tattoo, Dixie."

Slowly, she turned.

He sat up to get a better look before standing once more and stepping behind her.

Gently, he bunched her hair in his fist and lifted, giving himself an unimpeded view of her back. Running the length of her spine was the black outline of a stylized bird. Was it a swan? He wasn't sure, but the curved lines he'd seen at the gym above her tank top made up one of its wings, stretched up toward her neck. The ones he'd seen below her tank made up the other wing. The overall design had a simplistic elegance and sensuality, giving the suggestion of flight even as the bird stood upright.

It was gorgeous.

She was gorgeous.

And given what he'd said to her the night before, it seemed terribly significant that the only tattoo she had on her body was a bird.

Don't get on that plane, Grace. Fly with me instead.

"Does it represent anything in particular?" he asked. She jumped slightly as he traced the length of the tattoo with the tip of his index finger. She gave a long, drawn out moan when he leaned forward and began sprinkling kisses up and down the length of the tattoo.

"Not really," she said.

And he knew there was a story there. One she didn't want to share.

He'd give her that for now.

With one last kiss to her back, he straightened and reclined once again on the bed. "Go ahead and take a shower."

With a jerky nod, she headed into the bathroom, leaving the door open as he'd told her. He heard the shower turn on.

He blew out a breath even as he imagined her body

and that freaking fabulous tattoo glistening under the spray of the water. Groaning, he cupped himself through his jeans, imagining it was her stroking him. Fuck, when she'd been on her knees in front of him in that dance studio, it had taken all he'd had not to—

He heard her fumble a bottle and grinned. If she was half as torqued up as he was, she was probably cursing his ass about now. Best to get her mind on something else.

"Tell me about Lucy and Jericho," he said.

It didn't seem like she was going to respond, then she called back over the sound of running water. "After Lucy and her last boyfriend, Jamie, broke up, she came up with this theory."

"What theory?"

"That people with different backgrounds, like a jock and a brain, or a preschool teacher and a skydiver, can totally fool around with one another, but when it comes to long term commitments like should stay with like."

That didn't sound like the free spirited Lucy. Maybe he'd misheard her. "Like and like? Meaning what?"

"Both people should be preschool teachers. Or skydivers. You know, the same. In personality if not profession."

"Sounds boring," he said.

"Maybe. I thought Jamie and Lucy were so right for each other. They were completely different from one another, both professors but her wild and him more restrained. Even so, they lit up like Christmas trees whenever they were together."

"So you think her theory's all wrong?"

Only the sound of the shower came from the bathroom for a few moments. Then, Grace spoke again, her voice low. "How 'right' could they have been, given he broke up with her?"

"Are you saying the reason their relationship didn't last was because they weren't like one another?"

"Actually..." She hesitated, then the sound of the shower stopped.

Max worked hard to erase visions of a naked and dripping wet Grace from his mind. No time, he reminded himself. "Lucy never told us why Jamie dumped her," Grace said. "Just that he did, and that's when she came up with the whole 'like sticks with like' theory."

"You sure she wasn't talking about gender? Like with like, as in a woman with a woman? I mean, I know Lucy's not a lesbian, but is she bisexual?" Max asked.

Grace laughed. The sound was light and tinkling. "Does this go back to that male fantasy you were talking about earlier?"

"Everything goes back to that male fantasy."

She appeared in the doorway wearing a fuchsia top and flirty black skirt, a towel on her head turban-style.

"Have you actually ever had that fantasy fulfilled? I mean, in real life, not on a television or computer screen?"

The easy way she referred to porn made him wonder if she ever got off watching the stuff herself. He'd seen his fair share, but he couldn't recall a single scene, let alone one involving two women. All he could see was Grace.

"Max?"

"Huh?"

"Have you ever watched two women together? *Been* with two women?"

Holy hell. This conversation had taken a right turn to Interesting. "Yes. Does that turn you on?"

"Not at all."

His bullshit meter went into overdrive. What else was Grace lying to herself about? "Not even imagining you as one of the women?"

"I don't like to share," she said.

So if not two women, then... "So what about being with two men?" he asked.

Instead of denying anything, her expression softened and her eyes twinkled. "Isn't that every woman's fantasy? One man inside, the other man tending to whatever needs tending to?"

"We're talking about your fantasies right now."

"Then sure, I suppose that would feel nice. To have two men devoted to me. To my pleasure. But somehow I don't think it happens very often. Two hetero or even bisexual guys being comfortable enough to cross swords in bed? I bet you probably haven't even done it."

"You'd lose that bet."

The flirtatious light disappeared from her eyes, which grew wide, and she swallowed convulsively. Ha. He'd shocked her yet again.

"I'm not saying that's my thing—being with another guy and a woman. But my lover had a fantasy, and I made sure it came true for her. Part of that meant giving in to the fantasy myself."

"And?"

"And I was so turned on by the fact *she* was so amazingly turned on I came hard enough to strain a muscle in my neck."

"Are you saying you'd be willing to do it again? Because you shouldn't let your mouth write a check it can't cash."

He thought about it. "Is that what you want?"

"Answer my question first."

His chest tightened and he frowned. "I'm not certain I could do that with you."

Her brows raised in surprise. "Why not?"

"I don't know. You make me feel... possessive. I wouldn't want to share you with another man."

A hint of a smile formed at the side of her mouth.

"That doesn't mean I wouldn't ultimately do it. Or, failing that, that I wouldn't work twice as hard to make sure you were completely satisfied."

Grace took off the towel on her head, shook her hair out, then stepped toward him. "I have a confession to make..."

When she came close enough to stand before him, he deliberately didn't reach for her. His breathing went shallow. "And what confession might that be?"

"I don't want to be with two men. I—I just want to be with you. That would be fantasy enough, as far as I'm concerned."

"Fuck, Grace."

As if she realized just how vulnerable her confession made her, she laughed and stepped back. He instinctively followed her, and she held up a hand to ward him off. "Make-up. Hair. I'll be faster than a herd of turtles and then we can head to your parents' house, okay?"

Before he could respond, she high-tailed it back to the bathroom and he soon heard the blow dryer going. He fell back onto the bed with a groan and rubbed his palms over his face, then reached down to adjust himself inside his pants while her voice echoed inside his mind.

I just want to be with you. That would be fantasy enough, as far as I'm concerned.

Staring at the ceiling, he grinned.

He was no fantasy, and soon he was going to prove it to her.

Instead, he was hoping to be her dream come true.

"Light a fire under your ass, Dixie," he yelled.

He heard her giggle.

He'd been right before, back in the gym. Her giggle was fucking fantastic.

Even better, she knew what he was saying.

He wanted her to hurry because the sooner they got to his parents' house and back, the sooner they could get back to one another.

8

Max's Magic Rule #9:
Do what it takes to make the audience clap even louder.

Nerves danced in Grace's belly as she stared out the car window, watching the landscape fly past. Max had kept his foot on the gas ever since they'd left Vegas.

The farther they drove, the more nervous Grace became.

In a way, she felt like she'd be meeting Max's parents for the first time. Especially because Max said he'd never brought a woman to meet them before. What was up with that?

Had he simply not wanted to introduce his parents to a woman he knew wouldn't be in his life for long? Did that mean he'd never been in any kind of committed relationship?

She knew he was different with his mom and dad. Sweet. More loving. It simply emphasized in her mind all those layers Max had. And how she was pretty much disregarding those layers in her quest for an orgasm.

"So," Max said, interrupting her thoughts. "We've made progress with one of your goals. Have you made any progress with the baby plan?"

Surprised by the blunt way he brought it up, Grace searched his expression for any hint of mockery. All she saw was genuine curiosity. Relaxing back into her seat and welcoming the distraction, she said, "A little."

"Will you tell me about it?"

"If you're really interested, sure." Anything to take her mind off whether his mom would take one look at her and know she was using her son for sex. At that wince-worthy thought, she turned back to the window.

The desert shrubbery had switched from drab khaki green to something more verdant as they climbed into the foothills. Lovely. The elevation and vegetation reminded Grace a bit of where she'd grown up in Georgia. Different, but the same color green. For a moment, an image of her mama and daddy wrapped in each other's arms, Mama's head snuggled in Daddy's shoulder, came to mind.

Hot tears forced their way to the surface and she furiously blinked them away.

What was she doing here with Max? She was enjoying her time with him, yes, but it was also serving to remind her what she didn't have.

What she'd had as a young child had been precious. Her parents' marriage had been amazingly strong and beautiful. She hadn't been too young to forget how very much in love they were.

She could create her own memories with a son or daughter—she didn't need love and romance for that. She just needed healthy sperm and a man willing to be a father.

That man wasn't Max.

* * *

Max caught a glimpse of Grace out of the corner of his eye. She seemed withdrawn, lost in her own world. As much as he thought her plan to create a family was bullshit, he wanted to know more about her thought process, her plans. How else was he going to talk her out of them? "Grace?"

"Um… what is it you want to know?"

"I'm not even sure—this isn't a conversation I've had before. How do you find a baby daddy?"

"I've connected with a surrogacy agency to set me up with someone who has similar values and desires. It's essentially like a dating service, only…"

"Only instead of connecting with the intent of providing a baby and then walking away, you're interviewing with the intent to create a fake family."

"It's not fake," she said with frown. "The baby would have a real mother. A real father. They don't have to be married to be a family. Look at all the divorced families that still provide their children with stability and love. Sounds like you're implying anything other than a married man and woman isn't a family."

Max shook his head. "No way. That's unfair, Grace.

A family is a family, no matter what the structure is."

"That's my point. So long as the baby has parents who love it, what does it matter if the parents are married?"

"And what about agreeing on how to raise the child?"

"There are forms to fill out to ensure compatibility. Then contracts are created that specifically state major issues, such as to immunize or not to immunize, what religion the child will be raised with, private versus public schools, college savings plans, and so on."

He jerked the wheel, avoiding a pothole. They'd turned off the main road a few minutes ago, and here the asphalt wasn't as well tended. "Sounds like it will look great on paper. But what if the person you choose has the same compatible values as you do and follows the letter of the contract, but treats you distantly?"

She shook her head. "I'm still confused."

That was understandable, given her whole baby plan inherently involved distance between her and the baby's daddy. "What if the guy isn't respectful of you? What if he comes to pick up the kid and ignores you, or makes some negative comment about the mud puddle in the middle of the yard."

"What mud puddle?" she asked, her brow wrinkled up in confusion.

"When we were off tour, my mom would sometimes let Rhys and I dig a big hole in the front yard. We'd fill it with water from the garden hose, and play for hours. We'd end up coated in mud, our toys too, and there'd be a mud slick from the yard to the front door. Our dad would come home and see this gigantic mess. When my mom would come out to greet him, he'd wrap her in a big hug and ask her if we were having mud pies for dinner."

"I'm still not getting it," she said slowly.

He blew out a breath. "What happens if you make a mud hole and the kid's dad comes to pick him up, then bitches you out for getting the kid muddy or for mucking up your own front yard? What if he admonishes the kid for destroying a perfectly good yard, clothes and toys?"

Grace sat in silence, staring out the window again.

"My point," he said, quietly, "is you won't know how this guy's going to react when you build a mud puddle, and you certainly won't have any say in how he treats you. In what kind of behavior he models for your child. Is that what you want for your kid? Is that how you see 'family'?"

"People get married all the time without knowing everything about each other. There's nothing to say I couldn't be head over heels in love with someone who would bitch me out for getting the kids muddy someday. Having kids with someone is always a risk. I'm willing to take that risk even if you're not."

"Who says I'm not? You think I don't want to be a father some day?"

Her whipped around to face him and she looked shocked, which pissed him off. Jesus, what was it about him that made women so easily dismiss not only his potential to be a father, but his desire to want to be one in the first place?

"You just seem okay with your life the way it is, Max. You can't know what it's like to feel an emptiness that can't be filled."

His chest squeezed tight.

She was wrong. He felt that emptiness. Every day.

It seemed ever since he'd started this whole thing with Grace, he felt it more than ever. *Except* when he was with her.

Wasn't that what she wanted a baby for? To make her feel whole. Complete? No matter how true, that was a huge responsibility to put on a kid. She had to see that.

"So you think having a baby will make you happy, but what if it can't? What if it's missing a man's passion and love that makes you feel empty, Grace?"

"There will be time for that. After," she said. "But for having a baby? My time's limited. Every woman knows that."

"Usually they're not twenty-nine year old women."

"You know women, but you don't know anything about *being* a woman. So please, let's drop the subject."

They drove in silence for a few minutes before Max placed a hand on Grace's leg and squeezed. Thankfully, Grace placed her hand on his and squeezed back. He didn't let go and neither did she. "So, what happened back at the hotel room..." he said, feeling her out.

"What about it?"

"I didn't intend for it to happen, but it definitely was consistent with my plan to string things out and keep you guessing about O-time, don't you think?"

"O-time," she said. "What? Is that like circle time? Nap time? Snack time?"

He'd just learned something else about her that he liked—she didn't hold on to annoyance very long. He'd done as she asked and switched topics, and rather than continuing to light into him, she could let it go and tease with the best of them. He waggled his brows. "Nap time? No way. Snack time?" He glanced at her and grinned evilly. "I'm definitely planning on getting my fill of you."

She sucked in a breath. "Go on," she said. "What's your point? About the—" She waved her hand, making him laugh. "—stringing things along."

"When people start exploring sexuality, they generally begin with fooling around. You did it in college, before you had sex, right?"

She cast a quick glance at him. "Yes. Second base. Third base. That sort of thing."

"What did you consider pushing the envelope back then? What I did?"

"Kissing my breasts you mean?" She cleared her throat. "No. I'd say a guy touching my...." Her hand jerked, as if she was going to wave it, but she stayed the gesture, making him grin anyway. "Lady parts."

"Fingering you?"

After swallowing, she nodded.

"Remember how that felt? Experimenting. Seeing how far you could push things. Going to the brink but then not letting either of you go any further. Didn't you feel powerful? Did you have any doubt that when it happened, it would be incredible for you?"

She seemed to seriously consider his question before answering. "I remember feeling desperate. As if I was starving. Like if I didn't get him inside me, I'd implode. Like I'd climax the minute he entered me. But also that I didn't want it to end. I mean, I knew it would end. I knew we'd get there, but…"

"But it felt so good, to be on that edge. Because you could enjoy it all without fearing you'd get stuck there."

"Yes," she said. "It did feel good. Intense. But that was because I was inexperienced. I can't go back in time. No one can."

"You're wrong, Dixie. We can get you back to that place, where you're just feeling, not thinking. It's where you're in tune with my body and yours. When you're so immersed in the pleasure we're giving each other and an orgasm is a foregone conclusion."

"That, or we get me back to the places I've been since then. Feeling a whole lot of frustration. Frustration you'll feel too, by the way. Not just physical but…"

"But what?"

"You'll get tired of trying, that's all I'm saying, Max. But lucky for you, you have a deadline. One week. If you—if you find you're tired of things before then, all you have to do is tell me. Please tell me. I'd hate the idea of you—"

Her voice broke and she looked out the window.

"I'm not going to get tired of trying, Grace. God, I don't know how you can even think that."

She laughed bitterly. "And I don't know how you can say that with a straight face."

"Guess I'll just have to prove myself to you. How about we start right now?"

"What?"

"You liked what we did earlier."

"I think that was pretty obvious."

"Good."

"Why good?"

"Because we have a long drive ahead of us. Might as well take advantage of it."

* * *

"Just what are you referring to? Because I'm not keen on getting' into a car crash and being one of those couples that has to explain to an ER doctor how certain things ended up being where they shouldn't be."

He laughed but all Grace could think was, *Did I just refer to us as a couple? Get it together!*

"It really doesn't matter what you're keen on. I'm in control."

When she didn't respond, he prompted. "Grace?"

She stuck out her tongue. "Yes, you're the one behind the wheel now."

He looked over at her and grinned. "Bet that was hard for you to say."

The area between her thighs heated up, and she felt herself go wet. "You have no idea."

"You'd like it if I reached over and stroked you now, wouldn't you?" he asked.

Good Lord, would she ever. "No."

"That lie is going to cost you. Now try again."

"Fine. I'm turned on. I'd like it if you stroked me. So are you going to?"

"Nope."

Frustrated both sexually and by the conversation, she turned her attention to the view outside. "Forget your theory about stringing things along. I think you're just a natural born tease," she said.

"Want to know how I get the most intense orgasms?" he asked.

Her breath rushed out and she studied the landscape hard. "Not particularly."

"I'm ignoring that and telling you anyway. I hold off and hold off, sometimes all day long—"

"A whole day is holding off for you?"

He shot her a warning look but kept talking. "—until I have so much sexual energy inside me I practically explode when I do come."

She scowled. "Bully for you."

"Pouting?"

"No. I'm not only sexually frustrated here, I'm also getting jealous."

He laughed out loud at that, and she found herself loosening up again. She loved teasing him, and being teased by him, and it had nothing to do with sex. Even so, her mind went there. She'd loved teasing him in the dance studio, on the pole and off of it, and she wanted to do it again. This time, however, she wanted to take it all the way. Testing him, she placed her hand along the inside of his thigh. His muscles immediately clenched and his gaze snapped to hers.

"You should probably keep your eyes on the road, don't you think, Sugar?"

He immediately stared out the windshield. "Looks like you've already forgotten who's in charge."

More teasing, albeit in a much rougher voice than he'd used before. "I'm the one with my hands free, Max. And I'm seeing another opportunity to take control."

"That's not what we agreed to, Grace."

"I get that, but you're going to be working hard tonight. Maybe even all week. Don't you want to relax a little bit beforehand?"

"Talking to you relaxes me."

"I know a way to get you to relax without saying a word." She undid her seat belt.

"That's not safe," he said rather weakly.

"I bet you say that to all the girls who want to go down on you while you're driving." *Not.* She mentally snorted.

"I'm serious." But he didn't sound serious. He sounded intrigued in spite of himself. Tempted. And curious if she'd really do what she was hinting.

"If you're serious, then pull over and stop the car. I promise I'll put on my seatbelt and be a good little girl."

She waited. When he just kept driving, she grinned.

"Good choice, Max."

She took a quick glance around, saw they were fairly isolated on the desert highway with only one car coming up behind them and to the right. Max had slowed down significantly and the other car would soon be upon them. His car windows weren't tinted. If she ducked down, would the driver of the other car notice? The idea made her shiver.

She bent toward his lap, gasping when he fisted her hair in one hand and tugged her head up.

"What game are you playing, Grace?"

"No game. Honestly, I just want to do this. And you said I could, remember?"

He frowned, clearly not remembering.

"You said, 'You want to suck my dick? Suck it. But only because it will make you hot.' Well, I'm already hot, but that would make me hotter."

He swallowed hard and seemed to struggle for what to say next. "You sure you're not setting out to torture me, leave me high and dry as payback for trying to talk you out of your baby daddy scheme?"

"I'm thinking there's going to be a lot of people who are going to try and talk me out of it. And I guarantee you my response isn't going to be giving them a happy ending in a moving vehicle."

He loosened his hold on her hair and placed his hand back on the steering wheel. She took that as her cue to continue. He hissed in a breath as she unfastened his jeans, noting how the car suddenly lost acceleration before he steadied it out again. Gently, she lifted him out.

He was, in a word, luscious.

Or maybe magnificent was more appropriate.

Majestic?

Good Lord, whatever the word, Max Dalton did not disappoint in a single, solitary way.

He was thick and long and smooth, with a light dusting of hair at the base and a plum-shaped tip. With a small whimper of need, she bent forward and gave him a close-mouthed kiss. "God, Grace."

"Don't crash."

"Easy for you to say," he said. "If you're really concerned, you need to stop because I'm obviously not going to stop you."

She shook her head, allowing her hair to brush gently against him. Fascinated, she watched as he hardened even more. She stroked him lightly, then harder, making him gasp and bite his lip. The sight of his strong white teeth pressing down on his own flesh made her hunger spike. Quickly ducking her head, she sucked him into her mouth. Again, she started lightly, with gentle licks and kisses, before sucking harder and taking him steadily deeper.

She'd been at it several minutes when she couldn't resist looking up. He kept his gaze on the road, but his facial muscles were tense, the veins in his neck bulging, his breathing labored. When she combined her mouth with her hand and a sensuous little twist, he groaned like he was in pain, tilted his head back and took his right hand off the steering wheel to lightly cup the back of her head. He rested it there as she worked him. When she began teasing, taking in less and less of him until he almost slipped out of her mouth completely, his fingers tightened in her hair, communicating his dual pleasure and frustration. He let this go on a while, but eventually pushed her face forward, forcing her to take more of him. She didn't fight him, loving his unrepentant show of dominance.

With his rough touch, she became aware of more than his cock in her mouth or his responses. The vibration of the engine traveled through her body, making her shiver and ache. And just like she told him, she got so hot it was a wonder she didn't burst into flames. She began moving her mouth faster, sucking him harder, taking her cues from the consistent groans that now rent the air.

"Oh Grace. Baby... I'm going to come."

She'd already sensed that by the way his hips began to arch up, feeding her more of him, almost more than she could handle, but somehow she found a way to take everything he had to give her. Hearing him confess he was close to release was intoxicating. Their intimate little secret.

She murmured her encouragement, sucked harder, and with a few more hip thrusts and a muffled groan, he jerked, spurting into her mouth even as he trembled. She swallowed, enjoying his essence in a way she never had with another man.

When he was done, she rested her cheek against his thigh, licking her lips then smiling. Somehow he managed to keep driving, while she felt too stunned to move. Not because of what she'd done in a moving car—she'd done it before—but how close she felt to him. How proud she felt that she'd been able to please him. How utterly uninterested she was in anything he might feel obligated to give her in return. The pulses of sensation coursing through her body were enough on their own to make her want to purr. It was as if she'd truly committed the act for her sole pleasure, and how many people could say that with a straight face?

Even when she felt capable of moving away, she didn't want to. His hand remained on her head, his palm stroking her hair, and his thumb rubbing gentle circles on her cheek or tracing her ear. When his breathing returned to normal and the car went quiet, she forced herself to gently tuck him back into his pants, but left his zipper undone. Straightening, she returned to her seat and fastened her seat belt.

She felt flushed. She felt powerful. She felt like she was lit up from the inside out.

But she couldn't look at him. She was certain if she did he'd sense how hard it had been for her to pull away from him.

He reached out, took her hand, and placed it on his thigh again.

"Grace, look at me."

Biting her own lip, wishing she was biting *his*, she did as he said.

"That was amazing. Thank you."

"You don't have to thank me." She cleared her throat,

struggling for something witty to say. "So how'd it compare?"

He looked wary. "Compare to what?"

"Those orgasms you were telling me about, that were so intense because you made yourself wait?"

He grinned. "No comparison. That was the best damn orgasm I've ever had. For now." He lifted her hand to his mouth and kissed it. "The only way it will get better is when I'm locked inside you, feeling you come with me. And I swear to you, Grace, I want that. I need it. And I'm going to make damn sure it happens for the both of us."

Instead of rolling her eyes or snorting or arguing with him like she normally would, the words "I look forward to it," popped out of her mouth.

She actually meant it. Part of her was truly beginning to believe Max was going to get her there.

"And I look forward to you touching yourself. Right here and right now."

* * *

"There's no reciprocation needed, honey. I told you, that was just me wanting to do what I did."

"And I appreciate that, baby. But you wrestled control away from me. Time for me to take it back."

"Making myself come that way isn't guaranteed. I've never been able to do that with a man watching before." She felt stupid saying the words. They communicated something she wanted to deny. They communicated her inability to orgasm was so obviously not about biology but about her inability to trust. A man. A woman. It didn't matter. She might as well have held up a sign that said "Control AND Trust Issues."

But by the way he was looking at her, she obviously wasn't telling him anything he didn't already know.

"There you go again. Focusing on the orgasm as the goal. I didn't say I want you to make yourself come. I told you I want you to touch yourself."

He was back to his hold-off-on-the-end-goal-and-just-live-a-little theory. Which meant... "So just touch myself to do it?" Sounded like a waste of time to her... except, she reminded herself, Max would be sitting next to her watching.

Picturing it, her skin pretty much ignited.

"To make yourself feel good. To give me something fucking fantastic to look at while I drive."

Well there you go, but as always happened when he expressed his need for her so boldly, his words scared her even as they pleased her. She automatically tried to lighten things up. "You mean the scenery isn't doing it for you, Sugar?"

He didn't find her funny. "Take your panties off."

Slowly, she unbuckled her seatbelt again, raised her skirt, reached underneath and pulled off her pale pink thong. It was awkward, but she managed to remove them without flashing him.

"Now hitch your skirt up until I can see you."

Lifting her hips slightly, she tugged her skirt up,

stopping when she felt the cold leather on the back of her upper thighs. "Max—"

"Do it."

When she was completely bare to him, he reached out, caressed her just above her core then tugged her thighs farther apart.

"Fucking beautiful," he said, even as she moaned softly.

He withdrew his hand and reached for the radio, turning it on and flipping the channels until he found a song with a deep sexy beat. He raised the volume, then put both hands back on the steering wheel. "Now recline your seat back and touch yourself."

Not pulling her gaze away from his, she touched her thighs first. She knew he probably thought she was teasing, when the truth was she always started like that. When she finally trailed her fingers over her most sensitive flesh, she quivered. Max's eyes jerked back to the windshield for a quick check, then dropped back to her.

It reminded her they were in a moving vehicle. Once again doing something they probably shouldn't be doing.

And she didn't care. To prove it to herself and to him, she worked her clit. Her breath rushed in and out. Again, he glanced at the windshield. Again back to her. It started to become a little game. She waited for him to check the road to make sure they were safe. She *really* waited for him to look back. She wanted to keep him looking at her longer, so she started amping things up. She pushed a finger inside herself. Then two. She added another hand to the mix, so she could both thrust and rub.

Good Lord, it felt good. So good.

He looked away.

He looked back.

Looked away.

Back.

And it wasn't lost on her that as more time went by, he was having more trouble tearing his gaze away from her to check the road.

The next time he looked away, she closed her eyes because she couldn't help herself. She almost believed she *was* going to come. Only something wasn't right. She couldn't quite get there.

"Lift your right foot and rest it against the seat. Spread your thighs so you can really get in there."

Her eyes popped open and with a start she realized they were no longer moving. He'd pulled over to the side of the road. Occasionally, she could hear a car pass.

She hesitated and was about to pull her fingers away from herself, but he leaned over, gripping each of her wrists, keeping them exactly where they were.

She looked over his shoulder. One car passed. Then another. If drivers slowed down, and maybe even if they didn't, they'd get an eyeful.

"Do what I said, Grace. Now."

Her whole body jerked, not in fear or surprise, but in scream-worthy arousal.

With his hands still holding hers, she did what he said. She lifted her right leg and planted her foot on her seat.

His hands urged hers back into motion. Gently forced her fingers to thrust and rub again. The music was still playing, and his fingers no longer guided but simply held. He leaned in close, staring into her eyes one moment, looking down the next. Giving her his gaze and taking it away just as he had when he was driving. The game was on again, and she was waiting and waiting for his gaze to come back to her… to leave… to come back…

The pleasure wrapped her in an almost smothering embrace. Because of what she was doing. Because of what he was doing. Her and him. It felt good.

They felt good.

Without warning, she was almost there. Her body started trembling. Straining. She recognized the signs. She was going to come. With Max watching her. She was going to—

Her gaze locked on his even as her fingers froze. Her mind rebelled.

No.

She couldn't come. If she came, their week would be over. She wouldn't get to spend more time with him. She wouldn't be able to get to know him better. And she wanted to. She wanted more time with Max, and she didn't care if he made her come or not.

He was so right. There was pleasure in the journey and not just the destination.

She didn't want her journey with Max to end.

She tried to pull her hands away but he wouldn't let her.

"You're there, baby," he said, his hands guiding her again, this time his fingers brushing against her as well, until she had to hold back a scream. "Take it."

"Stop," she said. "Please stop," she choked out, and even she could hear the panic in her voice. Only she knew the true source behind her panic.

He hesitated and his grip lightened slightly, giving her the opportunity to pull away, quickly lower her legs and skirt, and curl towards the window. She pressed her forehead to the cool glass as she pressed her thighs together.

She wanted him inside her. She ached so badly. But this time she didn't care. She wasn't ready to let him go.

Not yet.

She heard him move and switch the music off.

"You okay?"

She nodded.

"You were there, Grace. Why'd you stop?"

She didn't turn to look at him and she didn't answer him for a long time. He didn't push. He gave her the time she needed. He'd told her before, but now she *got* it: as her lover, he'd give her *anything* she needed, even if that was space.

"You said stringing the pleasure out would make it better in the end."

"That's true, but you were *there*…"

At his obvious confusion, she forced herself to face him. She tried to come up with another excuse to protect herself. Somehow she managed to take a huge leap of faith instead. "You promised me something, Max, and I want it. Not some half-measure. The next time I come, I want it to be because you're touching me. If I can't have that, then I don't want it."

9

Max's Magic Rule #10:
Always have another trick up your sleeve.

Grace made Max stop at a gas station so she could wash up. She used the opportunity to take some deep breaths and compose herself so his mother wouldn't instantly know what they'd been doing on the drive. Since her confession about only wanting an orgasm if Max was touching her, Max had gone quiet. Maybe he was reading too much into what she'd said. Maybe he thought she'd get clingy at the end of their week together. To put him at ease, she started telling him the requirements she had for her baby's father, including a stable job that didn't involve a lot of traveling, as well as a large extended family. Though he nodded and responded here and there, his answers were terse.

Finally, he pulled into a neighborhood where the houses had big lawns and vast amounts of grass and trees between them. Being from overpriced-housing-and-space-deprived California, it wasn't the type of place she'd expect retirees to live. As they got out of the car, a fawn-colored Cocker Spaniel with feathered hair on its chest and legs ran up to greet them with a ball in its mouth. It dropped the ball at Max's feet and sat, its hinny wriggling and tail wagging like crazy.

Max laughed, crouched down and petted the dog. He didn't seem to mind when it covered his face with wet sloppy kisses. "This is Houdini. My parents got him when they moved in."

Grace bent to rub the dog behind his ears, laughing when he licked her hand then nudged the ball with his nose.

"Are they going to put him in a kennel while they're gone?"

"They're hiring a pet sitter to come to the house." He picked up Houdini's ball and waved it in front of the dog, who barked excitedly and spun in circles. Max hurled the ball towards a tree in the distance, and Houdini ran after it. Max turned to Grace with a grin. "I'd love to take him, but between all the performances…" He shrugged.

Despite the dismissive gesture, she wasn't fooled. Not being able to watch Houdini—not being able to have a dog period—was not something Max was okay with.

When Houdini brought the ball back, Max threw it again. He looked so carefree that she automatically wondered what else he didn't allow himself because of his commitments to the show. What other regrets did he try to hide behind a smile and shrug?

"Max," a woman called.

His parents walked down the long driveway toward them. Jack was fit, tall and handsome despite the fact he was losing his dark hair. What he had left of it seemed to stick up in random tufts. Rachel was beautiful, with an hour-glass figure and smooth skin that made her look closer to forty than sixty. She had the same light hair and eyes as her sons. Grace gave them what she hoped wasn't a nervous smile.

After hugging both his mother and father, Max turned and motioned for Grace to join them. "Mom. Dad. You remember Grace. She was in town visiting Melina and graciously offered to keep me company on the drive over."

Grace didn't miss the look Rachel quickly shot Jack before they both hugged her.

"Of course I remember Melina's beautiful friend from the wedding," Jack said.

"So wonderful to see you again," Rachel said. "And so nice of you to come along with Max. We know it's a long trip." She turned to Max. "I'm sorry for the trouble, sweetie. I know it was last minute and I appreciate you taking the long drive. I just really wanted Melina to have the baby blankets before we left, and with all the preparation we're doing for the trip…"

"Let alone all the arrangements we had to make for Houdini here," Jack said. "I'm telling you, Rachel, we should never have gotten him." In contrast to his words, however, Jack was petting Houdini and about to take over throwing the dog the ball.

Rachel patted her husband's shoulder. "You're just afraid you're going to miss your number one fan while we're gone. I'll have to make sure I keep you appropriately occupied so you won't." She winked at Max.

Instead of cringing at his mother's sexually-charged teasing, Max grinned. "Just leave the handcuffs at home this time, will you? We don't want another disaster on our hands."

Grace's eyes widened and her cheeks heated. She knew Max and his parents were close. She'd been close with her parents, too, but she couldn't imagine exchanging innuendos with them, no matter how old she was.

Rachel slapped Max's arm. "Max, stop. You're embarrassing Grace."

Max wrapped an arm around Grace's back and pulled her close to his side. "Grace isn't as easily shocked as you might think. Besides, I told you, if you flirt with Dad in front of me, I'm going to have to upstage you. It's in my nature."

Without taking her eyes off Max's arm, which was still around Grace, Rachel said, "I'm your mother, Maxwell. I know your nature by now. And I also know you have good taste. Both my boys do." Her gaze lifted and she winked at Grace.

"That we do." Max squeezed Grace's shoulder before dropping his arm.

As a group, they walked up the cobbled walkway toward the cottage-style ranch. The light blue shutters and wraparound porch lent themselves to the setting—so charming, so different from the bright lights and hectic energy of Vegas. Max looked totally at home. For a moment, it threw Grace. Made her wonder again—who was Max Dalton?

"How's Melina feeling?" Rachel asked, her expression shifting from delight to worry.

Grace frowned. "Is Melina not feeling well?" Was there something the others weren't telling her? Sure, Melina seemed tired after that massive shopping trip, but...

"She's feeling a little run down," Max said. "That's why Rhys wanted to spend the day with her today. He said he has some big meetings coming up, so he wants to give her some extra TLC."

Rachel stopped just outside the front door and turned toward Jack. "It's not too late for us to cancel our trip. If Melina's not feeling well—"

Max rested his hands on his mother's shoulders and gently turned her so she was facing him. "Mom, Melina's fine. You've been looking forward to this trip for a year—"

"That was before Melina got pregnant."

"—and there's no reason you can't go. The babies aren't due for another two months. You'll be back in two weeks. Enjoy yourself now because, as I told Grace earlier, you're not going to want to travel after the babies are born."

Rachel bit her lip. When she looked at her husband again, Jack stepped up and hugged her. "We're a plane ride away if they need us, Rachel," he said.

She nodded. Sighed. "Okay. It's just hard not to worry. About my boys. And about Melina." She patted Max's cheek. "I'll worry about your wife too, when the time comes."

"I know." He kissed her cheek. "Now, where are those blankets you've been working so hard on?"

His mom hooked her arm through his. "Let's go inside."

They walked into the house, modest in size and decoration—rustic, and with walls covered by photos of Max and Rhys, from young boys to adults. It was clear to Grace which twin was Max in the pictures—the one usually mugging it up for the cameras. Rachel beckoned them into the kitchen and poured a cup of coffee, which she held out to Jack. Grace took a moment to examine the numerous clippings stuck to the refrigerator with magnets. Each featured Max or Rhys or both. Many featured Max with young women, gazing adoringly at him or melted over his arm or shoulders.

"Rachel," a young girl's voice cried out just as a whirling ball of energy exploded through the back door.

"Grace, Max," Rachel said, smiling as she swung the girl who looked to be about four years old up into her arms. "This is Chloe. She belongs to Donna, our housekeeper and, for the next two weeks, Houdini's caretaker."

A young woman with the same strawberry blond hair and freckles as her daughter came into the kitchen after

Chloe, clutching a baby boy on her hip, a wide smile on her face. The baby didn't have much hair, but what he did have was dark. "Sorry, she's a little out of control. Chloe, what are you supposed to do when you come to Rachel and Jack's house?"

"Knock on the door and wait for permission to come in," the little girl said, patting Rachel's cheeks and gazing at her with adoration. "And I did. Yesterday."

Max laughed out loud, catching Chloe's attention. The girl, still in Rachel's arms, focused her gaze on him, but pulled in tighter to Rachel, and dropped the big grin.

"Chloe," Rachel said, "remember how I told you I have two boys? This is Max."

The little girl looked at Max, then at Grace, then back at Max again, twisting her body to meld closer to Rachel's, obviously uncomfortable. "He's not a kid. He's a grownup."

"Sorry," Donna said, apologizing again. "She doesn't do so well with strangers."

"It's okay," Max said. "Chloe, you're right, I'm definitely not a kid anymore. Both Rachel and Jack's kids grew up. But just because we're grownups doesn't mean we're not fun. In fact…" He took a step toward his mother, then reached a hand out, as if he was going to stroke Chloe's hair.

Grace held her breath. Even though she'd been an older child when her parents died, strangers approaching her always freaked her out. Max should know better than to come up to a kid so directly, especially one whose own mother said she was afraid of strangers.

But then he smoothed his hand over his mother's head, tweaked her ear, and held up a large silver dollar in his hand to show Chloe. "Check it out, Chloe. Did you know Rachel had a dollar in her ear?"

Chloe stared at the silver dollar with intensity, then swept her gaze back up to Max's face, a mixture of disbelief and concentration. "She didn't have money in her ear. You made that happen."

Max chuckled. "Yep. Know how?"

Chloe shook her head.

"Magic."

At that, the girl frowned, pinching her brows together. "There's no such thing as magic."

"You sure about that? Here," Max said. "Stick your fingers in your ears. See if there's any money there."

Promptly, Chloe stuffed her fingers in her ears, then pulled them out again, a satisfied look on her face. "No money."

"Bet you're wrong,"

The girl grinned. "No money," she shouted excitedly.

Max stretched his hands out, palms up, and let Chloe see he wasn't holding anything. Then he swept his hands over her ears and produced a silver dollar in each hand. "So what do you call this?" he asked.

A bright grin swept over Chloe's face. She grabbed the silver dollars, squirmed out of Rachel's arms and ran over to her mom. "Max made magic. He found money in my ears. Can I keep it?"

Donna started to shake her head, but Rachel said, "Of course you can. Max meant it as a gift. And a gift from Max is the best thing a girl can ever receive because he doesn't give gifts to just anyone. Just to those who are special. And you are special," Rachel said, tweaking Chloe's nose. Rachel glanced up at Grace and smiled, as if she was talking to her as well as Chloe.

Donna laughed and said, "Okay, so what do you say when someone gives you a gift?"

"Thank you," Chloe said sweetly before wrapping her arms around Max's knees, squeezing him tight. Grace felt warmth spread through her chest. She was moved by Max's actions, but also by Chloe's unreserved affection, as well as the message Max's mom had given the little girl. And Grace.

Rachel opened a drawer, took out a folded piece of paper and handed it to Donna. "Here are the emergency numbers for you, Donna, including our hotel and the vet. Thank you again for watching Houdini."

"Anytime, Rachel," Donna said, shifting the baby to the other hip. She turned to her daughter. "Chloe, it's time to say goodbye to Rachel."

"And Max," Chloe said promptly, then hugged Max again, who chuckled and ruffled her hair.

"I hope to see you again, Chloe," he said.

After Donna managed to drag her daughter out of the house, Rachel poured more coffee. "Help your father put away the outdoor furniture, would you, Max?"

Grace caught the silent look that passed between

Max's parents, which clearly communicated Rachel wanted to be alone with Grace. Tension slid up her spine and she felt herself blushing again, wondering if Max's mother suspected all the "gifts" Max had given her so far.

"No problem," Max said, but turned to face Grace and winked. "You want to come with me? I can show you the yard. My mom's a great gardener."

Bless Max's heart. He was giving her an out in case she didn't want to be alone with his mother. She took a quick peek at Rachel, who was fighting to hold back her laughter. Grace felt like laughing, too.

"Go help your father," Grace said quickly, "and maybe your mom will show me these baby blankets she made."

"They're in the guest room," Rachel said.

After Max and his father headed outside, Rachel gestured for Grace to follow her to a back room, where two large gift boxes sat on a bed. When Rachel pulled a quilted baby blanket out of one of the boxes, Grace caught her breath. It was beautiful. Hand quilted, with tiny stitches that had to have taken hours upon hours. The blanket bore Rhys and Melina's name and a large blank heart, which Rachel traced with one finger.

"Since Rhys and Melina waited to find out the sex of their babies, the baby's name will be placed in the heart once it's born," Rachel said.

"You did this?" Grace asked. "This must have taken months."

"Years, actually," Rachel said.

Grace looked up, puzzled. "Years?"

"A grandmother's love starts when the idea of a baby forms in her child's mind. Not when the baby is conceived. Or born. Rhys loved Melina for years, and I knew Melina felt the same way. That they dreamed of being a family long before they actually became pregnant."

Grace choked back a sob and fought against the stinging in her eyes.

Rachel was right. Melina had loved Rhys since she was fourteen. She'd just never believed Rhys could feel the same way. The day they married was the happiest of her life—until the day she found out she was pregnant. Now Melina, who was already close with her own parents, had twice as much family. That included Max.

Grace had friends, good friends, but she didn't have family. What would her life look like if her parents and their parents had lived? If a grandmother loved her when she was just a dream in her mother's heart?

She ran her thumb over a row of stitches that formed the intricate border of the heart. "Is the other one exactly the same?"

"Identical," Rachel said with a laugh. "Wishful thinking I guess."

The comment made sense, given Rhys and Max looked exactly alike. Funny, Grace usually didn't think about that. Max just seemed like Max. Not a twin but wholly unique.

"The babies will be lucky to be all wrapped up in

quilts so obviously made with love. Melina and Rhys are lucky, too. I'm sure they'll be grateful. Are they expecting the blankets, or is this a surprise?"

"Rhys and Melina know about the blankets, but Max doesn't know about his. Not yet."

Grace's eyes widened. Her first thought was, *Won't that be as useless as an ashtray on a motorcycle?* "You made a blanket for Max?"

For the first time, Rachel frowned. "I made blankets for both my boys."

"I'm sorry," Grace said quickly. "I didn't mean to imply... I mean, of course you'd make one for Max. Why wouldn't you?"

Rachel's expression smoothed and she smiled slightly. "I'm sure Max would recite several reasons. And I understand your reaction, Grace. Really. Despite the fact he's dated his fair share of women and sowed more than his fair share of oats, most people expect Rhys to be a great dad, and I'm sure he will be. It's Max who'll surprise everyone when he finally gets to be a parent. He'll be a fantastic uncle, but he'll be an even better father. Even if he doesn't quite believe it himself."

Grace couldn't imagine Max being insecure about anything, let alone whether he'd be a good father. Then again, she'd implied the same thing several times. She'd used Max's playboy reputation and celebrity status to judge him even as she'd selfishly sought to use them for her own pleasure.

Grace handed the quilt back to Rachel, who was

looking at her out of the corners of her eyes. Why? Because she wanted Grace to help convince Max he'd be a good father? Or because she wanted her to convince Max to be the father of *her* child?

She obviously had the wrong idea about them, just as Max had predicted.

"You know we're just friends," Grace said quickly.

"Oh, I know, dear. And sometimes that's often the best way to start. Friends first, lovers second. Of course, the opposite happened with Jack and me. We were lovers first, friends second, and it's turned out to be a fantastic relationship that's lasted forty years. Whatever it is you have with Max, don't underestimate it. I certainly won't."

Before a completely flummoxed Grace could respond, Rachel squeezed her arm. "Now, let's go see what the guys are up to."

* * *

Less than an hour later, Max and Grace were on the road back to Vegas. The more miles they traveled, the more intense the buzzing in Grace's stomach became. She squirmed in her seat, feeling jittery and hot. Somehow seeing Max with his parents, but also with Houdini and Chloe, made her feel as though she'd been granted a rare privilege. Exactly the type of "gifts" Rachel alluded to earlier. She suspected she'd gotten an up-close-and-personal glimpse of the "real" Max Dalton in a way most people never did.

And what she saw, she really, really liked.

Respected.

Desired.

She couldn't keep her eyes off Max. Her gaze fondled the strong column of his throat. The graceful competence of his hands on the steering wheel. The way his hair flirted with the tips of his ears so that her fingers itched to push it back, baring his flesh so she could nibble and lick to her heart's content.

Good Lord, she was turned on. More turned on than when she gave him a blow job. More turned on than when she touched herself with him watching. With Max, there didn't seem to be an end to the heights he could make her libido climb.

She glanced at the clock on the dashboard. His rehearsals usually started an hour before his first show, which began at eight o'clock. With the amount of time the drive would take, they maybe had an hour tops to spare.

Not long enough at all, but still time she didn't want to waste.

The buzzing inside her turned to tingling, and her breaths grew shallower. She suddenly felt light-headed, as though she would die if he didn't put his mouth on her. *Everywhere* on her.

"Max," she said. "Can you pull over?"

He looked over at her and frowned. "You feeling okay, Dixie?"

"I just really need you to pull over right now." She was breathing so fast she was on the verge of hyperventilating.

She sensed the car slow but not stop. "You look flushed. Let's find a place to get you a drink. There's probably a—"

"I don't want a drink, Max. I just want you to stop."

"Grace—"

"Do you want me to beg? Because if that's what you want, I will. I'll do anything' you want if you'll just kiss me. Because I really want you to kiss you right now. I *need* you to kiss me."

His body jerked and his knuckles whitened as he clutched the steering wheel. "Is kissing all you want?" he asked slowly, his voice deeper and rougher than just seconds before.

"I want whatever you'll give me."

His jaw flexed. The car suddenly swung to the right. Max slowed, edged the car off the highway, and came to a stop, sending dust in their wake. He glanced around until his gaze settled on a dirt road about a tenth of a mile up. "Hold on." Hitting the gas hard, he sent the car whipping forward. They careened down the dirt road for a few minutes until trees and brush hid them. Max slowed to a stop, put the car in park, then turned off the engine. Only then did he turn and look at her.

His eyes were feral.

His chest heaving.

His jaw clenched.

Faster than a hot knife through butter, she got her seat belt unfastened and practically threw herself at him.

Within seconds, they were outside the car, pressed against the hood, his mouth on hers, his hands buried in her hair, adjusting the angle of her head so he could kiss her deeper. She tugged his shirt out of his pants and immediately shoved her hands underneath, sighing with relief as she caressed the hard planes of his chest and brushed his nipples with the pads of her thumbs. He didn't bother taking anything off her, just shoved her skirt up and ripped off her pink thong. She gasped and he paused, lifting his head to stare down at her with hooded eyes.

"If you want something more romantic than this, tell me now."

Fast and furious, she thought, remembering what the brunette at Lodi's had told her.

"Do you—do you have a blanket in your car for this type of thing?"

It was the wrong thing to say. He jerked down her skirt then stepped back and ran his hands through his hair. "Fuck, Grace, regardless of what you think of me, I don't make a habit of pulling to the side of the road and having sex with women. In fact, this will be my first time."

He'd had a threesome but never...? She stepped closer and placed her palms on his shoulder. Went on her tiptoes to kiss him softly. "Well, I'm honored to be your first. Again. Now fuck me, Max. With your fingers. With your tongue. With everything you have."

"You mean that? You're going to take everything I have to give you?"

"Yes."

"Then tell me what your safe word is, Grace. I need to know you remember."

"Mango," she whispered.

Abruptly, he moved around her. Her heart squeezed with disappointment.

Until he opened his trunk and pulled out a snazzy-looking aluminum sun visor that was the size of a small blanket.

Grinning at her, he grabbed her hand and led her deeper into the trees until he found a spot he liked. He placed the sun visor on the ground.

Then he swept her into arms and laid her gently on top of it.

"What do you want to do first, baby?"

"I thought you were in control?"

"I am. And I'm choosing to ask you what you want to do first."

"Well, in that case, the first thing that comes to mind is you kissing me… in more than one place."

It started with stealth moves, soft and slow, but progressively became deeper and longer and harder until she was clawing at his clothes and her own. Soon nothing was between them and the sun but a smile, with him on his back and her positioned over him so they had their mouths on one another.

Lying outside naked, with his fingers and tongue inside her, with his cock in her mouth, she should have felt awkward. Self-conscious. All she felt was good. So good she never wanted it to end.

But it was going to.

Soon, if the tensing of her body was any indication. She was close.

And then she wasn't.

She got cold. She couldn't breathe. She pulled away from him. "Max, wait. You need to stop."

He didn't stop. He kept his face buried between her thighs, working her with fingers, tongue and teeth.

The cold started to recede. Her head fell back. She knew there was a reason she needed that cold. A reason to hold back from this man who had the power to hurt her more than any other man ever had.

She twisted, reached down, thrust her fingers in his hair and pulled hard. "Max. *Stop.*"

Twisting around so he was kneeling over her, his face above hers, he grabbed her wrists, and pinned them over her head with a one-handed grip. "I'm not going to stop, Grace, because you don't want me to stop."

"You have to—"

"You're scared. You're pulling back into your shell. But I'm not going to let you do it. I'm going to make you come."

She shook her head wildly even as a voice inside her head whispered, *Yes, make me come. Don't let me stop you. Give me what I really want, Max. Give me you.*

As if he read her mind, he said, "I'm going to force you to come."

Her pussy contracted at his words and a gush of liquid trailed down her thighs.

He saw it. He felt it when he inserted his hand between her thighs and began fondling her. "There's nothing you can do to stop me, Grace. You know why? Because it's what you want, but it's also what I want. What I want for you. And you are going to give it to me."

He said the last sentence in short staccato beats, loosening his hold on her at the end. Then he slowly let go of her wrists altogether, his eyes daring her to move them. She didn't. It was as if his words and the sheer power of his gaze and proximity continued to pin her down. Her body, bare from the waist down, was spread open for him, and she didn't have the energy or the brainpower to fight what was happening. He scooted down her body, keeping eye contact with her the whole time.

"Spread your legs wider," he commanded, then blew on her bare belly and pubic area. She jerked and whimpered, doing as he said, offering herself to him.

He gazed at her flesh until she was biting her lip to stop from screaming. Then he moved, burying his face between her thighs again, and she did scream.

Then he did exactly what he'd sworn he would.

He did everything she needed.

He sucked and nibbled on her clit. Licked her with long, strong strokes of his tongue and penetrated her with deep, slow thrusts of his fingers. He groaned and whispered to her as he did it, combining his beautiful voice with the sounds of raw, primal sex.

Her mind blanked, her body transforming into a fireball of pure sensation.

She forgot everything but what she was feeling and the fact it was Max making her feel it.

Before she even knew it was going to happen, he pushed her over the edge.

He made her forget her past and her insecurities, and all the times she'd told herself she shouldn't want or need things that normal people didn't want or need. He made her forget everything but him and the pleasure that built and built and built until she finally exploded into a million pieces.

Later, when she was able to breathe and move again, Grace scooted out of Max's embrace. He let her go, watching her warily as she pulled on her clothes. When she was done, she stepped toward the car. Suddenly, his arms were around her waist, pulling her close so her back was pressed to his front. His naked body pressed eagerly against hers, and she barely stopped herself from moaning in anguished delight.

"Are you okay?" he asked, his voice soft and hesitant.

She immediately felt like a bitch.

"Was I too rough? Did I—did I do something you didn't want?"

She twisted to look at him over her shoulder. "You did nothing wrong. You gave me exactly what I wanted, Max, and it was wonderful. I'm just... I'm just feeling a little shaken is all. You pack quite a punch."

When she turned to stare straight ahead again, he sighed and rested his chin on the top of her head.

She crossed her arms over his, then took one of his

hands, brought it to her lips and kissed it.

"You were right," she said quietly. "Even though we didn't string things out for long, the wait was well worth it."

"I second that," he said. He kissed Grace behind her right ear and continued to hold her. "Dixie—"

"I guess I can fly back to California earlier than I thought."

He stiffened. Then he turned her in his arms to face him. "We're not done, Grace."

"What do you mean?"

"You planned to stay the week. There's no reason you shouldn't."

"But you made me come," she said.

He smoothed her hair away from her face, then touched her lips with his fingertips, which still smelled and tasted like her. "I made you come with my fingers and tongue. But I haven't done my job until I've made you come every single way there is to do it. That didn't feel half as good as it will when my dick is inside you."

10

Max's Magic Rule #11:
Perfect the art of looking happy even
when you're miserable.

B y the time Max pulled up in front of Grace's hotel, he
had less than fifteen minutes to get to the theater and
prep before the show. It was probably for the best,
anyway. Grace was silently staring out the passenger
window, just as she had been doing for the last half of their
drive. Granted, she'd done it while he'd been holding her
hand—mainly because every time she tried to pull away,
he refused to let her—but despite allowing that physical
closeness, she was freaked out and scrambling to reinforce
all the walls he'd managed to partially break down.

Partially, he thought, because he hadn't even begun to
break down Grace's walls or see all of her.

Hell, this morning he didn't have a clue he was going
to see her, yet since then she'd pole- and lap-danced for
him, dry humped him, given him a blow job, touched

herself in front of him, and let him go down on her until she came. All that from and with the woman who'd not only never had an orgasm with a man before, but proclaimed sex wasn't the be-all-end-all—and was determined to devote all her future time and energy toward having a baby rather than finding a man who could satisfy her sexually, emotionally, romantically and in every other way that counted.

So now what?

Other than what he'd already told her, he had no clue. Other than intending to spend more time with her—making her come every way there was, and maybe even some ways that hadn't been thought of yet—Max wasn't sure what role he was going to be playing in Grace's life.

But he knew one thing.

If he had anything to say about it, he was damn well going to have a bigger role in her life than her best friend's brother-in-law.

He wasn't kidding himself. What they had right now—the passion and intoxication he felt just being with her—that wasn't going to last. Their intense sexual connection was going to burn out just like it had with every other woman he'd been with. But he liked and respected her. When this week was over, he didn't want to go back to being strangers who saw each other a couple of times a year then made polite small talk. He wanted a relationship with her, even if that relationship was friendship. It worked with Melina before she married Rhys. It could work with Grace, too.

She'd have been his friend a long time ago if he hadn't been so damn determined to stay away from her. And as her friend, he was more determined than ever to make her see how Operation Baby was the coward's way out.

If he failed? If he had to watch Grace grow plump with someone else's baby, and know that man was going to spend the next several decades sharing beautiful moments with her? He didn't want to think about that.

Because thinking about it pissed him off. It also made him feel sad. And he couldn't let himself feel either of those things.

About a half-hour ago, when he'd mentioned stopping by her hotel after his performance, she'd told him she was tired and needed a good night's sleep in order to be ready for her Skype appointment with a baby daddy candidate. His first instinct was to ask if she was crazy. *Even after proving you can have an orgasm with man, you're still going forward with your ludicrous plan?* His second instinct was to ask why she hadn't told him about the appointment earlier, but he didn't ask either one. Doing the first would just piss her off and likely make her bolt, something she was obviously far too willing to do. As for the second, he already knew why she hadn't mentioned it. She either didn't have an appointment, or she had an appointment and hadn't wanted to mention it, but changed her mind because doing so would now would buy her the time her panic wanted.

It was the last that made the most sense. Since he was

also shell-shocked from what happened between them, giving her space now seemed like the right thing to do. But that was only for tonight. Tomorrow he'd be back in her face, and that included talking to her before that Skype conversation.

Grace deserved better than an online-ordered baby-daddy. Both Grace and whatever child or children she'd have deserved a man in their lives who wanted to be there out of love and desire—not because of some prearranged coldly calculated bullshit. He should know. He'd been blessed with the best parents in the world. They modeled the type of relationship Max wanted if and when he ever found the right woman. The same type of relationship Rhys and Melina had.

Grace turned, looked at him and hesitantly smiled. "Thanks for everything, Max. It was fun." As soon as the words were out of her mouth, she rolled her eyes and laughed. "Well, I think we both know it was more than fun. I'll be busier than a cat on a hot tin roof tomorrow, otherwise I'd go to the theater with you."

"You saw the show the other night."

"You're just that good, Sug—I mean, honey." She lifted a hand and touched his lips, smiling when he kissed her. "Anyway, I know you've got to run. Have a great show tonight

"I'll try," he said. "Usually I love being on stage, but something tells me it won't compare to anything else I've done today."

She opened the car door, but when he moved to do the

same, she placed a staying hand on his arm. "No need to get out. Goodnight, Max."

"Goodnight," he said quietly. He watched her make her away into the hotel before he forced himself to drive away.

Later, backstage in his dressing room, Max took a quick shower and changed into his special show-ready tuxedo, still unable to get his mind off Grace. He replayed everything they'd talked about and done in and out of his car. How shy and wistful she'd looked at his parent's house. How afterwards she'd been literally shaking with her need for him. And how she'd initially fought her orgasm then surrendered herself to it so powerfully.

She'd exploded like fireworks on the Fourth of July—bright, beautiful, soaring and full of sparkle. He'd been so fucking turned on by how intensely she'd come, he'd almost come himself. But as amazing as her climax had been—and even though he'd been the one to give it to her—he couldn't wait to give her one when he was inside her. Sure, mouths and fingers and toys could get someone off, but what Grace wanted, what she needed, was to come with a cock rooted deep inside her. She needed to come the way nature had built her to come.

And so did he.

He just had to get through tonight's shows and then she was his.

* * *

Light pierced Grace's eyelids, waking her. Groaning, she realized she must have forgotten to pull the blackout blinds in her hotel room. She rubbed her eyes and sat up in bed.

Her big, empty bed, which didn't need to be empty.

Max could have been right here with her, finally sleeping after doing all kinds of wonderful things with her and to her last night.

Of course, he wasn't, and that was all her fault.

"I'm dumber than a June bug on a string," she muttered as she fell back on the bed.

But not really, the practical voice in her head reminded her. She was right to give them some space from one another. After the events of yesterday, she needed it. She was confused. Doubting what she was doing here and even what she was going to do after she left, and that included Operation Baby.

Were Melina, Lucy and Max right? Was having a baby right now a bad idea?

No. All she had to do was remember how she'd felt at the Dalton house yesterday, watching Max with his parents, and Chloe with Donna. She wanted that kind of relationship with a child. She wanted family, and no matter how much pleasure Max gave her this week, he couldn't give her that.

It was up to her to make it happen.

A knock sounded at the door. Her mind already on Max, her heart stuttered until she recalled arranging for breakfast delivery.

She brought in the tray, took a quick shower, then sat

cross-legged in the middle of the bed to eat. Next to her bagel and cream cheese sat one of the local papers. She spread cream cheese over her bagel, then opened the paper to the society section.

There, smiling wide at the camera, was Max. It was a photo of him and Elizabeth from that night outside Lodi's. Elizabeth looked gorgeous, wild-eyed and sexier than sin, her breasts pressed up against his arm so tight her dress gaped open. Not quite a nip-slip, but close.

And there was Grace, caught in a photo-bomb behind them, her devastation and confusion readily apparent.

Grace swallowed the large lump of bagel that stuck in her throat.

She looked like her heart had been broken.

If that wasn't a wakeup call to keep her emotional distance with Max, she didn't know what was.

A ping sounded on her phone. She grabbed it off the nightstand and read the text from the surrogacy agency. Her baby's potential father needed to reschedule their Skype interview—to a half hour from now.

She glanced around. It wouldn't take long to tidy her hotel room, but her hair was disastrous and she needed a little makeup.

Thirty minutes later, her hair pulled back in a French twist, and clad in her best professional button-up blouse and a pencil skirt, she sat in front of her laptop, screen open, nervously rubbing her sweaty palms on her thighs. Automatically, she set her phone to vibrate. The laptop screen beeped, then the smiling face of Robert

Montgomery appeared.

"You must be Grace," he said.

She studied him: thick blond hair professionally styled, a button-up in light blue, and he appeared to be seated in an office of some kind. On the walls behind him were various framed certificates or diplomas. A businessman then. Probably someone who'd be at every little league game or dance recital. Who'd play ball with his son after getting home from work, or be the carpool dad.

Not someone constantly playing the game. Always in the public eye and loving every minute of it.

Only it no longer seemed Max loved every minute of his life. He'd seemed happier throwing a ball with Houdini and spending time with her than she'd ever seen him on stage.

Yet…

She would *not* think of Max.

This moment was about Robert. And Operation Baby Daddy.

"Hello, Robert. It's so nice to meet your acquaintance." They spoke for a few minutes, exchanging pleasantries—careers, where they lived, favorite movies.

A vibration from her phone indicated a new text. Thinking of Melina and how worried Rhys was about her, she surreptitiously checked her phone.

Want to get naked tonight? It was Max.

She couldn't help herself. She smiled even as she forced her gaze back to the computer screen, where Robert was elaborating on his days on a row team at Harvard.

Quickly, she texted back: *Sure.*

Boring response. Text me something hot.

Robert was talking about his own childhood and Grace fought to pay attention.

"Would you agree consistency is important?" he asked.

Yes, she thought. Consistency would be great. She'd finally had an orgasm with a man's fingers and tongue inside her last night. When she and Max got naked together tonight, she was hoping for the same result—only she wanted his cock involved. Staring at the computer screen, Grace said, "If you mean in a shared parenting arrangement, yes. I think a child should have equal time with both parents."

Robert frowned. "I meant consistency as in going to bed on time every night, even on weekends. Eating the same well-balanced diet week to week. An exact form of punishment and consequences at each home."

Eating the same diet every week? She'd go crazy if she had to do that. What fun would it be if you couldn't have pancakes for dinner every once in a while? Or a burger for breakfast? And what was that about punishment?

Are you wearing lace panties again?

Her cheeks flushed and her breathing escalated. She relived the moment Max ripped her lace panties off the night before and went down on her. The fact that Robert was still frowning, studying her as if he could read her mind, made her wriggle in her seat to ease the ache steadily building between her thighs.

She couldn't imagine Max, let alone the Max who'd played with Houdini and Chloe yesterday, talking about eating the same thing or planning out ways to consistently discipline his child. He was too fun. Too vibrant. Too spontaneous for that. Look what happened when she'd begged him to pull over and kiss her.

He'd acted.

He'd sensed she needed more than that.

And he'd given it to her.

Robert didn't look like he could rip a pair of panties off anyone, no matter how turned on he was. But then again, that wasn't the job he was interviewing for.

She needed to focus on Robert, not on Max's naughty texts.

She texted Max back anyway.

Cotton underwear.

I don't believe you.

He shouldn't, she thought with a smile. She always wore lace panties.

I'm in boring business attire.

Nothing about you could ever be boring, Dixie. Why business attire?

I'm Skyping with a potential candidate.

When he didn't text back right away, she said to Robert, "I suppose we'd have to hone in on what each of us thinks is important. Make sure we're in agreement with how to raise the child. There are parenting classes—"

"I'm not taking any parenting class," Robert said. "I will be raising the child the way my parents raised me."

Grace frowned. Was she supposed to know what that meant?

I thought that was scheduled for later?

He called early.

Is he everything you want?

No, she thought.

Not sure. He just said he'd raise the child the way his parents raised him. Which means a consistent diet and punishment. ☹

He's an ass. Get rid of him. Now. If you don't do as I say, I'll punish you tonight.

She'd been thinking of getting rid of Robert-the-ass, too, but the moment Max mentioned punishment...

No, no. Stop thinking about Max tying you up and spanking you. Of making you feel so damn good it actually hurt. That wasn't what a normal woman planning a family would want.

No matter how fabulous it was last night or is going to be tonight, she had to think of the future. You don't have to love Robert, just make sure he'll be a good father. She wasn't going to make snap judgments.

She smiled sweetly at Robert. "I'd like to discuss what I consider important in raising a child."

Take off your panties. Finger your clit in a slow circle and imagine it's my tongue.

A shiver ran through her, culminating at her core, which went from hot to incinerating.

Stop sexting me, you pig.

Take them off.

Will you leave me alone if I do?

He didn't respond and she read both his silent dare and his refusal to agree to anything. It just ratcheted up her desire even more. But she'd already had one naked picture used against her and that had resulted in sexual misconduct charges at work. Did she really want to risk putting another picture out there?

Grace bit her lip. It wasn't that she didn't trust Max exactly. She'd trusted him enough to give him a blow job in a moving car. To beg him to kiss her and fuck her at the side of the road.

Her phone vibrated again.

I won't ever do anything to hurt you.

Grace trembled and her knees went a little weak. Her fingers hovered over her phone before she quickly punched out: *What if I want you to hurt me in a good way?*

Almost a full minute went by before he responded.

Did writing that make you wet?

Not wet. Wetter. Soaking.

"Grace?" She heard the male voice, but because it didn't belong to Max, she was momentarily confused. It took all her effort to direct her attention back to her computer.

"Are you okay?"

"Yes, I'm just having trouble with how inflexible you seem."

"Well, you're a woman. Women follow the man's

lead. I mean—" Robert leaned forward into his computer camera, close enough that his face nearly filled her screen, bringing her attention back to him and away from Max's texts.

"The agency said you were from the South," Robert said. "I figured you'd act like a Southern woman."

Her spine stiffened and she smacked her palms down on either side of the computer. Max had turned her on with his raunchy texts, but this man was eradicating her arousal with his sexist attitude.

"If by acting like a Southern woman you mean subservient to men," she said, "you're in the wrong century."

"I disagree."

He could disagree all he wanted. If he truly thought he was getting a baby from her, he was dumber than a soup sandwich.

Grace tuned him out and instead looked at her phone. Quickly, she texted Max: *He thinks I should act like a subservient Southern woman.*

Don't hang up on him. Take off your panties while he's still on the line, then text me a picture of your beautiful body.

Robert's voice brought her attention back to the computer screen. "So I'll make the decisions, then. We're in agreement?"

They were in agreement if she was a complete idiot and wanted a male chauvinist pig straight from the sixties to help raise her child. If Robert was any indication, it wasn't going to be easy finding her baby daddy.

Grace. Panties. Pussy. Now.

She normally hated it when a man used the "p" word, but with Max... he had a gift for knowing when to use dirty talk and when to use a more subtle hand. He had the same wonderful instincts when it came to using his body.

She couldn't help it. Couldn't stop herself. She pushed the rolling office chair back from the desk. Keeping her eyes on Robert and trying to be as discreet as possible, she pulled her skirt up, wriggled her black lace panties off, spread her thighs and, holding her phone strategically under the desk, took a picture.

Then hit SEND.

11

Max's Magic Rule #12:
Enjoy the applause while it lasts… because it always ends.

After that night's magic show ended and Max signed programs and tickets for his fans— he politely refused to sign various body parts offered by several women—he headed straight for Grace's hotel. He'd thought of her throughout the day—far too much, especially after she'd texted that mind blowing picture of the tender wet flesh between her legs. He'd never had a woman who could distract him when he was on stage, but he'd had to concentrate extra hard to keep focused. That worried him.

He'd only been with Grace a few days and going to bed without her last night had been painful. He hadn't been able to stop thinking of how she'd felt and tasted. How her expression had twisted and her body had shaken from the intensity of her climax. He wanted all that to happen when he was inside her. Even worse, he couldn't foresee a time he didn't want more of her. More time. More sex. More of whatever he could get. She was an intoxicating bundle of contradictions, a challenge but also fun, sexy, sweet. Most of all, being with her felt natural, as though the rest of his life was some kind of sham, and he could only let down his guard and be himself when he was with her. Like when they were in the car together. Or at his parents.

What the hell was up with that?

He was still contemplating the question when he pulled up in front of the hotel and handed his keys to the valet.

He could contemplate it all night. It wasn't going to stop him from finally getting inside her.

In the elevator, he texted to let her know he was on his way. Still, he was surprised when she yanked the door open before he could knock.

He was even more surprised to see her eyes puffy and red, as if she'd been crying.

"Tonight isn't the best time for us to continue this sex thing, Max," she said, her voice shaking, her gaze fixed to the floor by his feet.

Instead of pushing past and entering her room, he placed one hand on the doorway and leaned close. Something was up, and it didn't have anything to do with them. Did that guy on Skype something to upset her? Did he see what Grace was doing with her phone and give her a bad time about it?

Max told Grace before that they didn't know each

other yet—not well, at any rate—but he knew her well enough to know something hurt her, and badly. And whether she knew it about him or not, that was not something he was going to allow.

No one hurt his family. Or his friends. And as he'd already established in his own mind earlier that day, Grace was his friend.

"Let me in, Dixie," he said quietly.

She shook her head and bit her lip.

"Grace. Invite me in." He didn't take a step forward, but leaned in close enough for her to breathe in his scent. When she didn't back up, he lowered his head, touched his forehead to hers, and waited.

She didn't push him away. Didn't back up. Instead, she stood there for several moments, then whispered, "Come in."

In less than two minutes, he entered, shot the deadbolt, and ordered a bottle of California old vine zinfandel, macaroni and cheese and chocolate ice cream— his comfort foods of choice. Then he guided Grace toward the bed. Sitting with his back against the headboard, he pulled her into his arms. Grace leaned into his embrace but still avoided looking at him.

"So," he said, "we can sit here all night, and even fall asleep this way, with me holding you and you being silent, or you can tell me what's going on. It's up to you. This isn't something I'm taking control over. This is up to you, baby. But just know—I'm a good listener."

Grace snuffled and buried her head against his chest.

"One more thing I didn't know about you."

He let out a light chuckle. "You've learned a lot about me in the past couple of days. What else are you referring to?"

"Your mom told me something I should have known about you already."

"And that would be…"

She shook her head. "Never mind. I'll tell you another time."

"Wait a second," Max said. "You can't just—"

A knock sounded at the door. Gently, he disengaged himself and stood, but warned her, "We'll get back to that."

"Another time," she said.

He opened the door to the bellman, who set up the food then accepted his tip with a grin and a "Love your show, dude."

"Thanks," Max said.

"Hmm. That's weird," Grace said when they were alone again.

"That a bellman has seen my show?"

"That a *guy* complimented your show. In the time I've known you, you seem to attract only female fans. Beautiful female fans."

"Are you a fan, Grace?" he asked quietly.

She looked startled and pressed her lips together. Finally, she said, "You're a great magician, Max. A great lover." Before he could respond, she turned toward the food. "I'm famished. And thirsty." He watched as she downed a glass of wine before diving into the food.

"How did you know?" she asked.

"What?"

She waved a fork at the tray. "What comfort foods I like."

He shrugged. "I just ordered what I'd want if I was upset over something."

"You get upset?"

The question pissed him off, especially given her telling statement that he was a great magician and lover but nothing else. She obviously thought he was shallow, hard-hearted and emotionally closed off.

But then he looked at her and saw only teasing on her face.

She'd said his mother had revealed something about him that she should have known already. Since his mom would only reveal good things about him, maybe Grace didn't see him the way the rest of the world did. Maybe she just didn't want to admit how much she liked him because that would leave her emotionally vulnerable. After all, he hadn't exactly declared his intentions to remain in her life once this was all over.

"Food doing the trick?"

She nodded, set aside the tray, then cleared her throat. When she said nothing, he grabbed the bowl of ice cream and two spoons, and hopped back on the bed, this time leaning against the headboard next to Grace, who snuggled in and grabbed a spoon. "So, you being upset... Does it have to do with Operation Baby? Did the ass on Skype say something to make you feel bad?" he asked.

"No. I hung up on him right after I took that picture and sent it to you."

"That picture was the highlight of my day, you know. But we'll get back to that later, too. Tell me why you were crying."

"It's about my job. I don't know if you're aware of it, but I'm on administrative leave right now."

"I didn't know. Is that how you're able to take a week off? Because you're on leave?"

Sighing, she dug into the ice cream, then ate a few bites before responding. "There's a sexual misconduct suit against me. A graduate student named Logan Cooper filed it after a faculty party."

"Was he flunking out and needed to blackmail you?"

Her eyes widened. "You're not going to ask if the charges are legitimate?"

He stared at her. "Seriously?"

"Well, you don't really know that much about me—"

"I know enough, Grace. Enough to know you would never act inappropriately with one of your students. You can cover your body with tats and piercings and vajazzle, but you're a class act all the way."

Her face reflected startled pleasure before she frowned. "Vajazzle?"

"You know… embellishments for…" He waved his hand, making her giggle. "What? I'm being serious. It's a thing."

"You'd be the guy to know." Her smile dimmed.

"You're right. I'd never do anything inappropriate with a student. Not intentionally anyway. But what happened was my fault."

"How?"

"I did something, and Logan took it the wrong way. Quicker than a knife fight in a phone booth could start, he went to the dean and I was put on leave. I had someone, a witness who said he was going to come forward and explain that Logan misunderstood what happened. But I checked my emails tonight while you were doing your magic show and... well this witness is backing out."

"And you're afraid if the witness doesn't come forward, you might get fired?"

"Not really."

"I'm confused."

"I don't want my professional reputation stained, believe me I don't, but I'm leaving the job to focus on my plan anyway. This witness... Well, I guess I'm more upset about why he won't come forward than the fact that he won't."

He took the spoon she was waving about out of her hand and put the ice cream on the nightstand, then laced his fingers through hers. Stroking her knuckles with the pad of his thumb, he said, "What was it you did that Logan Cooper took the wrong way?"

Grace let out a deep sigh. "We were at a party— faculty and graduate students. I was his counselor during his undergrad program, and continued to advise him when he got into grad school. I knew he had a bit of a crush on me, but it seemed cute. Naïve, almost. At least, that's how it seemed at first. But I should have known better. He complained about his teachers a lot. In fact, he complained a lot period. I swear, if he had a ham under both arms he'd cry 'cause he had no bread. Anyway, he'd come on to me before, but he did so again at this party."

"You turned him down."

"Of course. I mean, he was hot in a young college student way, but as I already said, a bit irritating. And as a member of the university staff, I was in a position of trust. I'd never cross lines with a student, but I blurred those lines at the party."

"Blurred?"

She pulled her hand away and shifted off to the side so they were no longer touching. "There was someone else there, someone I'd... slept with. One of the professors, Steven LaBrecht. What we had wasn't anything more than sex, but he was a nice guy and he'd been hinting he was interested in getting together again. That he wanted to help me..." She waved her hand. "...You know."

"Keep going."

"I was wearing a wrap-around dress. And when I sat, my dress slid partway open and showed... pretty much everything. I was wearing a thong. I didn't mean for it to happen, but as soon as it did..."

"It turned you on, wondering if others would see."

She stayed silent several seconds. "I wasn't thinking about Logan at all, but I caught Steven's eye and he saw me and, well, I let my dress gap open a little too long.

Logan must have seen what was happening. He took a picture with his phone and turned it in as evidence that I was flirting with him."

"And Steven was going to be your witness to say you'd been flirting with *him*?"

Grace winced. "I know. Still tacky, but better the ethics committee know I'm just a skank rather than a skank who'd come onto a student." Grace's voice had grown harsh, and she wouldn't look at him, so Max cupped her chin and made her.

"Don't ever call yourself a skank or anything derogatory again, do you hear me?"

"Max—"

"Tell me you hear me, Grace."

"I hear you."

"Did you want Logan to see you with your thong showing?"

"No. I didn't want anyone but Steven to see me. The way I was positioned, I didn't think anyone else could."

"Did you want Logan to take a photo of you?"

She shook her head. "No, of course not. But in Logan's photo, people were milling behind me, and I had a martini in my hand. It all looked pretty damning. And you can't forget... I did get turned on by the possibility of someone seeing me."

"Someone. Steven. Not a student whose advances you already turned down."

"It was irresponsible of me."

"Maybe. It was also irresponsible for you to give me a

hummer while I was driving, but I wouldn't change that for the world. That's life, Grace. Sometimes you just have to live in the moment. Sometimes doing that will come back to bite you. It doesn't mean you did anything immoral or that someone is justified in throwing a mistake in your face, lying about it, and trying to get you fired because you wouldn't go out with him."

"That makes sense, I suppose."

"So what? The college believed him?"

"He even said the idea of going into a back room and fooling around came from me. That I suggested it and then flashed him to provoke him into having sex with me. I don't think the board would have believed him if it hadn't been for that photograph. Or if Steven had come forward."

"So why isn't he coming forward?"

"He has a new girlfriend. He doesn't want her to learn he's into kink, and he's afraid that's what will happen. That's his right, but it just…"

"It makes you feel even more ashamed of what you did. Like there's more reason to hide it."

"Yes," she whispered.

"Get that shit out of your head. You're intelligent, beautiful, healthy, and have great sexual energy. I understand why this Steven guy has some concerns about coming clean, but that's because the world can be harsh. It has nothing to do with who you are and whether you should be ashamed."

She let out a rough laugh. "Sex is supposed to happen in the privacy of one's own bedroom, not in public.

Getting off on the possibility of someone catching you naked is wrong. It was wrong at that party, and it was wrong today, when I texted you that photo while I was Skyping with Robert—"

"You're making yourself sound like an old man wearing a raincoat and flashing innocent bystanders on the street. You're not, Grace. You're a beautiful woman with a healthy sex drive and you're not afraid to explore it. At least, not when you trust yourself and the man you're with."

A sob caught in her throat and his chest ached with her pain.

"Why can't I get turned on in bed, with candlelight and a great guy? Why do I need a clit ring and pole dancing and blowing you in the car where people on the road can see I have a cock in my mouth? Why do I need kink? Why can't I be normal?"

There. *There* was her truth. She didn't think she was normal. Because of how hard it was for her to orgasm with a man and because of what it took to get her close. This was about her wanting to have a baby so she wouldn't be alone, yes, but also so she could be normal. This was about her not realizing how fucking amazing she was. How beautiful her sexuality was. He pulled her in tight and let her silently sob until the soft cotton of his button-down shirt lay damp against his chest.

"Don't let someone like Logan Cooper have that kind of power over you. You've got to be proud of who you are and own it."

She nodded, then pulled back slightly to look at him. "Do you believe that about yourself or just about others?"

"What?"

"Do you love being a performer so much that it's worth giving up having a dog like Houdini?"

He frowned and released her. "I enjoy being a performer. And I have responsibilities to the crew and my family. I have an intense lifestyle that doesn't make having a dog practical."

"That's not what I asked. Do you love your job enough that it's worth the sacrifices you're making?"

"What other sacrifices are you talking about?"

"You tell me."

"I would, but there aren't any. This is the life I want. I only have to worry about myself. I get to do what I want. With who I want. For how long I want. Then when I'm ready to move on, I do. Can't get much better than that."

She closed her eyes, as if his words landed a physical blow. "That doesn't sound like someone who wants to be a parent someday."

"When the time is right for me to be a parent, I'll know. It's not now and I'm not going to rush things just to prove I can be a good parent or have a wonderful family someday."

"So you think that's what I'm doing?" She stood, distancing herself further. At that moment, that's what he wanted too.

"You already know it is, Grace."

"Thank you for being so sweet but I think you should

leave. Like I said, I'm not really in the mood for sex. And that goes double now."

He clenched his teeth in frustration. "I didn't mean to make you feel worse."

"I butted into your business when I have no right to. We're not even friends. We're just fuck buddies, and ones with an upcoming expiration date."

He froze. "We're not friends?"

"Well..."

He got to his feet. "I guess I was thinking differently." He strode toward the door but turned to her before opening it. "I consider you my friend, Grace, and I was hoping that would continue past this week. I wasn't lying when I said you were amazing. Everything about you is special. When you find the right guy, making love in a bed with candlelight will do it for you. You just have to believe it will happen." He opened the door, pausing when she called his name.

"I think you're special, too. I didn't mean to imply you aren't."

His mouth twisted bitterly. "No matter how special you think I am, you don't even consider us friends."

"I misspoke—"

She hadn't. She'd spoken the truth. *Her* truth. "That's understandable. You're tired. And frankly, so am I. So tired I think I could sleep for years."

"Stay, Max. We don't have to have sex. You said we could sleep together. Let's talk first and then—"

She looked so upset he couldn't help himself. He

strode back to her and tipped her chin up with the touch of a finger. Gently, he gave her a soft. "It's okay, Dixie. Just get some sleep."

"Did Max Dalton just tell the woman he's vowed to give an orgasm to in every way possible to go to sleep?" She tried to joke, but it was clear from her expression she still felt bad for saying they weren't friends.

The truth hurt, right?

She'd hammered home the lesson Nancy Morrison taught him long ago. He wanted to give her space and comfort; she thought he was all about sex.

"Like I said, get some rest, Grace. I'll see you tomorrow."

He left. But when he did, he leaned back against the closed door. It was several minutes before he felt capable of moving. And several minutes after that before he knew what he needed to do.

* * *

The next day, Melina called. After reassuring Grace she was fine and she'd enjoyed a wonderful day with Rhys, she asked Grace to come over. Since Grace hadn't heard from Max and he hadn't returned her calls or texts, Grace jumped at the chance. Now she was sitting on Melina's couch, carefully folding freshly laundered onesies. So tiny, so soft... just the sight and touch of the little pieces of baby clothes made her insides tug with longing.

Her biological clock was ticking all right.

And at the same time, every time she thought of Max, she either felt aroused or guilty. Or aroused *and* guilty. She'd hurt his feelings last night when she'd said they weren't friends. But didn't he realize no sane single woman would *want* to be just friends, unless, like Melina, she had a dream man of her own that looked exactly like him?

"Have you heard anything from the university about Logan's complaint?" Melina asked.

Grace hesitated, feeling drained by all the drama the topic already caused last night. "The ethics committee hasn't made a ruling yet."

"And you're sure, even once you have the baby, you don't want to go back to work? Perhaps take an extended leave of absence rather than give up your job altogether?"

Melina's words caused a jolt to go through her. She'd referred to "the baby" as if he or she was a foregone conclusion, which was her tacit way of telling Grace she was going to support her in her plan. She smiled at her friend and blinked back the sting of tears in her eyes.

Melina covered Grace's hand with one of her own. "You've always supported Lucy and I, no matter what we were pursuing. I'm going to do the same for you. And I'm excited our babies will only be a year or two behind one another. I just wish…"

"What?"

"I just wish I knew you were going to be happy in your love life, too. But you're right. It'll come. And who knows, the right man might be under your nose already."

Which was Melina's subtle way of prodding her for information about Max. Not that she knew what Grace and Max had been doing. Max had promised to keep their arrangement a secret and she trusted him to do that. But Melina wasn't stupid. She knew Max tracked Grace down at that bar two nights ago and that immediately afterward Grace had extended her trip. Melina wasn't going to pressure Grace for information, but she was clearly jonesing for her friend and brother-in-law to get together, as in fall in love, not just have sex.

For a moment, Grace opened herself to the fantasy of being in a committed relationship with Max. Of having a child with him. A child who would love her from day one. The latter, at least, was possible.

A child she wouldn't have to fear would get bored with her and leave, or make every day a dream come true only to die...

She mentally winced. She knew what her thoughts meant. That she was a coward. But they also made her practical.

If her parents hadn't waited so long to have her, they could have watched her in dance recitals in grade school. Celebrated with her at her high school and college graduations. Been there to hold her and let her cry with her first heartbreak.

But time had cost not just them, but her all those opportunities. All those years she could have loved and been loved in return.

She didn't want to make the same mistake her mama

and daddy had—holding back on having a child until age compromised everything. Now was the time. The time to build her own family, no matter what form it took.

She looked at Melina's round belly, then stroked the pile of baby clothes next to her. Robert What's-his-Name had been a dud but the agency promised other candidates. Hopefully not all the men interested would be as sanctimonious.

A sudden gasp from Melina made Grace whip her head around. Her friend stood in the middle of the living room, one hand clutched tight to her belly, the other gripping the back of a chair. Her eyes were closed and she wore an intense grimace.

Grace's heart stuttered against her ribs. She stood and rushed to Melina. "Oh, God. Are you in labor?"

"I can't be," Melina said, eyes still closed. "I'm not due for another two months. It's probably just false labor."

"Here, let me help you to the couch." Grace slid her hand under Melina's elbow and guided her to where she'd just been sitting.

Almost ten minutes after that, Melina gasped again, and this time her face went white. Her gasp was followed by a guttural growl.

When she'd calmed, Grace called the hospital and explained what was happening. The nurse told her to come in if the contractions continued.

"I'm sure I'm fine. My water hasn't broken," Melina said. Another contraction took her. Then another. She let out a loud groan and screwed her eyes shut.

"I'm taking you to the hospital. Now." Grace found her purse and pulled out her phone.

"Braxton Hicks. I'm sure that's what this is. But maybe it's time to call Rhys." Melina was pale, her expression scared.

Finally! She'd wanted to call Rhys twenty minutes ago but Melina had refused. With shaking hands, she flipped to Rhys's cell number and hit dial. It went straight to voicemail. She left a brief message that she was taking his wife to the hospital because of what could be preterm labor.

Thirty minutes later, Grace paced next to Melina, who lay in a hospital bed, covered in monitoring equipment. They still hadn't heard from Rhys. The equipment showed the babies were fine, but the doctor hadn't said whether this was false labor or premature contractions.

"Are you sure you don't know where your husband is?" Grace asked, forcing tension from her voice. No sense in freaking out an already slightly freaked Melina. She sat next to her friend, stroking her arm in what she hoped was a reassuring manner.

"He had an appointment, that's all I know."

Melina gasped in pain again. Grace swept her gaze to the monitors—another contraction.

Maybe Max would know where his brother was.

She pulled her phone out and found his number. The naughty texts from yesterday were still there, but she ignored them. Max didn't answer either, but she left a detailed message, letting him know Melina was in the hospital and that she couldn't get ahold of his brother.

Moments later, Melina's doctor arrived and explained she was going to administer meds to stop Melina's contractions. She also said not to worry. That Melina and the babies were doing fine and weren't in danger.

It was almost an hour before her cell rang. She cast a quick glance at the caller ID: Max.

When she answered the call, he didn't wait for her to speak. "Rhys there?"

"We haven't been able to reach him."

"I have no clue where he is. How's Melina?" His voice was tight and rough. Throaty, as though full of emotion.

"She's fine. The doctor put her on medication to stop the contractions."

"The babies?"

Grace blew out a puff of air. "The babies are fine, too. Heart rates are normal, and everything looked good on the ultrasound. They're sleeping through the whole thing. Where are you?"

"I was in a meeting with our landlord. Jeremy spent half the time asking questions about Elizabeth and our photos in the paper. He was leaning towards letting us renew our lease... "

"Well go back then."

"'Fuck that. I'll be there as soon as I can."

His vehemence caught her off-guard. "That's not necessary."

"Screw what's necessary. You focus on Melina and

I'll keep trying to get ahold of my brother on my way over."

She glanced at the clock on the wall. Still early afternoon. He said he'd almost convinced Jeremy to renew the lease, and she knew how important that was to everyone involved in the show.

"Max, we're fine on our own. You don't have to come. Don't jeopardize your career for something we don't even know is serious or not."

"Dixie, the last thing I give a fuck about right now is my career. I'm certainly not going to be MIA when Melina's in the hospital and pregnant with my future nieces or nephews. I'll see you in fifteen minutes."

Max clicked out of the call, leaving Grace to stare blankly at the phone. Max rushing over to the hospital wasn't what she'd anticipated. She'd thought he'd make a couple of calls, put out a couple of texts, not walk away from the negotiating table.

Again, it proved how little she knew about Max and how much she'd underestimated him.

She turned to Melina. "Max doesn't know where Rhys is, but he's going to find him. He'll be here soon."

12

Max's Magic Rule #13:
If you get stage fright,
ock onto one person in the audience.

Max punched the button in the hospital elevator, his thoughts split between worry for Melina and anger at Grace. Since Grace assured him Melina was going to be fine, anger was winning out. He'd do anything for his family. Why didn't Grace see that? How could she doubt for even a second that he'd drop everything the minute he heard Melina was in the hospital?

The fact she *could* think that made him even more determined to end things with her. He'd given her what she wanted so why risk exposing himself to yet more evidence of her low opinion of him?

Quickly, he found Melina's room. When he saw her, his heart slowed. She was pale and had a limp arm wrapped around her belly, but she and Grace were smiling. She smiled even harder when she saw him, holding out her arms.

Grace smiled, too, but her smile faded when Max didn't reciprocate. She stood, giving up her spot next to Melina on the bed.

Max hugged Melina, pulled back then kissed her forehead.

"Thank God you're okay." Gently, he laid his palm on the bulge of Melina's stomach through her hospital gown and bed sheet. "Hey, babies."

Melina covered his hand with hers. "Max, you didn't need to come. The doctor has already given me something to stop the contractions."

"You're my sister now," Max said with a frown, acutely aware of how rough his voice had grown. "Even if you weren't, you're my friend. *You* know I'd be here."

Grace sucked in a breath. When he glanced up, her expression was stiff. Hurt.

Max sighed and shook his head slightly in apology. In case she didn't get the message, he said, "Hi Grace. Thanks for watching over Melina."

"No need to thank me," she said. "She's my best friend."

Melina flashed Grace another smile before turning back to Max. "Grace said you were in the middle of meeting with Jeremy. I'd hate for you to lose the theater because of me."

"That's not going to happen. Rhys—"

"He called a few minutes ago and is on his way," Melina said.

"Where was—?"

"Melina!"

His brother's voice sounded behind him.

Max spun around to see Rhys rushing through the doorway, his face pale and haggard, eyes frantic. "Ladybug," he whispered, his gaze fixed on the face of his wife.

"I'm okay, sweetie. And the babies are okay, too."

Now it was Max who stood, making room for Rhys to sit on the bed.

Just as Max had done, Rhys placed his hand on Melina's protruding stomach and gently caressed it. After leaning forward and giving her a soft kiss on the lips, he cast a glance around the room, taking in the beeping monitors and the IV in Melina's arm. "You said on the phone the doctor gave you meds to stop the contractions. You haven't had any more pain?"

"Absolutely none."

Max felt the air go in and out of his lungs more easily and he noticed Rhys's shoulders relax. Still, the fact he hadn't been able to reach his brother during a medical emergency pissed him off. "Where the hell were you, Rhys? Why weren't you with Melina?"

His brother frowned. "I was out looking for another theater for the show, so we wouldn't have to deal with Jeremy's bullshit any longer."

"You picked *now* to go hunting for a new venue? Yesterday you said Melina wasn't feeling well."

"Max—" Melina said.

"Your wife was probably in preterm labor, you dickhead."

"You think I would've left if I thought there was a chance in hell of her—"

"Rhys, Max didn't mean to imply that," Grace said quietly. She moved next to Max. "He knows how much you love Melina." Although she didn't take Max's hand, she stood close enough that he could feel her pressing against his side. She was taking his back, he realized. "He was just frantic when he couldn't reach you. We all were."

Rhys took a deep breath and turned to his wife. "Baby, I thought I was just a phone call away. I wasn't that far—just about two miles, in the Pixie Dust Hotel. The manager called earlier this morning to tell me their headliner was going on tour in Europe and we could have the venue if conditions were met. I was there, looking at the stage and backstage area." He swore quietly, then dipped his head to kiss Melina's lips then her belly. "I didn't realize there was no cell service in the theater. I should have checked to make sure. I am so, so sorry."

Melina laughed, the sound light and sweet. She stroked her husband's cheek. "You're here now. That's all that matters. Besides, Grace was with me. She knew exactly what to do. I was in excellent hands."

Max didn't hesitate. He reached down and took Grace's hand.

He hoped the gesture conveyed everything he wanted it to, including that he was sorry. That he admired her for being such a sweet and loyal friend to Melina. That he thought she was an incredible woman, and would be an amazing mother—he just wanted her to wait until the time and *the man* was right.

She looked at him with uncertainty then smiled and leaned in closer. Relief made him slightly dizzy.

When he looked up, both Rhys and Melina were staring at their joined hands.

Remembering his promise to keep their arrangement a secret, Max let go and took several steps away from her.

"The Pixie Dust Theater is gorgeous," Melina said. "What happened?"

"Unfortunately, even after all this, the venue won't work—not enough room under the stage for some of our tricks. For now, Jeremy's still got us on the hook." He looked at Max. "I really wanted the new venue to work," he said quietly. "You shouldn't have to play the media on a constant basis just to keep the lease agreement in place. That sucks for you."

Surprise shut down any response Max could have made. He'd always thought Rhys and his parents believed playing the charming playboy was easy for him. Rhys going out on his own and trying to find a new venue spoke volumes.

"How'd the meeting with Jeremy go today?" Rhys asked.

Max shook his head. "Let's talk about that later." Rhys wouldn't give a shit that Max left Jeremy hanging in the wind to race over here, even if that meant losing their lease as of yesterday, but the last thing he wanted was to add more to his brother's worries. Max wanted all of Rhys's focus where it belonged—on Melina and their babies, not on him or the show.

Grace said something to Melina and he looked at her again.

All day he'd planned what he'd say to her. How he'd tell her they were over. The thought of doing so had seemed difficult before. It seemed almost impossible now.

A rush of emotion swirled through him as he gazed at her. Awareness. Attraction. Respect. *Longing*.

That was a complication he didn't like. He'd started to care far too much about what Grace thought of him, and he wasn't big on being disappointed. In her eyes, he'd never be a man worthy enough to build a life with.

A bustling sounded at the doorway and he turned to see a doctor in a white coat, stethoscope around her neck and a chart in her hands, entering Melina's room.

After introducing herself and getting Melina's permission to speak in front of Max and Grace, the doctor flipped through the chart.

"You were definitely in preterm labor, Mrs. Dalton," Dr. Ellis said.

"Meaning?" Rhys asked.

"Melina's body thinks it's ready to have the babies. We've put her on medication but I'm going to recommend she stays in the hospital for the next few days while we get her stabilized."

* * *

After the doctor left, Grace breathed in deeply, the scent of cleanser reminding her where she was, as though the beeping monitors weren't proof enough. Thank God she'd been there to help Melina get to the hospital. And thank God Rhys showed up. Even though she'd been handling things and trying to hold it together beforehand, Melina had seemed to relax substantially once her husband appeared in the doorway.

It wasn't lost on Grace that she'd been hiding her own anxiety and stress, but felt immeasurably better after Max stormed into the room, even with his brooding expression and fisted hands, and the way he initially ignored her.

Now Max and Rhys spoke quietly, making arrangements for Melina's stay in the hospital. Watching them, she remembered her conversation with Max about whether she'd want two men to pleasure her. She doubted she'd ever actually do it, but the fantasy was hot as hell. The only thing hotter than imagining being taken by two men was imagining being taken by Max and his identical twin.

There'd be two pairs of green eyes to gaze into. Two sets of strong hands. Two muscled chests to caress and mouths to kiss. Two...

Max glanced up and cocked a questioning brow at her. Flushing, Grace looked away.

Mortification swept through her. What wrong with her? Melina was in the hospital and here she was fantasizing about her friend's husband doing her right along with Max.

She was a horrible, horrible person.

With her friend's pregnancy at risk, her quest for an orgasm, even if it had been partially achieved, seemed all the more ridiculous.

More than ever, the scare they'd all had tonight proved what mattered most was family. It was also a reminder that she'd wronged Max by doubting he could be more than a good lover.

Time and again, she'd told herself he was the man the media presented to the world—the man he presented to the media.

A playboy.

A bad boy.

Hell, he'd even called himself those things.

But those monikers weren't accurate. No, Max may have dated numerous women, and may have used the media's attention to pump up his own reputation, but deep down, his family came first. He cared deeply—about his mother, his father, his brother, and now his sister-in-law and soon-to-be-born nieces or nephews.

She watched Max reach out and stroke a strand of hair behind Melina's ears. Melina was right. If the way he treated his parents, Rhys and Melina, and yes, Grace, was any indication, Max was going to make a wonderful husband and father someday.

It just sucked that it wouldn't be with her.

That meant she needed to stop wasting their time. She needed to push forward with her plan. When the time was right, she'd tell Max. Let him know he was off the hook.

"What can we do, Grace and I?" Max asked Rhys.

Grace started. That Max included her in his question surprised her. He'd referred to them as a "we," reinforcing the conclusion Rhys and Melina would have jumped to when he'd reached out and held her hand.

They weren't a "we." Not an "us." And yet when she glanced at him, she realized he was staring at her as if the word "we" was on purpose.

She cleared her throat. "Yes... What do you need done? I'm happy to help."

Rhys ran a hand through his hair. "I can't think of anything."

Melina jabbed him in the ribs with an elbow. "Uh... hello? Nursery. Cribs. Disaster zone?"

Rhys flashed her a grin, then turned to Max. "I started the project yesterday, but I was distracted by my beautiful wife. The pieces are still all over the nursery. Do you think you and Grace could put cribs together?"

Max looked at Grace. "Do you know how to use those weird hex screwdriver things?"

She couldn't help it—she giggled. "I think between the two of us, we can figure out how to put together a couple of cribs. After all, neither of us has a beautiful wife to distract us."

Something dark flashed in Max's eyes, then was gone. "We'll do it," he said to Rhys. "Need anything else?"

"We need bedding for the babies, too," Melina said. "I have a bunch of clothes and diapers, but other than the quilts, no sheets or blankets."

"We'll take care of that once we're done with the cribs." He bent to give Melina a light kiss on the cheek. "And we'll be back later tonight to check on you."

Another use of the word "we," Grace noted. An odd tingle shot up her tummy and into her chest. In past relationships, the use of the word "we" had signaled a turning point—a moment when the relationship deepened from dating to a full-on connection. Was Max even aware of what he was saying or how it could be construed?

She gave herself a mental head-shake. She was reading way too much into a casual use of a pronoun. She may have finally admitted Max Dalton had much more depth than she'd originally given him credit for, but that didn't change anything. He'd offered to give her orgasms in a variety of ways. He seemed to like her and enjoy her company. But he'd liked and enjoyed the company of many, many women over the years, and he'd continue to do so.

13

Max's Magic Rule #14:
For good or bad, an audience can turn on you at any time.

The house was quiet—too quiet, Grace thought as she and Max walked into Melina and Rhys's place. The ticking of a clock in the kitchen was the only sound. Eerie, given that hours earlier her and Melina's laughter had filled the small home.

"I'll probably need your help," Max said, bumping into her as she came to a stop in the doorway of the nursery.

The room was a disaster. Crumpled instructions were scattered on the floor, as were slats, boards, screws and nuts. She nudged a board with her foot. "No problem, I'm happy to help. Looks like Rhys left us a bit of a mess," she said. "I imagine it would be hard to put a crib together with just one person."

Max barked out a quick laugh. "Yeah, especially when that one person is me."

She glanced at him and was surprised to see his face lined with tension instead of humor, the way she'd anticipated. "What do you mean?"

Max shrugged. "Rhys is the one that designs the props we need for the show. When it comes to inanimate objects, I'm great with my hands once something's built, but..." He shrugged. "Good thing I'm just the looks of the two of us or we'd be stuck with just cards and scarves rather than the intricate stuff Rhys creates."

"Max," she said quietly. "You're not just a sexy and good-looking guy. You're every bit as talented as Rhys. I'm ashamed if I ever implied otherwise..."

He stiffened and his eyes widened before his expression went blank. "Thanks. Now, how do we get started?" He focused on the crib parts, picking up a piece at random.

He's insecure and afraid, she realized. Just as insecure and afraid as I am. How is that possible?

"Max—" She stopped when he shook his head.

"Grace," he said. "I think, despite what you said the other day, you know we're friends. So given we're friends, let's just focus on the cribs, yeah?"

She wanted to shout no. She wanted to insist they talk about *him* and *her* and how much she liked him and how, if she thought it was really possible, she'd want to be more than his friend. Much, much more. Instead, she picked up the crib assembly instructions. "Here, take this and see what you can puzzle out. I'll gather up the hardware."

"Hardware?"

"Nuts. Bolts. Those hex screwdriver things you mentioned."

"Gotcha. I get the wood and you get to screw."

She laughed.

Five minutes later, Grace watched as Max studied the lengths of wood and the plethora of metal bits she'd carefully placed in front of him, explaining where they all went and how to use the hex driver. He held up two identical screws. "What the fuck? Didn't I already do this step?"

"Problems, Sugar?" Grace drawled, secretly pleased by how out of sorts Max seemed and how willing he was to let her see that. She suspected that wouldn't be the case with just anyone.

He pretended to look indignant. "Of course not."

Without being asked, Grace came over and started to help him assemble the crib. He'd admitted how bad he was at building things. Apparently that hadn't been much of an exaggeration.

After a few minutes of them working silently, Max cleared his throat. "So we never really talked about that Skype conversation you had earlier. Still determined to go through with Operation Baby?"

Tension tightened her spine. She wasn't so sure she was but he didn't need to know that. "I really don't want to argue with you about it, Max."

"I don't want to argue either. I'm really interested. Maybe... maybe I can even help."

"Help?" Her hands froze, then she moved again,

carefully laying out the odds and ends that confused Max to no end.

He shrugged. "Sure. I mean... I know guys..."

"You know guys..." What did he mean?

He cleared his throat again, obviously uncomfortable with the way the conversation was going, but apparently willing to persevere. "I mean, men who might want to make a family. Men maybe a bit more your style."

"You're pimping me out?"

She was joking, but when Max slapped a crib part to the ground and furrowed his brow, she worried he'd taken her seriously.

"Are you still determined to find someone to co-parent with, or has that changed at all?"

"Changed, how?" Now she was really confused. What was Max asking?

"I mean, have you reconsidered waiting for more? Love. Romance. In addition to..." He waved his hand, but this time she didn't even smile at their private joke. When she just stared at him, he blew out a sharp breath. "Never mind. Let's just get these damned cribs put together—and safely, might I add—and get to the baby store. Don't we need to buy bedding? Or is it bunting? That's a thing, right? A baby thing?"

"Yes," she said slowly. "Bunting is a baby thing, or at least it is in nursery rhymes." She hesitated, wondering if Max's questions could possibly be motivated by self-interest in finding love and romance and passion *with her*? But that kind of thinking was just heartbreak waiting to happen.

"I'm going to contact the agency," she said, "and explain how Robert wasn't anywhere close to what I wanted in a father for my child. But I'll admit, talking to him, it's given me second thoughts about having a baby with a stranger." How practical her plan had seemed when she'd first come up with it. And yet now, watching Melina and Rhys, becoming aware of the real man Max was behind the mask he presented to the public, she felt confused and uncertain. What would it be like to get pregnant by a man she loved? What would it be like to have the father of her children rush to her bedside when labor started, to kiss her belly and brush her hair from her face? How wonderful would it be if that man was Max?

"Grace?"

She realized she'd zoned out, staring out the windows at the darkened sky. Flashing a quick glance at Max, she noticed how intently he stared at her—as if he'd somehow entered into her mind and had heard her thoughts. But if he'd done that, surely he'd be laughing himself silly. "Maybe you all have been right. I searched for years to find the right man to give me an orgasm. How could I possibility think it would be easy to find an intelligent, educated, career-oriented man who wants a child but not the hassle of a relationship with the child's mom, beyond parenting?" She shook her head. "Sometimes I think I really am a slice short of an apple pie.'""

His expression turned fierce. "Hey stop it. You're not a slice short of anything. You just want to be happy and fulfilled, and you're willing to put your heart into it and take risks. That's admirable." His expression twisted. "Not many people do that."

"You do."

Once again, his expression went blank and for the first time, she realized how much practice he had at doing it. At performing in general. He was good at turning on and off, and concealing his feelings.

How much of Max was an act and how much of himself did he hide without even knowing he was doing it?

She shifted closer toward him. "Max. Are you unhappy in Vegas?"

"I like Vegas. I like being close to Rhys and Melina and knowing their kids are going to have some stability *and* adventure in their lives."

"But?"

"But sometimes I want more. Doesn't everyone?"

"Sure, but more of what? Money? Women? Fame?"

His mouth twisted and she mentally winced.

She didn't mean to, but she kept hurting him. "Do you want the love and family that Rhys and Melina are building together? Because sometimes it seems like you do, and maybe you don't think you can have it. Kind of how you accepted not being able to watch Houdini while your parents are gone."

"It's not the same thing. I—oh shit. My parents. I've got to call them. Tell them what's going on."

"Won't they just worry?"

"It's Melina," he said simply.

She nodded. "Right."

He got to his feet, pulled out his phone, then hesitated. "Grace?"

"Yes?"

"I enjoy talking to you. I want to keep doing it." His mouth twisted wryly. "Among other things, of course. Can we continue this conversation later?"

She bit her lip. "Yes, I'd like that, Max."

Max left the nursery to call his parents and was back within ten minutes.

"Are they already on a flight back?"

"I convinced them to wait until we have more information from the doctor." He rubbed his hands together. "So let's get these cribs together."

She turned back to the crib parts, stiffening when he said, "Unless you want to tell me why you blushed so hard when you were looking at Rhys and me at the hospital earlier?"

Her back to him, she closed her eyes before pasting a smile on her face and turning around. She handed him two blocks of wood and several screws.

He laughed.

She didn't.

But she smiled for a good long time as they got to work.

* * *

A few hours later, Grace stood with her jaw just about to

her knees while Max covered the baby store counter with items. Not just sheets and blankets but rattles and teething toys and board books. With each article he placed on the counter, he smiled as if seeing himself playing with the babies or reading them the books.

As the clerk rang up the purchases, Grace noticed a tiny ballerina outfit. A pink tulle ballet skirt banded a white long-sleeved onesie. For some reason, it made her think of the dance and acrobatic show that had moved in next door to Max's theater, the same one that contributed to their reduced ticket sales. She knew Max and Rhys's biggest concern was getting Jeremy to renew their lease. Then they intended to brainstorm ways to boost sales. Their late night show already included adult humor and even some topless action by Max's beautiful assistants, but she couldn't help thinking of the phrase "fighting fire with fire."

"Have you ever thought about adding an acrobatic act, or dancers to your show?" she asked.

Pulling out his wallet from his back pocket, Max hesitated. "No. Magic's always been the focus. I'm not sure I want it to be different."

"Just because something's always been one way doesn't mean a bit of change won't do it good or result in something even better. Maybe it's time to start looking at expanding the show to attract people with varied interests. Bring in people who aren't already sold on the allure of magic." Maybe it's time to start thinking about yourself differently, she thought, remembering how he'd indicated wanting more in his life.

He handed the clerk his credit card. "Go on."

"Tell me the truth. Were you happiest performing with Rhys or are you happier now?"

"Rhys is still plenty involved with the act—"

"That's not what I asked."

"I don't want him to ever feel guilty about doing what he needs to do to make himself and Melina happy."

"Max, that's the last thing I want. This is just you and me talking."

The clerk slipped the receipt closer to Max and he signed. "Then yes, I was happier performing with Rhys. It makes sense. More time with him. Less pressure on me. But I'm handling it."

"Of course you are. But what about modifying the act a little? Making it about a troupe instead of carrying everything on your shoulders." She rested a hand on his arm. "The success of the act has been your responsibility for a while now. I see it, Melina sees it, and even Rhys sees it. That's why he's trying to find another theater, isn't it?"

"Seems to be," Max said.

"It's not all up to you to fix things. You deserve to be happy, too, you know."

The clerk placed the bagged items in front of them. Max swept the packages off the countertop, not letting Grace carry any. "If I can fix anything, I will, especially with the babies on the way. But I'll think about what you said, Grace. I'm not sure I have the time to start investigating dance troupes, though."

"If 'ifs' and 'buts' were candy and nuts we'd all have a Merry Christmas. You've got to make the time for this, Max. I know a woman who runs a dance studio right here in Vegas. She's my lawyer's sister. I can put you in touch, if you want."

He grinned. "Candy and nuts, huh?" Out front, Max popped the trunk to his car and placed the packages inside. Before shutting it, he leaned against the back end of the car, folded his arms over his chest and looked at her. "Sounds like a fancy way of saying you want me to get off my ass so you can help me out. Does this mean we really are friends?"

I don't want to be your friend, she instantly thought. I want to be more. But she'd settle for that. "You've helped me. It's the least I can do to help you. I'm not sure if I've even given you anything that will work, but it's an idea."

He reached out, cupping her chin in his hand. She caught her breath and held it, heard the pounding in her ears as her heart rate intensified. Max pulled her closer to him until their hips touched. Her hands found his arms.

And then he kissed her.

Deep.

Long.

Hard.

There, on the side of the street, in front of the baby boutique, Max Dalton kissed Grace Sinclair with the tenderness of a lover.

Not a tomcat.

Not a bad boy.

But a man capable of putting his family before his career.

A man who loved his parents, who wanted a dog, and who made her feel whole.

A man capable of making all of Grace's dreams come true, whether he wanted to or not.

14

Max's Magic Rule #15:
The best performances happen when
you're not trying so hard.

After dropping off the baby supplies, Max and Grace stopped by the hospital to check on Melina, who was resting peacefully with Rhys by her side. For over an hour, Grace talked with her friends, noticing how Max, who sat beside her, couldn't seem to keep his hands off her. Whether it was to stroke her hair or rub her back or hold her hand, he didn't seem to care what message he might be communicating, either to her, Melina or Rhys.

And what he was communicating was that he cared for Grace and enjoyed her company.

It began to dawn on Grace that not only had she been wrong about what kind of man Max was, but maybe she'd been wrong about whether he'd want to build something even more special than friendship with her.

Suddenly, there was no longer a doubt in her mind it

was what she wanted.

As they walked to the hospital parking lot after saying their goodbyes, Grace stopped beside Max's car, took a deep breath and said, "In case you're interested, I want more than just an orgasm from you."

Max tilted his head to the side and frowned. "You mean you're considering me for the position of your baby's father?"

"No," she said quickly, wincing when he frowned and his eyes blazed. "Not that you wouldn't make a wonderful father. But I need to think about some things. Put my baby plan on hold."

His shoulders seemed to relax slightly. "Why?"

"I think you and Melina and Lucy might have been right," she whispered. "I mean, I still want a family. A baby. Sooner than later."

"Is there a 'but' coming?"

"*But* I think I was rushing into having a baby because I was lonely. All my life I've just wanted to be normal. My parents died when I was ten. My body refused to give me an orgasm with a man. Not normal. And I guess I saw the same thing happening down the line with a family. I was so afraid I wouldn't find the right man that I wanted to skip over any pressure to do so."

"And now?"

She glanced away but forced herself to say, "Now I'm thinking I've found the right man after all."

He folded his arms across his chest. Not encouraging. "Why the sudden change of heart."

"It's actually not that sudden," she said. "I've always liked you, but your reputation scared me. It still does. But if you feel the same way, if you want to give us a try beyond sex... I don't know, maybe we can run us up a flag pole and see what salutes."

He failed to crack a smile. "Say it straight."

"What?" *I've made a mistake. He's just standing there, when he has to know how hard this is.*

But maybe that's what he needs. To know someone cares enough, wants him enough, to get through a little discomfort to get him.

"Tell me exactly what you're saying so there can't be any confusion."

"I'm saying I want to get to know you better. I want to spend time with you. A lot more time. I'm saying if you gave me a chance, it would be easy to fall in love with you." She resisted glancing away at her discomfort. "I know that sounds silly. We've only been hanging out a few days but—" She lost the battle and her gaze darted to the sidewalk at her feet.

"Eyes on me, Grace."

When she raised her head, he was finally smiling. "It's not silly."

"Then what is it?"

He strode toward her. "It's fucking fantastic." Gripping her arms, he pulled her into his body so the breath whooshed out of her. He hugged her tight, then pulled back and kissed her deeply. "Do I look scared to you?" he asked after he raised his head.

"You look happy."

And she *felt* happy. Stunned by the knowledge Max actually wanted more from her than just sex. Even if it didn't last long, she was taking the ride.

"You say that now, but wait until I get you back to my place."

"What will I be saying then?"

"For starters, how about Please, More, Harder, and Please."

She giggled, feeling more carefree than she could ever remember. "You said please more than once."

"So will you. Now *please*, can we get in the car so we can get started?"

She nodded, then clasped his hands in hers. "We can go back to your place and just talk all night. If that's what it takes to prove I respect you and think of you as more than just a sex object, then definitely."

He raised their hands and kissed hers. "If I say thank you for the offer but now that I know you want more, I'm more than happy for you to think of me as a sex object, will that be okay?"

"To quote someone awesome I know, that would be fucking fantastic."

* * *

The drive from the hospital to Max's condo was significantly different than the drive to his parents' house. Shorter, of course, but almost transcendent, as though they were traveling in their own private bubble. As he drove, Max never stopped touching Grace, whether it was holding her hand or caressing her thigh while they were moving, or pulling her in for a kiss every time they stopped at a red light.

She began to crave those brief stops far more than she'd ever thought possible.

She wanted to hit every red light in Vegas just so she could experience an endless variety of Max Dalton kisses, from sweet to blazing hot. She liked that he kept her guessing about what was coming, never knowing if this time he'd nip her lip or plunge his tongue in her mouth or tease her with the barest of forays. The silence in the car added to the intimate atmosphere. Grace felt drugged on the look, the smell and taste of him.

She'd never ached this badly for a man.

She was confident she'd never feel this way about another man again.

And she hoped she wouldn't have the chance to find out.

The next time Max stopped, Grace decided to take the kind of kiss she wanted, and it was full-throttle. When she pulled back, Max looked as dazed as she felt. She turned toward the windshield, expecting to see a green light and angry drivers barreling around them. Instead, they were pulled up in front of Max's condo.

"You didn't tell me we were here."

"You kind of distracted me."

"Just kind of?"

"Let's go inside and I'll let you *definitely* distract me. Sound good?"

"Depends. Does anything go?"

"Baby, when it comes to you, I want everything. And I'm more than prepared to return the favor."

* * *

At Max's words, Grace's eyes actually glazed over. With a muttered curse, he got out of the car, opened her door and helped her out. As soon as they were inside, she dropped her purse and he pushed her up against the door. Hands clamped on her hips, he took her mouth even as he shook with the intensity of his feelings. He could barely believe she was here, not just in his arms but in his life, wanting more from him than just sex.

Their tongues tangled and her hips undulated against him in an uninhibited display of desire. He wanted to rip off their clothes and nail her against the door. Hammer into her. Fuck her until he got her out of his system and then do it all over again.

And he would.

But first he was going to give her something else. Something he'd never given a woman before.

He was going to give her all of him exactly the way she needed it. And that was going to require a little more finesse. He pulled away, smiling when her mouth followed his and she linked her fingers behind his neck, refusing to let him go. He rewarded her by cupping her breasts and playing with her nipples, wishing he could make their clothes disappear on command so he could get to the delicate piercings that drove him fucking insane.

When he finally tore his mouth from hers, she lifted her lashes and stared at him in confusion, her cheeks flushed and her breathing ragged. "Why'd you stop?"

"Because we're going upstairs, and while I'd normally carry you there, I need you to stay here while I take care of a few things." Her eyes instantly rounded and he smothered a laugh, picturing the wild assortment of *things* that must be running through her mind. "Don't worry. You already told me you're not into whips and chains."

She bit her lip. "If that's what you like… "

He kissed the tip of her nose. "Let's just start with you and me tonight."

She shivered at his implication they'd be working their way to other things. With a smile and sigh, she leaned back against the door.

"Give me a few minutes and then come up," he said.

She nodded and he headed upstairs to his bedroom. He immediately opened his closet and pulled out the box he used to hold various shit he accumulated over the years, mainly things his mom and Melina gave him and he was too sentimental to throw out. He grinned as he grabbed several scented candles, then tossed the box back onto the shelf. He reached into his pocket and took out the lighter he always carried simply because he used it in a variety of magic tricks. Lighting the candles, he positioned them next to the bed.

Grace wanted to have sex in a bed with lit candles around her. He was giving her that. But that was the only bit of 'normalcy' he was going to allow her. Fuck normal. He wanted Grace, kink and all, challenging him and making him work for everything she could give him.

Hearing a noise, he turned. Grace stood in the doorway, eyes wide with disbelief. "Max?" She blinked a couple of times, her voice rough with emotion.

He strode up to her and swung her into his arms. "I know it's just a few feet, but I've wanted to carry you like this for a helluva long time," he said. Bending, he kissed her as he walked. Then he gently lowered her.

He slipped her shirt over her head then undressed the rest of her, thoroughly kissing each patch of exposed skin before baring the next. He spent a long time at her breasts, sucking her nipples hard and tonguing her piercings until she was shifting restlessly, alternately pulling him into her body and pushing at his shoulders, not wanting him to stop but also wanting him to move on.

He urged her onto her stomach and focused on her tattoo, kissing down her spine from the top of one bird's wing to the bottom of the other. He straightened and ran one finger down the same trail. "This tattoo. What does it mean to you, Grace?"

She stiffened and turned her face into the sheets.

"Dixie?"

She took a deep breath. Released it. Turned her head so he could once again see her sweet profile but kept her eyes closed.

"It's a peacock," she said quietly. "Peacocks are beautiful but their plumage and dazzling color? It's all show. They look like they'd be able to fly forever, but they can't. They can only fly a very short distance."

So he'd been right in his interpretation; the tattoo on her back represented both flight and inaction. To Grace, she was a peacock, a grounded bird always longing to fly a little longer. A little farther.

He leaned down to kiss her lips and closed eyelids. Then he kissed up and down her spine once more. When he was done, he said, "Maybe ordinary peacocks can't fly for long. But don't forget I'm a magician, Dixie. Together we'll fly so high you'll think we've gone to heaven."

She turned over to face him and he lowered his head, kissing her again and again until all hints of sadness left her. "Undress me," he said even as he unsnapped her jeans and began to tug them down her legs. Eagerly, she obeyed.

Soon they were both naked and he was kneeling next to her. He felt his expression turn savage as he took her in. Her tousled hair, beautiful eyes, and puffy lips. Her tight pink nipples, creamy flesh and closely trimmed patch of blond fuzz at the juncture of her thighs.

"Fucking beautiful," he growled. He gripped his dick and pumped it several times, once again overcome by the need to shove himself inside her but still fighting it. She watched and lifted her hands to cup her breasts, fingers closing around her piercings to delicately tug.

His breath froze in his chest.

"Spread your legs for me," he said. "Show me your

pussy."

Her body jerked and her eyes went round but she immediately obeyed, spreading her bent knees wide so he could see her slick pink lips and the tiny hoop piercing the hood of her clit. His fist picked up speed and his mouth began to water. Abruptly, he covered her body with his, fists braced into the mattress as he took her mouth. When she was lost in his kiss, tongue dueling with his for dominance, he lowered himself so his chest pressed into hers and his hips forced her thighs even farther apart. She gave a keening cry as her tight little nipples stabbed into his chest.

He ripped his mouth away. "Jesus, you're hot, Grace. I bet you're so hot between your legs you'd burn me if I touched you."

"I am. I will. Please, honey. Touch me. Lick me."

He smoothed his palm over her hair and teased, "I am touching you."

"No," she said. "Touch me like you mean it. Like you need me. Like you'll starve without me."

"I *have* been starving without you. It's only been the past few days I've felt sated. Even if all we did was talk, you've given me more than any other woman ever has."

Joy sparkled in her eyes and he managed to smile at her before they kissed again. When her breathing grew ragged, he pulled back. His mouth latched on to her turgid nipple even as he dipped his fingers into the wet slit between her thighs. A smothered cry tore from her chest.

God, she was so wet. He inserted a finger inside her,

then two, and her engorged flesh hugged him. Adrenaline raced through him. Using his thumb, he rubbed circles around her clit, occasionally flicking her piercing. Beneath him, her body jerked again and again, performing a sexy little dance he was orchestrating. Unable to resist, he released her nipple with a soft pop, withdrew his hand from between her legs, and touched her lower lip, forcing her to taste herself. Her tongue immediately came out to swipe at him. Gently, he pushed two fingers into her mouth, and she sucked them. He shuddered, feeling the suction in his cock.

With his free hand, he cupped her breasts. Then he kissed his way down her body, nudging her legs farther and farther apart before settling one over each of his shoulders.

Gently, he caught her clit ring between his teeth and tugged.

She hissed and buried her hands in his hair. "Lord, Max. That feels so good."

"The pleasure's just begun, Dixie," he said.

Then he went to work to prove it to her.

* * *

Max's tongue swirled and probed her moist flesh, and Grace could barely contain the scream rising in her throat. She suspected once she started screaming, she wouldn't be able to stop. His hard body, his wicked mouth, his talented fingers—they were all driving her out of her mind with desire. And every time her eyes caught on the flickering candles surrounding his bed, her desire ratcheted up several notches, as did her affection for him.

He remembered what she'd said about wanting to have sex in a bed with candlelight. This man, this playboy who could have any woman he wanted, was taking the time to give her not only what her body needed, but what her heart did, too.

Right then and there, she fell in love with him and she had to bite her lip to stop herself from saying it.

When he sucked her clit, she clutched the bed linens beneath her and writhed. The tension built inside her and she held her breath, knowing the pleasure he was giving her was too intense to last much longer. But she needed it to last. She needed to make him feel as good as he was making her feel.

She tugged on his hair. "Max, wait."

His hands moved from her breasts to cup her ass, lifting her higher as he continued to eat her out. She felt the beginnings of an orgasm twitch through her and pushed it back.

He lifted his head. "Stop fighting it, Dixie. I want you to come in my mouth."

"I want that, too. But right now I want to come with you inside me. Please, Max. You said you'd give me that and I need it."

He stared at her, green eyes burning bright, then his hands clamped around her hips. She let out a surprised squeal when he flipped their positions. She blinked when she found herself straddling his gorgeous body. "Then take me, Grace. Take all of me."

She grinned at the challenge in his voice, then she took him.

She started with his nipples, laving and sucking the flat brown disks even as she cupped his balls and he stroked her back, whispering how sexy she was. How badly he wanted to fuck her. How he couldn't wait until she shuddered and came.

With a soft moan, she kissed her way down his muscled chest, rigid stomach and lean hips. Then her mouth covered the flared, engorged crest of his dick. Pleasure seemed to dance across his body as she blew him, alternating between soft sucks and deep pulls that took him down her throat. He shouted and bucked several times, almost making her gag, but she kept at it, remembering how his muscles had tightened before he'd come inside her mouth while he'd been driving, and how she'd eagerly drawn the pulsing jets of release from him. She loved how he tasted, clean but with a hint of spice.

"Grace, stop," he said. "Fuck, baby, your mouth is so hot. So good. But I'm too close. I want you to fuck me. I *need* you to fuck me."

She lifted her head, slowly sliding him out of her mouth. "I am fucking you," she said.

And even though his expression was tight, his face flushed, his eyes nearly desperate with lust, her magic man teased her, tossing her earlier words back at her.

"No," he said. "Fuck me like you mean it. Like you

need me. Like you'll starve without me."

"I *have* been starving without you, Max. But I'm not going to starve anymore. You're gonna fill me up."

She shifted until she was straddling him, gripping his dick and sliding the head of him through her slick folds. Teasing him just a little bit more with a taste of heaven.

* * *

Grace was killing him but he didn't care. He was going to savor every second of it.

Pulling her closer and burying his mouth in the side of her throat, he groaned at the slick wet glide of her over his erection. Wildness shuddered through him and his hips involuntarily jerked, seeking entrance into her body.

He forced himself to pull away.

She whimpered in distress.

"Shhh, baby, wait. I need to take care of you." He grabbed a condom from the nightstand, ripped the package open and quickly rolled on the rubber. When he was done, he leaned up, kissed her and cupped her face in his hands.

"Now that that's done, I need you to give it to me. Not Max. Not Sugar. Say it. Give me what I need."

Her eyes widened with understanding. "Honey," she said, and he immediately smiled. Once again, he got her in position above him, pressed the head of his dick against her saturated flesh and swirled himself against her. A rivulet of sweat ran down his spine.

"Please. Honey, you're making me feel so good. Give

me more. Please," she said, her words coming out as gasping cries, growing keener as he started to push inside.

She arched her back. Ran her tongue over her lips. Cupped her breasts. And before he could stop her, she pushed herself down on him. His shout mingled with her ragged moan.

The damp heat of her pussy was like a brand.

Eyes locked with hers, he thrust up, his flesh cleaving hers, her liquid heat surrounding him. Her tight flesh swallowing his dick inch by slow inch.

Once he was seated deep inside her, he clutched her hips and rocked her against him gently, knowing she was stuffed full and would feel him rubbing against her G-spot. She tossed her head and her expression tightened into one of pained pleasure, and it was so fucking beautiful he groaned. Forcing his hands away from her, he lowered his arms by his side until his palms touched the bed. "Ride me."

Shifting, she sat up and braced her arms on his chest, lifting herself up until only the tip of him was inside her. Then she lowered herself, swallowing him once again in her snug grip.

Up.

Then down.

Up. Down.

Again and again she took him, working his flesh deep inside her as he watched, transfixed by her beauty and fighting to stop himself from exploding.

When he was almost there and he could feel her

muscles tensing in preparation for her orgasm, he lifted his hand and cupped the back of her neck, drawing her head down so he could swallow her whimpers of pleasure. Pulling back, he locked gazes with her. "Come for me now, Grace. Give yourself to me and I swear, I'll do everything in my power to give you the world."

The orgasm ripped through her and she screamed, her inner walls clamping around his dick so hard that pleasure stabbed at his balls and he immediately followed her over the edge. His teeth snapped together and his body convulsed as he poured himself into her. Even though he could barely keep them open, his eyes stayed on Grace, watching every spasm shimmy through her until she collapsed against him.

Feeling shell-shocked, he wrapped his arms around her and hugged her close.

He caressed her back. Smoothed her hair. Kissed the top of her head.

And the entire time, he thought: What the hell had just happened? Because that wasn't sex.

No, it was far more than that.

Even as his thoughts scared the shit out of him, he couldn't wait to do it all over again.

Their bodies cooled and their breathing evened out before she stirred in his arms. Her fingers smoothed over his shoulders in a contented, kneading motion before she pushed herself up to look at him. Still inside her, his dick twitched and began to harden again.

"You did it," she said. "You made me come with you

inside me and you didn't need to hold me down or fuck me in public to do it. You did it in a bed, with lit candles around me."

"*We* did it," he said softly. "And I loved everything we did. But don't think it's always going to be like this. Because I want to fuck you every way there is, clean and dirty, slow and fast, achingly soft and head-bangingly furious. I want you to tell me everything you've ever wanted and I want to give it to you. Never be ashamed of who you are and what you like, Grace, because you're exactly what I need. In case you don't get that, I'm going to prove it to you tonight. Repeatedly."

15

Max's Magic Rule #16:
No matter how successful you become,
don't forget your friends.

The next morning, Grace woke to the smell of coffee and bacon, two of her favorite things, but she didn't smile until Max leaned down and kissed her shoulder. "Mmm," she said without opening her eyes. She stretched, enjoying all the small tingles and aches that lingered from the night before. "I was right."

"About what?"

"There's nothing you can't give a woman in bed."

When he didn't respond, she cracked her eyes, then opened them all the way. He was sitting beside her, a cup of coffee in one hand, and a worried expression on his face. "Hey. What happened? Did Chevrolet stop making trucks?" Sitting up and tugging the sheet around her, she cupped his face. "Honey, you're amazing. In bed and out. I'm happier than a tornado in a trailer park right now. But I was referring to you serving me breakfast in bed. I thought you believed I want *you*, not just your sexual prowess."

He set the cup of coffee down on the nightstand, right next to a plate that held an omelet and bacon. He rubbed the back of his neck before kissing her lightly, as if to reassure both of them. "I do. It's just a hard habit to break, thinking everyone sees me as a…well, a…"

She arched a brow. "Man-whore?"

He narrowed his eyes at her. "Funny. Melina once called me that."

She laughed. "If she did, I'm sure it was in the most loving way possible."

"Well, the only time I ever want you to call me that is when *you* can say it lovingly." He rested his forehead against hers. "Because it's going to be very easy to fall in love with you, too, Grace. In fact, I think I'm more than halfway there."

"Max—"

The phone rang from the other room and he frowned. "That's my cell. It might be Rhys. Don't move."

When he left, she flopped back on the bed and stared at the ceiling. Then a grin split her face and she had to stop herself from leaping to her feet and dancing right then and there.

"Grace," Max said. She looked up, immediately tensing. The worried expression was back.

"Melina—"

He shook his head. "No, she's fine. I'm sorry. I shouldn't have made you think…" He ran a hand through his hair.

"What is it?"

"That was Elizabeth on the phone."

Elizabeth. As in Elizabeth Parker, the hot blond actress he'd kissed in front of Lodi's? She looked away but the distress she was feeling must have been obvious.

"Hey," Max said, rushing to her side. "Look at me, Dixie."

When she did, he cupped her face. "I am crazy about you. You have nothing to worry about with Elizabeth. We're just friends."

Friends who'd had sex with each other. Friends who'd been photographed in a passionate embrace just days ago. But it wasn't like she didn't have a past, too. And he'd so easily believed in her innocence against Logan Cooper's accusations. She needed to believe in him, too.

"Okay," she said. "So why do you look so worried?"

"Elizabeth was just about to board a plane to Vegas when she called and it's probably getting ready to take off."

Good Lord. Did this have to do with their plan? Had she called to arrange another photo op with Max? Because she knew Max wasn't exactly hers, but she felt like he was. She didn't want another woman's anything on him, and she certainly didn't want photos of it splashed all over the papers. "So you and she..." She waved her hand in a circle but he grabbed it and squeezed gently.

"This has nothing to do with our plan. She was upset. She said she's about to cave and beg her cheating ex for

259

another chance."

"And she doesn't have anyone else to go to?"

He winced. "I know it's bad timing but…" Again he ran his hands through his hair.

"But she's your friend," she said.

"Yes. She is. But she's *just* a friend. And you're going to be so much more than that to me. You already are. If it makes you uncomfortable I won't pick her up."

She didn't want him to go, of course, but the whole reason she was here with him right now was because she knew what a great guy he was. A great guy would be there for his friend. "You should go."

"Are you saying you're not uncomfortable with the idea?"

"I'm saying I trust you, Max. That I wasn't lying when I said I wanted more than sex from you. I want… I want to build something special with you. Something lasting."

"I want that, too."

She nodded and forced a big smile. "So how much time do you have?"

"How much time do *we* have. And the better question is how much 'special' can we fit into two hours?"

"I don't know, but I'm looking forward to finding out."

"What about your breakfast?"

"I'll take my eggs and coffee cold. So long as I get you while you're hot."

* * *

At Max's request, Grace stayed at his condo after he left to pick up Elizabeth at the airport. He promised he'd be back in a few hours, after he had a chance to talk with her. Grace used the opportunity to visit Melina, who was doing great and would be going home the next day. She was just saying her goodbyes when Max called.

"Hey," she said. "Everything okay?"

"With Elizabeth? I'm hoping it will be soon."

"Does that mean you'll be back in time for a late lunch?"

"I'm not sure. Things are a little… complicated. But will you wait for me at my place?"

His serious tone finally registered. It seemed more than just serious because his friend was having troubles. It sounded like he wanted her to wait for him so he could have a talk with her about something she wouldn't want to talk about.

She glanced at Melina and Rhys, whose heads were bent in conversation. She hadn't told them about Elizabeth's impromptu visit, just that Max had business to take care of and would be by later. Then she'd dodged Melina's insistent questions about what was going on with her and Max. But she'd also blushed the whole time, making Melina laugh and only press harder until Rhys had said gently, "Ladybug, drop it. They'll tell us in their own time."

She caught them looking at her as she talked to Max

and stuck her tongue out at them even as she turned away. The playful gesture, however, contrasted sharply with the worry Max's demeanor and words had caused within her.

"Grace, will you wait for me?"

"Of course. But what's wrong? You're worrying me."

She heard him exhale loudly, as if gathering his courage. "I told you, you have nothing to worry about as far as Elizabeth goes. Problem is, she got off the plane wasted and I've been trying to sober her up while at the same time keeping her off the radar."

Poor Elizabeth, she thought. It was bad enough to be going through such a tough time without having to worry about bad press. "Anything else?"

"She showed me a paper she bought at the airport. We're in it, Grace. Someone took a picture of us kissing outside the baby store."

She breathed a sigh of relief. That wasn't great news, but it wasn't horrible either.

"Grace, I'm sorry. I promised to keep things between us private and—"

"Max," she said as she deliberately turned to face Melina and Rhys. "We kissed on the street." Melina and Rhys grinned and gave one another a high five. Melina even did a little jig in bed, which made Grace nod and smile. "It's not your fault. And I'm not upset. I mean, the two of us...if we're going to be together... People will find out. By the way, I just outed us to Melina and Rhys. They seem pleased as punch about it."

For the first time, his tone lightened. "Good. Now I

can kiss you wherever and whenever I like."

"As if anything's changed," she teased.

"I'll see you soon, Dixie."

"See you soon," she said.

But hours later, even after wrapping up her visit with a very happy Melina and Rhys, visiting the gym and watching a movie from Max's DVD collection, Max still hadn't returned.

Now it was six p.m., about seven hours after Max left for the airport to pick up Elizabeth. She'd just put another movie into the DVD player when someone knocked on Max's door.

She opened it to a nice looking man with curly dark hair. He wore a dress shirt and tie, a camera hanging from his shoulder, and a lanyard around his neck with some kind of ID. He was holding a pencil and pad of paper. "Ms. Sinclair, I'm Jeff Michaels with the *Vegas Scoop*."

Grace moved to shut the door. Michaels stuck his foot into the doorway to block her.

Grace's brows snapped down. "Move your foot. You have no business being here."

"You're sleeping with Max Dalton, a celebrity around here, and he's sleeping with Elizabeth Parker, an even bigger celebrity."

She didn't mean for it to come out. It just did. "Max is not sleeping with Elizabeth."

Michaels smirked. "Sorry, but he is. I just came from seeing them check into a hotel near the airport."

She lifted her chin. "I didn't just fall off the turnip

truck. You think I'll just take your word on that?" Besides, even if he was telling the truth, Max had said Elizabeth was drunk and he'd needed to take her someplace away from prying eyes. A hotel would certainly qualify.

Michaels held up his camera and showed her the screen.

He'd taken a picture of Max and Elizabeth in what appeared to be a full-on clinch, but could very well have been a hug between friends—if one of those friends was extremely upset. In the image, Max wore the same dark slacks and mint green shirt he had on when he'd left. And there was a little time stamp at the bottom of the screen indicating it was taken about three hours earlier, right around the time Max called her.

It would have been easy for her to jump to conclusions but, with the whole fiasco with Logan Cooper still fresh in her mind, she didn't. Instead, she remembered Max saying it would be easy to fall in love with her and she focused on that.

She focused on the fact she already loved him.

The reporter, however, wouldn't give up. "I followed the two of you here earlier. When Dalton left, I went with him. After I saw him with Elizabeth, I figured I'd come back and see if you were still here..."

"So you could hurt me? Sorry, you've failed. I know what kind of man Max is and that's all that matters. You can print whatever you want about him. I won't think any less of him."

Michaels finally withdrew his foot from the doorway.

"Does that mean you have no comment about the story I'm about to break?"

"There is no story."

"But there is. There's the story about how Elizabeth Parker couldn't keep her husband satisfied in bed and she's seeking solace in the arms of an old boyfriend, only he's cheating on her with a woman who likes sex so much, she harassed one of her students. A woman who likes sex so much she texted a naked picture of herself to Max Dalton's cell phone."

16

Max's Magic Rule #17:
Know when to pack up your things and get off stage.

Three days later

Grace closed the trunk of her car after shoving the last few things from her office inside. Before getting behind the wheel, she texted Melina the ruling by the university's ethics committee. She copied Lucy and Rhys on the message. She thought about adding Max, as well, but ultimately didn't.

She did, however, scroll to the messages they'd sexted one another during her Skype interview.

She should have deleted them. She didn't. She couldn't.

She hadn't seen him since that day he'd left to pick up Elizabeth from the airport. Once Michaels had told her the subject of his article and that it involved information derived from her texts with Max, she'd driven back to her hotel, packed up her things then stopped by the hospital to say goodbye to Melina and Rhys, swearing she'd fly down as soon as the babies were born.

She didn't leave Max a note. Didn't phone him.

And although he'd been blowing up her phone since she'd left, she'd refused to answer.

She wanted to. She had to force herself not to because she was afraid she'd cave.

She loved Max. She didn't believe he'd betrayed her with Elizabeth.

But Michaels' visit had clarified the real reason she and Max couldn't be together.

It wasn't that he was a playboy and wouldn't want to have a relationship with her. It was because he was a celebrity, one whose private life would constantly be fair game to the media. He was also a man who made all the kink she'd been born with go into hyper drive.

That's not what she wanted.

She wanted love. She wanted family. But most of all she wanted a normal life.

Now that she'd left Vegas, she was several steps closer to getting it.

For now, the fiasco with Logan Cooper was over.

The university's ethics committee had ruled in her favor. In the end, they'd decided Grace's behavior at the campus mixer had been unwise but not unethical. A huge factor in the committee's decision was that, after Grace's lawyer forwarded him the article Michaels had run in *The Scoop*, Steven LaBrecht had come forward to testify on her behalf after all. She and Steven had gone to coffee after he gave his statement to the committee, and Steven said the woman he was dating was sticking by him. Grace was glad.

There was still the lawsuit against the university to contend with, but her lawyer was confident that given Steven's statement, it would eventually be settled or dismissed outright. And although she'd had to deal with a bevy of reporters trying to follow-up on Michaels's story once she'd returned to California, they'd soon lost interest in her once they'd realized Max wasn't going to show and that she refused to say a word about him. It helped that both Elizabeth and Max had seemed to disappear as well. There were all kinds of speculations online that they'd flown to the Caribbean to try to undo the damage Grace did to their budding relationship. Grace knew from Melina that was far from the truth. Elizabeth was holed up somewhere even Melina didn't know of, and Max had gone off by himself to stay at his parents' house.

At least he'd be able to spend some quality time with Houdini, she thought. That would be good for him. And she wanted what was good for Max.

She just knew what was good for *her* and that was for them to stay away from one another.

Michaels's article wasn't as bad as it could have been. Although it referred to her and Max sexting one another, it didn't include any of the actual texts, or the photo she'd texted. In the end, it was just another tabloid article that could have been based in truth or completely fabricated.

Now Grace was headed home. She'd quit her job at the university as planned, but she'd also dropped Operation Baby. If she'd learned one thing during her time with Max, it was that she didn't know what she wanted. Acting rashly by bringing a baby into the world under those circumstances was not okay.

Grace was intent on getting inside her car when she sensed movement behind her.

She turned and saw Max.

She nearly whimpered in combined excitement and regret. He looked good, but he also looked tired. Haggard. Worn-out and drained. Much the same way Rhys had looked when he'd rushed to the hospital the day Melina had those contractions.

Max's expression never changed to joy or relief the way Rhys's had. He stood several feet away, arms crossed over his chest, scowling.

She barely resisted throwing herself at him.

It had only been three days and she missed him. Longed for him. Every minute of every day, but especially at night, when she was haunted with memories of them being in each other's arms.

She finally asked, "Melina's okay?" even though she knew she was. If something was wrong or if Melina had gone into labor, Rhys would have called or texted her.

He didn't reply.

"What brings you here, Max?"

Her words seemed to snap him out of a trance. He strode toward her. Then to her utter shock he bent low, put his shoulder to her belly and straightened, carrying her away from her car. It took several seconds before she could speak. "What are you doing?"

"Bringing you some place you can't run away from me. I'm a magician. I have an assortment of ties and handcuffs. Too bad I didn't know when I left my place to see Elizabeth that you were going to run. I would've tied you to the bed."

Having reached his car and unlocked the doors with his beeper, he threw open the passenger door and stooped down to gently deposit her inside. "Stay," he said, pointing at her.

As if she was freaking Houdini.

Fortunately for him and unfortunately for her, she was in such shock over what he'd just done and said, he was able to get behind the wheel and start driving before she recovered.

"Are you crazy?"

"Crazy pissed, crazy frustrated, crazy to have ever gotten involved with you. Take your pick," he said.

That made her mouth snap shut. She knew it was stupid, but his comment hurt.

He seemed to get that. Sighing, he said, "In case you're wondering, I'm also still crazy about you. And I know you're still crazy about me."

His bright green eyes lasered into her, holding so much resolve that she had to turn away and glance out the window.

"You're wrong, Max," she said quietly.

"No, *you're* wrong if you think I'm letting you walk away from me."

Her head snapped around and she stared at his profile as he drove. "'Letting me'? We're not in bed, Max, and last time I checked, you no longer have any control over me."

"I can change that."

She shivered and her core began to throb. Max had always been more than his fair share of bad boy, but she'd never seen him this dominant before. She wanted to keep fighting him on principle, but she could plainly see how hurt he was just beneath the surface of his anger.

She'd done that.

She didn't want to hurt either one of them anymore.

Time to try logic and honesty. Max was reasonable and they hadn't been together that long. She'd just explain why this wasn't going to work for her, like she should've in the first place, and he'd be reasonable. He had so many women who wanted to be with him. He didn't need her complicating his life.

"You're right. I am crazy about you. But you can't give me what I need. I want a family. I want stability. I want a nice, normal, peaceful life. As a visit from a certain reporter proved you come with drama, not peace."

"You need some drama."

"Not that much. Good Lord, Max, they crucified me in that article. The things they said... About the lawsuit... About those texts..."

"It was Jeremy. He took my phone during a

performance one night. Read through it. He needed the money, and he knew Michaels worked for *The Scoop*. He called him. Thankfully, he knew better than to actually forward our texts to him."

"Jeremy? Your landlord."

"Ex-landlord."

"Oh no, Max. You didn't give up your lease for me, did you?"

"Are you serious?"

"No I—"

"Are you fucking serious?"

Stunned, she stopped talking.

He pulled the car into a strip mall parking lot and turned to face her. "Dixie, the guy stole my phone and used personal and private information to hurt you. Breaking our lease was the least of what Rhys and I did to him."

Her eyes rounded and he shook his head. "We didn't hurt him even though we really wanted to. Can't take the risk of Rhys not being around for his babies. And I didn't want to take the risk of not being around when you came to your senses."

"I've retained my senses, Max. That picture I sent you..."

"I deleted it off my phone right after you sent it. Jeremy never saw it."

"You deleted it but not the texts."

"The photo... I didn't want to risk someone seeing it and tracking it back to you. The texts I took a calculated risk on. Turned out to be the wrong decision and I'm sorry about that. But like I told you before: sometimes to live a full life, you've got to take risks and those risks are going to backfire on you. Doesn't mean you stop taking risks."

She wanted to believe that, but she couldn't. "You and I won't work. I wish that wasn't the case, but if wishes were fishes we'd all cast our nets. You're in the spotlight and I'm just a normal girl who craves family—"

"Bullshit. You're not 'normal' no matter how much you want to be. And that's a good thing, Grace. You want a family, but you also want love. You want excitement. You want kink. I can give you all of that if you'll let me."

"No."

He stared at her. Took her hands and kissed them, just as he'd done in the past. "I know it sucked, having that reporter blindside you. I know you were humiliated. But it wasn't me who did that to you, Grace. And right now you're telling me I'm not worth the drama, even if said drama wasn't my fault."

She wanted so badly to reassure him but she couldn't. He was right. She *wasn't* normal—her propensity for kink and the risks she took proved that—but she wanted to be normal. To be normal, she needed a normal life. Not a life in Vegas dating a celebrity magician.

"The drama wasn't your fault, Max. It's just… it's just who you are. It's all you'll ever be."

He looked like she'd stabbed him. "Right." He stared at their joined hands for several seconds before letting go. He started driving again, executing an abrupt U-turn and heading back in the direction of the university. "God, I never learn. First Nancy and now, eleven years later, you. I thought I'd learned my lesson."

She didn't know who Nancy was, but the way he said her name, she knew she didn't want to be compared to her. "Max, I'm sorry," she said when he pulled up next to her car. "We want different things…"

"Don't play that card, Grace. You're scared. You opened up to me, and then you had to deal with some ugly stuff, and you're afraid there's going to be more ugly stuff. But what you're most afraid of? You're afraid I'm going to hurt you."

"And that's so outside the realm of possibility? You've left plenty of women behind, Max."

"I have. But when I walked away, I did it knowing I never promised them I wouldn't. I never lied to any of those women. But you lied. You told me you respected me. That you wanted to build something special with me."

"Honey, I didn't lie. All that was true. It *is* true. But we're too different."

"Again, bullshit, Grace. Now get out. Go pursue your normal life. Just remember, when you're bored out of your fucking mind and realize you could have had more, everything, just remember *you're* the one who walked away. And now you've done it twice."

She hesitated. Struggled with indecision. Then she got out of the car.

As soon as she shut the door, Max drove off.

17

Max's Magic Rule #18:
Leave your heart on the stage every single time.

"You're out of your mind," Lucy said, even as she took out the clothes Grace put in a suitcase. As soon as Melina had the babies and Grace held them, she was headed for the Caribbean. She'd bought her ticket and everything. But first, she had to get Lucy to stop unpacking her stuff.

She took the clothes Lucy put back in her drawer and put them in her suitcase again. "Lucy, stop. I told you I don't want to talk about it."

"And you thought that was actually going to shut me up? You two are perfect for one another." Lucy made a grab for Grace's clothes again, but Grace shut the lid just in time. Quickly, she closed the zipper before turning back to her friend.

"How can you say that? His lifestyle got me crucified in the papers. Half of Vegas knows about the sexual misconduct charges—"

"That your employer found had no merit."

"—and that I texted Max a picture of my private parts."

Lucy pursed her lips. "*The Scoop* is tabloid trash. No one believes what it actually prints. And even if someone did, you're a sexually active female. In the grand scheme of things, it's not that shocking. What *is* shocking is you actually believing the article is the reason you're running from Max."

"It is the reason."

"It's a convenient excuse to take the easy road instead of taking a risk."

Grace whirled on Lucy. "You're one to talk."

Lucy scowled. "What does that mean?"

"It means you're dating Jericho and sticking by your 'like-should-be-with-like' theory—which by the way is further proof that Max and I would be a disaster together—because it's the easy road. You'd rather do that than deal with the fact you were crazy about Jamie and heartbroken when he left you."

Lucy jerked back. "First, Max and you *are* alike, whether you want to admit it or not," she said quietly. "You're both loving and intensely loyal and smart and ambitious, and you've both got enough kink in you to fill Caesar's Palace. Second, Jamie didn't break up with me." Lucy sat down on Grace's bed, her expression crumpling. She wiped furiously at the tears pooling in her eyes. "But he made it so I had no choice but to break up with him."

Shocked by both Lucy's admission and the fact she was crying—she'd never seen Lucy cry before—Grace sat next to her and placed a hand on her arm. "Tell me."

"He lied. About who he is. What he does."

"He's not really a professor?"

"He is, but there's so much more to his life than that. He comes from wealth. He's so stinking rich, it's obscene."

"Oh," Grace said.

You'd never know it, but Lucy came from money, too. And she hated it. Her father and mother controlled her, made her feel bad for not fitting into the high society crowd, said hateful things about her choices in hairstyles, career, men and practically everything else. Lucy left that behind when she was sixteen and never looked back.

"But Jamie's not like that. He's working as a college professor. He's never treated you with disrespect."

"He tried telling me what to wear. Thought I dressed too revealing."

"That's probably because he was jealous."

"He didn't like me going out to clubs. He wanted to stay home all the time and wanted me to do the same."

"He didn't want to share you."

She shook her head. "No. It wasn't jealousy. It was image he was worried about. Even if it was jealousy, I'm no man's possession. And most important, he's a liar. Everything I thought I knew about him wasn't true."

"Not everything. Certainly not the way he felt about you."

"You're wrong. I walked away and he never called me. Not once. That tells me how he felt about me."

"That doesn't mean he doesn't care about you, Lucy. That he didn't love you. He probably still loves you."

"It means he wasn't willing to fight for what we had, and to me, that's the same thing. And I'm betting Max feels the same way."

Grace pulled back and stood. "That's not fair." Even as she said the words, she remembered one of her mama's favorite sayings: *Fare is what you pay to ride the bus.*

"It wasn't meant to be," Lucy said. "It was meant to shake some sense into you before you lose the best thing that's ever happened to you."

"He's drama, Lucy."

"And you love drama, Grace. At least the kind Max can give you. He'll try his best to protect you from the kind you don't like. Obviously he won't always succeed. But he'll never stop trying. He'll always be by your side, getting kicked in the teeth right along with you. Too bad he can't say the same thing about you."

She must have looked crushed because Lucy stood and folded her in her arms. "I'm sorry for being harsh, Grace, but let's not forget: Jamie lied to me. Max has never lied to you. Not about who he is. Not about how he feels about you. What happened sucked, but it sucked for both of you. And you ran from him like it was all his fault."

Now she was the one fighting back tears. "That's not what I meant to communicate. I'm just scared, Lucy. He amps-up everything inside me, the good and the bad."

Lucy pulled back and shook her. "You don't have a bad bone in your body."

"I want to be normal," she whispered. "Like Melina. I want to have love and a family. I want people to respect me."

"First, Melina is far from normal. Second, you have all that already. In case you don't get it, me and Melina and Rhys and their babies, we're your family. We always have been. Max will be, too, if you give him the chance."

Staring into Lucy's eyes, she finally accepted it. She'd had her family all along. Why hadn't she seen it before? "I messed up, didn't I?"

"You freaked. It's understandable. The question is what are you going to do now?"

"The last time I saw Max he was as mad as a mule chewing on bumblebees. With good reason. I left Vegas, refused to answer his calls then turned him away like a lily livered coward. What can I do?"

"Take a lesson from the Daltons and prepare to give the performance of a lifetime. Roll up your sleeves and make the biggest play of your life and show Max how you feel. Anything coming to mind?"

She thought about her time with Max. Both the confidence and the insecurities he'd shown her. And how she wanted to give him everything he thought he couldn't have—including her. "Actually, a couple of things do. But I'm going to need a lot of help."

* * *

"I told you I can take care of the new theater search, Rhys. You should be with Melina."

"Melina's fine, Max. Mom and Dad are with her."

Only because they'd cut their trip short, but once Melina had gone to the hospital, none of them had really expected anything different. "But *you're* not with her."

"We're going to check out the Paradise Theater when we have a chance. You've always loved it and now it's vacant."

"It also costs a fortune to rent."

"I told you, I'm working on an investor who's interested. He just needs us to give him a game plan for a fresh act, and to come up with that game plan, I need you to take a look at the theater and work up some new tricks with me. The tour won't take long. We'll just check out the place. See if it has what we need and whether it inspires us."

"Fine." Max grumbled as they entered the theater. Part of him wished Rhys would just leave him alone but the other part was grateful his brother was still pushing forward. Given how devastated he'd been after seeing Grace, Max should be lying around watching TV, drinking beer and eating pizza all day. But he had his family and those babies to think of, so he had to get his ass in gear some time.

He forced himself to focus on the theater lobby. It was a beauty, with wood, stone and crown molding. The theater itself was huge, with lots of space under the stage and in the wings, which was critical for an act like theirs that required large set pieces and trap doors. He felt a jolt of excitement he hadn't felt since before Grace left.

"Look," he said. "We don't know what we need yet so we might be going about this backwards. I told you Grace's suggestion about working with a dance troupe and I think we need to give that more thought. Maybe we should wait before looking at theaters."

"I completely agree that Grace's suggestion has merit, but the theater is available now. We need to act before someone else does. Ah, here we are.

Rhys opened the huge doors that led into the theater itself.

"Looks like we might be too late already," Max said.

There were people on the stage, some stretching and some dancing. "Sorry, Rhys. I know how much—"

"Max Dalton?"

He turned toward the woman who'd called him and was now moving toward him with long, graceful strides. She was wearing a leotard and tights.

"Yes?" he said.

She held out her hand. "I'm Louisa James. I run a local dance studio."

Max shook her hand. "Right. My brother and I were just going to—" He turned to introduce the woman to Rhys, but his brother had disappeared. What the hell?

He turned back to Ms. James. "I'm sorry to disturb you. I'll just be going."

"Oh you didn't disturb us. We're here for you. Grace arranged for it."

"Grace?" He looked around, his pulse escalating at the idea of seeing her, even as he wondered again what the hell was going on.

"She told me you were interested in incorporating some dance and acrobatics into your magic act. She arranged for me to bring several dancers so we can talk about different options."

Max couldn't believe it. The last time he'd seen her, Grace had wanted nothing to do with his 'drama'. So why had she arranged for all this?

The answer was obvious.

Grace was afraid of taking a risk on him as a lover and partner. She refused to see herself as normal, kink and all. But she was a good person. A good friend. She cared about Melina and Rhys and their future. Hell, she probably cared about Max, too. Just not enough. "When did Grace contact you?"

"A few days ago."

After he'd acted like a caveman, carried her to his car, then practically kicked her out of it because she'd hurt his feelings.

"Is Grace here?"

"No but she is in Vegas. She said she'd stop by later. Shall we talk things out?"

Grace was in Vegas. He was going to see her. He didn't know if that was a good idea or not, and he didn't care. "Yes, let's do that."

Hours later, Max sat alone in the quiet theater waiting for Grace. Louisa James and her dancers had shown him some definite possibilities for making the show bigger than ever. They'd already scheduled a time to meet again. Even if it turned out Rhys and Max couldn't afford to lease the Paradise Theater, there were others . . .

But where was Grace?

He wanted to thank her. He wanted to ask her what all this meant. He wanted to know if she'd changed her mind about giving them another chance.

But she'd hurt him. Far more than Nancy Morrison ever had. Could he really set himself up for that kind of hurt again?

He knew now Nancy's rejection all those years ago had more to do with her own insecurities than it had him. She'd talked a good game, but when he replayed her words, he saw how many of them focused on her fear that he'd get bored and move on to someone else. He hadn't seen it then and he'd let her walk away. He'd done the same with Grace.

He hadn't wanted to, but the bottom line was he couldn't be with a woman who didn't believe in what they had enough to fight for it. To fight *for him*.

He heard Grace's footsteps before he saw her. When he looked up, she was only several steps away, carrying a gift box in her hands. She looked good. She always looked good. But she also looked uncertain.

She sat next to him.

"How'd it go with Louisa?" she asked.

"We're going to collaborate together. Thank you, Grace."

"You're welcome." She cleared her throat. "How are you?"

"I'm okay."

"Mmm." She traced the edge of the box she carried. "That's too bad. Because I'm miserable without you. I was kind of hoping you were the same."

He remained silent. Waiting. And hoping, as well.

"You know how badly I want to be normal, Max," she said.

He sighed and took her hands in his, the box balanced on her thighs while their joined hands rested on top of it. "You're more fabulous than normal can ever be, Grace. I know you don't believe that and, as we've already established, I can't give you normal. Not with this life. So why are you here?"

"Because I can give *you* some normal." He tried to pull away, but she tightened her grip on him. "I've been trying so hard to reject the kinky, adventurous side of me that sometimes I forget it's just *a part* of me, not all of me. There's more to me than that, just like there's more to you than being a performer. We've got layers, you and I."

"Agreed."

"I think, between the two of us, if you're willing to try again, we can have it all. I can support your career and your lifestyle, Max. That's why I brought Louisa here. We can give each other the sexual excitement we need. But we can also give each other normal, too. Stability. Comfort.

Security. Love. And eventually, if everything works out well and you want it, a family."

"Why are you sure we can have it when you weren't sure before. What's changed?"

"I've had time to talk to friends, to family, who refused to let me resign myself to a lifetime of missing you. And that's what I'll have without you, Max. A whole lot of missing you."

He brought her hands to his mouth so he could kiss them. "I've missed you, too, Dixie."

She leaned forward, obviously wanting him to kiss her on the mouth as much as he wanted to do it, but the box on her lap got in the way. When she pulled back, he tapped on the box lid. "Is there something inside there you want to show me?"

She looked uncertain. "Maybe there's no need. I kind of brought it as back-up, just in case you needed to be convinced how serious I am about you, but now it seems like overkill."

"Grace, you rented a theater and had a dance troupe show up for me. I'm pretty sure nothing in that box is going to blow my mind."

"Okay." She lifted the lid and took out a blanket.

He sucked in his breath. He'd been wrong.

She had blown his mind.

The blanket Grace held looked similar to the ones his mom had given Rhys and Melina for the babies. He reached out to touch it. It was soft. Almost as soft as Grace's skin. He traced the outline of his and Grace's names above a blank heart where a baby's name was supposed to go.

"It's not the real one," she said. "Your mom has yours safely at home."

His mom made him one? He shouldn't be surprised, but he was.

"I had this one made because I wanted you to know this is what I want. Our names on a baby blanket that your mom makes for us. With our baby's name in a heart underneath ours. I want time to explore our relationship and enjoy one another. But eventually, when we're ready, I want to build a family with you."

"I want that, too," he said in a gravelly voice. "And Grace, I don't need to be a magician to make it happen. You worked your way into my heart back at Lodi's. You've never left. And until the time comes that we're ready to have a baby, I'll be your family. For now and forever."

EPILOGUE

Max's Magic Rule #19:
Visualize a standing O, prepare for it, perform,
and reap the rewards.

Two months later, Max was in the Paradise Theater helping choreograph a new set that combined the Dalton Brothers' magic tricks with a stunning acrobatic number courtesy of Louisa's dance troupe. He'd just called for a break and was speaking to the show's biggest investor—Jamie Whitcomb, Lucy's ex—when the theater doors were flung open and Lucy came running down the aisle. When she stopped in front of them, she kept her gaze glued to Max as if Jamie didn't exist. Jamie, however, looked at Lucy as if he wanted to throw her over his shoulder and head for the nearest bed. Actually, he looked as though any horizontal spot would do.

"Rhys and Melina are on their way to the hospital." Lucy grabbed Max by the shirtfront and shook him even as she grinned and bounced up and down. "The babies are coming. Let's go, Max."

"I'll get Grace and meet you in the parking lot," Max said, not even bothering to hide his own grin. *This is it,* he thought. *Soon I'll be holding my nieces or nephews.*

With a nod, Lucy turned to head outside, but froze when Jamie cupped her elbow.

"I'll drive you to the hospital," he said.

Lucy jerked away from his touch and narrowed her eyes. "If you want company, you can always hire a chauffer. Hell, you can hire ten. I'd rather walk down the Strip naked than go anywhere with you."

Jamie's fists clenched and his jaw ticked. "Damn it, Lucy. You're being ridiculous. My money's good enough to invest in this theater but nothing else?"

"I didn't ask you to invest in the theater. Melina did. I simply told her I had no objection to her asking you. And I don't. I have no objection because you mean nothing to me. You mean less than nothing."

He crossed his arms. "If Melina wasn't in labor I'd make you eat those words, Luce."

"Dream on, Jamie." She headed toward the door, calling, "Let's *go,* Max!"

Max placed a hand on Jamie's shoulder. "I'm sorry, man, but I've gotta go."

"I'll meet you there," Jamie said.

Max wasn't surprised Jamie was going to the hospital since he and Melina were friends before he'd started dating Lucy. He just hoped the two of them could keep *their* particular brand of drama under control when they got there.

Since Grace wasn't working right now, she spent a lot of time at the theater. She planned on spending more time helping Melina with the babies, but she was going to have to fight Max's and Melina's moms for that honor. Max found her talking to one of the dancers. "It's time, Grace. Melina's at the hospital."

"Good Lord." She said a quick goodbye to the other woman, grabbed Max's hand and began dragging him to the back door. When they got to his car, however, she stopped.

"Melina's going to be a mama," Grace said as tears filled her eyes.

Max hugged her close. "Your time will come, Grace."

She laughed and shook her head. "I'm not thinking about myself. Family surrounds me and I know I'll have more someday. It's just... Rhys and Melina... They're perfect together. And now their lives are going to be even more perfect."

"If anyone knows about perfection, it's you, Dixie," he whispered as he ran his knuckles down her cheek.

She smiled, pressed a soft kiss on his jaw, then threw open the passenger door. "Come on! The babies are coming."

* * *

A week later, Max and Grace had tears in their eyes but for slightly different reasons. Rhys had convinced Melina and both sets of grandparents to go out to dinner, leaving Max and Grace alone with his niece and nephew for the first time. Now, settled into the rocking chair in the nursery, Max cradled a baby in each arm, his expression one of utter adoration.

Grace was quite familiar with that look since Max pinned it on her frequently.

Not a day passed that she didn't feel like the luckiest woman in the world because of it.

That's why her tears were ones of happiness *and* regret. It scared her sometimes, how close she'd been to losing him.

Max sensed her mood and looked up from the babies to frown at her. "Dixie, what's wrong?"

She reached out and smoothed the downy hair on each of the baby's heads. Then she cupped Max's face in both hands, leaned down and gave him a soft kiss.

He immediately angled his head and deepened their lip action, only pulling back when Charlie squeaked. She giggled when Tabitha gurgled in response. "I was right," she said. "They're perfect."

Max sobered. "Tell me," he said.

"I'm so happy," she said. "And I know with you in my life, I'm only going to be happier. I just can't believe I was such a fool. That I didn't see everything you were from the beginning. What if I never came to my senses? What if I let you get away?"

"That was never going to happen. You saw me, Grace," he said. "Long before you walked into Lodi's."

"What do you mean?"

"No way you would've approached me the way you did unless you knew I had more to offer than my—"

She slapped her hand over his mouth. "Don't you dare," she said. "Not in front of the babies."

He puckered his lips and kissed her palm. When she removed it, he said, "All right. I'll wait until we're alone to start the dirty talk. Or on second thought, maybe I'll let you do all the talking tonight."

"You're just saying that because hearing me talk southern gets you hot."

"Everything about you gets me hot, but yeah, the way you talk, Dixie? It made me hard and got me hot before I ever laid eyes on you."

"The time we talked, that first night on the phone, before you dragged Melina onstage to make her grand play for Rhys?"

"How did you know?"

"Because that's when I fell for you, too. You don't need an accent, Max. I knew the moment we spoke you were the one. I was just too scared to admit it."

"And now?"

"Now I just want to see you holding these darling babies, hoping that one day I'll be lucky enough to be carrying your baby inside me. I love you, Max."

It was the first time she said it even though she'd been certain of her feelings for quite some time. She hadn't been so certain what Max's response would be.

But she should've known Max would beat her to the

punch.

"Reach into my shirt pocket, Dixie."

She did and pulled out a playing card.

The queen of hearts.

On it he'd written, "I love you, too, Grace."

She blinked back even more tears and whispered, "Gimme some sugar, magic man."

He did.

And she knew, no matter what, even when things weren't perfect between them, her life with Max would *always* be sweet.

BOOKS BY VIRNA

THE BEDDING THE BACHELORS SERIES
Book 1: Bedding The Wrong Brother (Rhys)
Book 2: Bedding The Bad Boy (Max)
Book 3: Bedding The Billionaire (Jamie)
Book 4: Bedding The Best Friend (Ryan)
Book 5: Bedding The Biker Next Door (Cole)
Book 6: Bedding The Bodyguard (Luke)
Book 7: Bedding The Best Man
Book 8: Bedding The Boss**

HOME TO GREEN VALLEY SERIES
Book 1: What Love Can Do (Quinn)
Book 2: The Way Love Goes (Conor)
Book 3: I'm Gonna Love You (Brady)
Book 4: Best Of My Love (Riley)
Book 5: Because You Love Me (Sean)

SAY YOU LOVE ME SERIES
Book 1: Say It Sexy
Book 2: Say It Sweet

ROCK CANDY SERIES
Book 1: Rock Strong
Book 2: Rock Dirty
Book 3: Rock Wild**
Book 4: Rock Free**

**Coming Soon

BEDDING THE BACHELOR SERIES

Bedding The Wrong Brother
(Bedding the Bachelors Book 1)

Determined to find her inner sex diva, Melina Parker enlists her childhood friend, Max Dalton, to tutor her after hours. Instead, she ends up in the wrong bed and gets a lesson in passion from Max's twin brother, Rhys Dalton, a man Melina's always secretly wanted but never thought she could have.

This #1 Bestselling Contemporary Romance is rated HHH ("Heat, Heart & HEA") and involves a bed mix-up, hot identical twins, sex lessons, naughty word games, light restraint, a shy sex bomb who's afraid she's boring and a playboy hero determined to prove she's got everything he'll ever need.

Bedding The Billionaire
(Bedding the Bachelors Book 3)

Free-spirited Lucy Conrad enjoys her friends but keeps others at a distance, especially her affluent and judgmental family...and the billionaire she once dated, Jamie

Whitcomb. Despite their explosive chemistry, experience has proven she'll never fit into his world.

Charismatic Jamie enjoys work, women, and wealth. When duty demands he take over running the family business, he jumps in full-throttle; his only regret is Lucy's refusal to take the ride with him.

Then tragedy strikes and Lucy realizes that in order to gain custody of her orphaned niece, she must prove she can fit back into the high-society world she once rejected. The solution? Accept Jamie's make-believe marriage proposal, and be seen as the type of mother her niece deserves. Respectable. Controlled. Willing to play the game.

With her faux-fiancé by her side, Lucy exchanges dirty martinis and leather for champagne and silk. But when the passion between Lucy and Jamie only grows greater, they have to make a choice: back away from each other and not get hurt...or risk everything for the kind of love money can't buy.

Bedding The Best Friend
(Bedding the Bachelors Book 4)

As the new year approaches, nice girl Annie O'Roarke finds herself bored and lonely. She wants more excitement. More adventure. And more sex...even if it won't be with her secret crush, her best friend, Ryan Hennessey. Annie's determined to be "bad" for once in her life, and that includes completing her "naughty" list in a city where being bad is just an ordinary day: Vegas.

Ryan Hennessey is a firefighter who relishes his time off with Annie. Annie's the only person he can count on and he'd never jeopardize their friendship. Then Ryan discovers Annie's "naughty" list. Although he's stunned Annie is raring to explore her wilder side, he doesn't trust anyone else to keep her safe.

So long as he's there to protect her, Ryan's going to teach Annie the true key to being a bad girl.

A bad girl takes what she wants.

Will Annie be brave enough to act on the passion that sizzles between her and Ryan? And will Ryan convince himself and Annie that love is worth gambling for?

Bedding The Biker Next Door
(Bedding The Bachelors Book 5)

Jill Jones has good friends, a great job, and a steady amount of dates. What she doesn't have is a kinky or wild bone in her body—or so she thinks. Then she meets a handsome tattooed biker who lights her on fire. Suddenly she's saying yes to all sorts of things, starting with a night in bed, no strings attached.

A security expert, Cole Novak protects others for a living, but he's weighed down by grief that he couldn't save the most important person in his life. Then he meets Jill, and for one night she brings color back into his world…only to walk away, plunging him back into the now-familiar darkness.

Soon Cole discovers that Jill is closer than he realized—living in the very house he plans to sell in order to leave the past behind. With the wild woman of his dreams suddenly the girl next door, will Cole still sell the place and move away, or will he soak in more of Jill and open his heart to hope and love?

Bedding The Bodyguard
(Bedding The Bachelors Book 6)

Hollywood actress Kat Bailey is on track to win an Oscar, but in the past year she's been embroiled in a nude photo scandal, threatened by a fan of her cheating ex, and run off the road in what could have been a deliberate act. Now she's renting a cabin in Lake Tahoe, considering the pros of leaving acting—including living a normal life for a change.

Bodyguard Luke Indigo initially turned down protecting Kat because he worried his intense attraction to her could compromise the job. But when he learns Kat has gone into hiding, Luke's sense of duty has him following her to Tahoe. Once there, he pretends to be a vacationing neighbor in order to stay close and protect her. As they spend time together, Luke learns Kat's charm is more than skin deep. She's smart. She's kind. And she's oh so sexy.

Kat's intrigued by the steely-eyed man who exudes danger but touches her so tenderly. Even better, he seems to have no idea who she is, making her think she's finally found a man who wants her for herself rather than her fame.

However, when Kat learns Luke is the same bodyguard her manager tried to hire to protect her, she fears ambition not love has been his agenda all along. Can Luke convince Kat that he'd protect her no matter whether he's hired to or not….and can he convince her that he wants her: body, heart, and soul?

Bedding The Best Man
(Bedding the Bachelors Book 7)

Rough-around-the-edges Gabe Nolan grew up poor in a bad neighborhood and literally fought his way to the top, learning discipline through boxing and earning a college degree. Now the owner of the nation's most popular chain of sports adventure stores, he enjoys wealth and women, but neither can diminish the pain of losing the girl of his dreams to his best friend.

Brianne Whitcomb is all set to marry Eric, a man who's perfect for her in every way—except for the fact he's not Gabe. But Gabe didn't fight for her when he had the chance, and it's obvious he views her only as a friend. He's even agreed to be Eric's Best Man. Only when Eric fails to show up for the wedding, Gabe takes on a new role: Brianne's confidante and shoulder-to-cry-on. The more time they spend together, the more friendship turns into an irresistibly tempting passion.

With no idea if or when Eric will return, Gabe and Brianne tentatively explore whether their physical attraction can lead to something lasting. But Gabe's fear that he'll never be good enough is the toughest opponent of all. Will Gabe take on the fight of his life to win Brianne's love?

HOME TO GREEN VALLEY SERIES

What Love Can Do
(Home To Green Valley Book 1)

Ireland has always been home for the five O'Neill brothers, but several tragedies, including the recent death of their mother, have them feeling lost. After making an unexpected discovery, eldest son and former rugby player Quinn O'Neill heads to Forestville, California, in the enchanted river valley where his mother grew up. There, he hopes to learn more about his family and explore the possibility of settling someplace new.

Traveling the world before opening her own bakery is Lillian Parker's dream, and she's one step closer to achieving it after winning an internship with a world-famous pastry chef in Miami. Unfortunately, Lillian's mother is pressuring her to stay in Forestville and help run the family B&B. Then a handsome Irishman blows through the door with charm and sex appeal to spare, and suddenly Lillian's not sure what she wants.

Sparks instantly fly, and Lillian finds herself agreeing to show Quinn around the area. Soon their building feelings have them wishing for more time together. But Quinn's just beginning to explore the magic of Green Valley wine country, and Lillian needs to stretch her wings. Even worse, exposed secrets pit Lillian's family against Quinn's, creating thorns in their blooming love.

Can passion survive conflicting family loyalties? And can love bond Quinn and Lillian together forever when dreams of adventure versus home and hearth threaten to keep them apart?

The Way Love Goes
(Home To Green Valley Book 2)

A middle child of five Irish brothers, Conor O'Neill always enjoyed life footloose and fancy free. Then Con's mother dies and he's never felt so lost. With his oldest brother, Con explores new possibilities in Green Valley, California, where his mother grew up. Finding inspiration in the great, wide Pacific, Con opens a surf shop in nearby Timber Cove where he meets the classiest lass he's ever seen.

Madlyn Sanchez is surprised when the Irish surfer seems to take a liking to her. Older than him, a high-strung wedding planner, she couldn't be more different than Conor. But the two have one thing in common—they're both looking to start over. Before Madlyn knows it, they kick off an unlikely, passionate romance. But when

Madlyn's responsibilities in San Francisco can no longer be ignored, she kisses Con goodbye and wishes him well.

Missing Madlyn more than he ever thought possible, knowing he's let one too many opportunities pass him by, Conor closes up shop to go after her. In San Francisco, however, he discovers the truth behind Madlyn's real life—a child and an ex-husband still in residence. Con just learned to commit to one woman—can he commit to a child as well?

In no time at all, mother and son have Conor's heart. But can an Irish rogue who once cherished his freedom convince the love of his life he's more than ready to put down roots while still teaching her to fly?

I'm Gonna Love You
(Home To Green Valley Book 3)

Steadfast and pragmatic Brady O'Neill, second eldest of five Irish brothers, never thought he'd leave Dublin. But after the death of his daughter and his parents, and the loss of his wife, Brady realizes he can no longer live in the city where he experienced his greatest joys and deepest heartaches. Moving to America, he joins his brothers in Forestville, California, to open a family restaurant. What he doesn't expect is the spark he feels when he meets Anna Kincaid, a confident, gorgeous woman with enough sass to sink a ship.

Owner of a local eco-adventure tour company, Anna Kincaid is familiar with all that is Forestville. So when recent Irish arrival, the insanely handsome and sexy Brady O'Neill, wants to visit the vineyard where his mother grew up, she agrees to be his guide. Soon, Brady's showing his appreciation with more than flirtatious smiles and mind-boggling kisses.

The chemistry between them may be explosive, but tensions heighten when Anna's recklessness puts her in danger. Brady's lost too much already; and a risk-taking woman with an impetuous nature could cost him yet again. Will Brady risk giving all he is to Anna? And will Anna learn that there's no greater excitement in the world than taking a chance on love?

Best Of My Love
(Home To Green Valley Book 4)

Irish charmer Riley O'Neill never thought he'd fall for one woman so soon after moving to America. After all, his brothers were all about love and commitment these days, and *someone* had to keep the ladies satisfied. However, after months of keeping Erica Underwood in the friend-zone, Riley has a decision to make—continue to enjoy variety, get back together with his ex-girlfriend in Ireland who's wanting a second chance, or finally make his move on Erica, the one woman he can't get out of his mind.

After a short holiday in Ireland, Riley returns to California wine country and suddenly he's treating Erica different. Teasing glances and lingering touches indicate he's ready to be more than friends, but Erica's worked hard to get over her crush on Riley. She's started seeing another man and when Riley finally declares his feelings, she's convinced he's only attracted to the challenge she now represents.

But Riley's not giving up on Erica, and he sets out on a mission to prove they're perfect for one another, in bed and out. Soon, they're inseparable, and their passion burns wild and hot. Until a phone call from Riley's ex Lucy threatens to destroy everything...

Will Riley and Erica crumble in the face of unexpected challenges, or will their love bring out the best in both of them and lead them to happily ever after?

Because You Love Me
(Home To Green Valley Book 5)

Readers have fallen in love with the Irish O'Neill brothers...now it's time for Sean O'Neill's story!

Sean and his four brothers moved from Dublin, Ireland to California wine country. One by one, the O'Neill brothers have fallen for the women of their dreams. Now it's Sean's turn, and he's determined to convince Juliana Madison, his college English professor, that he's not just a younger man—he's definitely the man for her.

Now that classes are over, will Juliana play it safe or will she give in to her attraction to the brown-eyed Irish lad whose tender words and strong arms fill her with joy and make her believe in love again?

SAY YOU LOVE ME SERIES

Say It Sexy
(Say You Love Me Book 1)

This life I'm relishing--the women, booze, and parties-- won't last forever. But while it does, I'll take it all in with no regrets. Pleasure stands paramount. When I party, I forget all the trash that's happened in the past. It's the same when I'm acting, when I become someone else, someone not afraid to feel or make others feel. It's what I live for: The next party. The next role. The next girl.

That's my life. That's the way I want it to be.

Except now I've met Gwen...

Garrick Maze, young Hollywood's hottest bad boy, just landed the male lead in a new network television series. Known for indulging in wild parties, casual hook-ups, and fast cars, he spends his days on set and his nights on the town. Love's the last thing on his mind, especially when it comes to his ice queen female lead.

Gwendolyn Vickers intends to be America's next celebrity sweetheart and that means keeping her public image pristine. The last thing she needs is to be linked to trouble-making heartthrob Garrick Maze. But he's shamelessly flirty and sexy as sin. Her body craves him. Soon, so does her heart.

When secrets from the past clash with the bright lights of fame, Gwen realizes there's more to Garrick than washboard abs and sex appeal. He'll prove that when it comes to mixing mind-blowing pleasure with true love, he's not about to let her down.

Say It Sweet
(Say You Love Me Book 2)

Outwardly, Erica Ellis seems to have it all. At twenty-three years old, she's already hit the *New York Times* bestseller list and her breakout novel is being made into a network television series. But even after collecting her cushy advance for Book 2, she can't seem to forget the struggles of her past or stop longing for the sexy and sweet man who views her only as a friend.

A former fighter turned actor, Shane Mason hides his pain behind a good-guy façade just like he hides his growing feelings for Erica. The willowy blonde is way out of his league…or so he thinks, until an unexpected hookup at a party has him thinking he and Erica might just be perfect for each other.

Only it turns out Erica doesn't remember the night they spent together. Now Shane has a choice—walk away or let Erica see all that he is and can be to her: a nice guy and a bad boy. A friend, fighter, and lover.

ROCK CANDY SERIES

Rock Strong
(Rock Candy Book 1)

I've seen and done it all--sex, drugs, rock-n-roll, and then some. I've made the cover of Rolling Stone. I've won Best Rock Performance at the Grammy's. I'm living a life of fame, wild tours, crazy money, and insanely hot women. But the one woman I can't get is prim and proper cellist, Abby Chan--gorgeous, natural, talented as all sin. The first time we met, I knew we would be something special. She's not convinced, but I am.

Now I'm going to prove she's all the woman a wild man like me will ever need...

Liam Collier, sexy and enigmatic frontman for Point Break, the world's hottest rock band, is at the top of his game. With two songs in the Billboard Top 10, he's a rock-and-roll bad boy, known for his trademark falsetto as well as his proclivity for partying and hooking up with gorgeous women. For Liam, falling in love was something he figured would happen far off in the future--not on the first day of his first world tour. And not with his super sexy but extremely reserved background cellist.

With a Master of Music degree from Juilliard School of Music, Abby Chan is on the road to becoming a cellist for the New York Philharmonic Orchestra. But to pay back her expensive education, first she has to travel another kind of road--a gig playing cello for the North American leg of a garish rock band's world tour. She'd expected hard work and long hours, but what she never expected was the intensity of her reactions to Liam Collier. He's sweet. He's hot. And despite being surrounded by roadies and the world's most beautiful women, he's set his sights on her.

When classical music meets rock and prim propriety meets a carefree attitude, Abby and Liam venture outside their comfort zones. What they discover is that living wild is the perfect preparation for flying high--on love.

Rock Dirty
(Rock Candy Book 2)

As one of the hottest drummers in the world, Tucker "The F***er" Benning lives life hard. But when his band's world tour is cancelled, Tucker finds himself stuck in an airport with no destination in mind...until he spots a red-headed knockout hurrying through the airport on her way to Paris, France. She's classy, sexy, and turns heads. Why not buy a first class ticket and follow her? That's when the real fun begins.

Dominique "Nikki" Lorenz, heiress to her mother's magazine empire, is headed to Paris, hoping to leave behind her celebutante tabloid reputation and make a new name for herself. She's amused when the famous Tucker Benning sits next to her and starts flirting—could he *be* any more of a rock star? But when he presents a naughty proposal, she figures why not have one last wild experience before settling down?

Once they land in Paris, though, Nikki makes a stand—no more naughty stuff. She has a fresh and clean reputation to build, and being seen with Tucker won't help. Yet Tucker's bad boy allure is impossible to resist and so is his softer side, which makes her feel cherished and worthy.

Tucker has a decision to make—does he fight for his band, or does he commit to the woman he's come to care about, a woman who longs for love and stability his rock star lifestyle can't give?

Tucker's life has always been about fame, fun, and f***ing around. But now Nikki needs him and he'll do whatever it takes to win her heart…including fighting dirty. Because love is worth risking everything.

ABOUT THE AUTHOR

Virna DePaul is a *New York Times* and *USA Today* bestselling author of steamy, suspenseful fiction. Whether it's vampires, a Para-Ops team, hot cops or swoon-worthy identical twin brothers, her stories center around complex individuals willing to overcome incredible odds for love. Bedding The Wrong Brother, which begins the Bedding The Bachelors Series, is a #1 Bestselling Contemporary Romance and a USA Today Bestseller.

Virna loves to hear from readers at www.virnadepaul.com.

CONTACT VIRNA HERE
Website: www.virnadepaul.com
Twitter: @virnadepaul
Email: virna@virnadepaul.com
Facebook Fan Page: www.facebook.com/booksthatrock

44195713R00177

Made in the USA
Middletown, DE
31 May 2017